ALSO BY IAN MOORE

Death and Croissants
Death and Fromage
Death at the Chateau
Death and Papa Noël
The Man Who Didn't Burn

A JUGE LOMBARD MYSTERY

DEAD BEHIND THE EYES

IAN MOORE

DUCKWORTH

First published in 2024 by Duckworth, an imprint of Duckworth Books Ltd
1 Golden Court, Richmond, TW9 1EU, United Kingdom
www.duckworthbooks.co.uk

For bulk and special sales please contact
info@duckworthbooks.com

A catalogue record for this book is available from the British Library

Printed and bound in Great Britain by Clays Ltd, Elcograf S.p.A.

Hardback ISBN: 978-0-71565-553-5
Ebook ISBN: 978-0-71565-552-8

Cover design and illustration by Andrew Smith

For Charlotte, my oldest friend who also
refuses to read my books

Chapter 1

Sometimes he would dart down a quiet backstreet. Then next he might nonchalantly saunter across a crowded market square. It was a game he liked to play. Nobody physically followed anyone anymore; there was no need to with electronic surveillance. These days, people were always, always telling you where they were.

But best not to take chances.

Besides which it was fun, it gave him an extra frisson of excitement. It added to the danger of the rendezvous he was scurrying, sometimes strolling, to make. The freedom and the power he was exercising. He felt good like this, working off his dinner as he went. His circuitous route sometimes took him in the opposite direction to where he was actually going; if someone recognised him that was an extra layer of protection.

The thought of protection made him check in his pockets again. Yes, he had them. Extra thick too. This wasn't about sexual gratification, this was more about the theatre, the experience and, again, the power. He could hardly contain himself.

He took a right into the rue des Tanneurs, out of the narrow streets and medieval buildings of the old town of

Tours, and into some of the uglier tower blocks. His lip curled in disgust and he was barely able to look at the box square buildings. He knew from experience that this was where the lowlife bred, a battery-farmed population of people who rarely stood a chance and who behaved accordingly. There are those who have and those who don't, that was just the natural order of things. Society is a pyramid and he was at the top. He crossed the road heading for the car park under the Pont Napoléon, even taking his car keys out of his pocket, overacting the moment but still, despite his jittery physical excitement, retaining an element of caution.

He walked past his car parked under the trees in the far corner of the gravelled parking area and tip-toed over the syringes and condoms that lay scattered and discarded. *It couldn't get much seedier than this*, he thought. It was just perfect.

He saw her before she saw him. She was drawing on a cigarette and the glow of the tip was visible in the twilight, as were her white stiletto shoes, which made her look taller than she was. Her legs, pale and dimpled with cellulite, stuck out below a blue leather miniskirt with a front zip. Her jacket, which was too small, looked leather as well but wasn't, the collar turned up and nestled under her high red hair. She disgusted him and, again, that was perfect. His breathing got heavier as he walked quickly towards her, not bothering to see if there was anyone else about. His furious desire overriding his usual care.

He grabbed her by the elbow to guide her down to the privacy of the riverbank, but she was stronger than him. Startled she turned on him quickly and raised a fist. He ducked and winced in anticipation of the blow that didn't come.

'You're late,' she said aggressively.

'I know.'

She relaxed and lowered her fist, breaking into a smile showing remarkably good teeth. 'You shouldn't go sneaking up on people like that!' she said warmly. 'You'll get yourself hurt.'

'I've never done this before,' he lied. 'Sorry.'

'No harm done. Got the money?' He gave her a few bills which she counted just to make sure. It felt even grubbier than he'd imagined it, a grim, soulless transaction, nothing more. And therefore everything he had wanted it to be. 'Where do you want to go?' she asked, zipping the money into a leatherette pocket and lowering the zip on her jacket to show a stretch-marked cleavage.

'Down here is as good a place as any,' he replied, his confidence restored.

'True, it's almost a home from home,' she said coldly. 'But quiet 'cos it's early.'

She turned to walk down the bank, showing surprising agility and balance despite her footwear, holding on to branches as she descended, avoiding the rocks and exposed roots like a skilful sailor through a reef. He followed, less sure-footed despite the fact that he knew the path well; it was well trodden anyway but he had done his research when he had first had the idea of these arrangements. It wasn't something he did often, maybe now more regularly than at first, but the feeling it gave him was becoming addictive. He liked to thrust power on the contemptible weak.

She knelt down before him and began to unzip his trousers. From where he stood, he could hear the traffic of the busy city centre but could see nothing other than trees and nobody, unless they had specifically been searching, could see him. She didn't matter. She was just a vassal.

'Hold on,' she said irritably. 'My hands got dirty coming down the bank. I'm going to wash them.'

'It's not a problem for me,' he said, a hint of desperation in his voice.

'Well, it is for me!' She stood up and walked quickly to the river's edge, bending down again, her skirt stretching to breaking point. 'I may not be a high-class hooker, but I am a clean one!' she cackled as she dipped her hands into water.

'I really...' he began, but was cut off by her piercing scream. She fell back on to the ground and scrabbled like a crab up the bank. Startled and suddenly vulnerable he helped her up roughly. 'What is it?' he hissed.

She pointed at the water's edge, her eyes wide with fear, a hand over her mouth. His hand. He turned to look, annoyance his overriding emotion until he saw what she saw. It was a body, snagged on a low branch, bobbing gently in the ripples like a log.

'Go,' he said. 'Get out of here.' She stared at him in fear. 'Now!' he said with real menace. 'You were never here. I was never here. Go.'

She ran up the bank and he heard her running across the gravel. Waiting a moment to see if her scream had alerted anyone else, he stood absolutely still. He had a choice to make. Cautiously moving towards the river, he got out his phone and turned on the flashlight. The body, a man, was face down, arms outstretched. The legs pointing out into the River Loire, the head hidden in the overgrown riverbank. He bent down to take a closer look at the corpse, parting the grass and branches that covered the shoulders and the head.

He fell backwards.

There was no head.

Chapter 2

Juge d'Instruction Matthieu Lombard went from the bottom of the bleached stone steps of the Palais de Justice straight on to the running board of the bus opposite without interrupting his stride. It was, he reflected, one of life's pleasing small victories and, today, a very necessary one. The morning's frustrations, the starvation of his role and intellect, had taken their toll, so he'd walked out in search of a change of scenery and found himself on a bus. The almost aggressively cool air-conditioning, battling the heat of an early July morning, was a welcome change from the stifling mustiness of his office, and it felt like the cobwebs were being literally blown away. Not his irritation though, that was building like the sand in the bottom of a timer.

It wasn't supposed to happen like that today. He was aware – at least it had been pointed out to him – that he could be naïve, trusting, but he'd convinced himself that the meeting, scheduled for 10 am sharp, was going to change things. No one was enjoying or gaining from the status quo, it was time to bring Lombard back into the fold, stop throwing him scraps and use the talent that was there. He had reckoned without the insidious cunning of the department head, who had been called away urgently to a conference.

The insult was clear to Lombard. *I mean*, he thought, *who goes to a conference urgently?*

Procureur D'Archambeau, presumably right now en route to this crucial talking shop, had so far tried several different ways to get rid of Lombard: trumped-up charges of evidence tampering, early retirement – *very* early retirement in his view – on compassionate grounds, forced grief counselling, which had nearly succeeded, and now, and so far the most torturous of all, they were trying to bore him into submission.

The idea was to make him jump, the *procureur* not having the political support to push the high-profile *juge*. Lombard had a track record of success in prominent investigations and didn't care whose toes got trodden on to find the truth. He was therefore the living embodiment of the powerful and independent investigating magistrate and that made him popular with the public, but not with his more politically motivated colleagues who felt eclipsed by him. Being half-English played against him too, as it meant he was only half-French, to some French a heinous crime, in the same way that being only *half*-English was to some English. They now wanted him out, and felt they had the leverage too. What the seethingly ambitious D'Archambeau failed to grasp, however, was just how much he, Juge Matthieu Lombard, was now enjoying his recently crowned status as a right royal pain in the backside and had no intention of jumping anywhere.

There were plenty of seats available on the bus, pre-lunch and post rush hour, but he preferred to stand. He'd been at his desk all morning dealing with the paperwork that was supposed to be the most important part of his job and so was enjoying the sway of the bus as he calmed a little. He had no idea what impulse had driven him to leap on to the bus in the first place, other than it was there at the right time and seemed somehow meant for him. *Kismet*, he thought. Acting on pleasing impulse. He must remember to tell his counsellor that, maybe even praise him for it.

A young man sat near him, his head nodding under enormous headphones, which he seemed reluctant to remove as Lombard tried to get his attention. Eventually he did so, obviously recognising a persuasiveness that was hard to ignore.

'Sorry to bother you.' Lombard smiled warmly. 'What line is this?'

The young man threw him a look suggesting that even though Lombard wasn't dressed as your usual bus-hopping lunatic, he was certainly behaving like one. He put the headphones back on his ears before answering.

'Eleven,' he said, and stared out of the window to avoid any further interaction.

The minutiae-, trivia-obsessed Lombard could now reel off all the stops between place Jean-Jaurès, where he'd got on, and the terminus at Mareuil. He even briefly felt like doing so to the young man, but decided that was pushing his faux eccentricity a little too far. So he was heading north, that meant past Les Halles, past the place de la Victoire, over the Loire at Pont Napoléon, along Saint-Cyr-sur-Loire and up through Fondettes. It was tempting to get off at the Espace Naturel du Val de Choisille, where Madeleine and he used to go sometimes on fabulously indulgent, and sometimes very physical, picnics. Would that be a good idea? His counsellor would probably not approve. Lombard wasn't sure he did either, but he had nothing more interesting to do.

Chapter 3

Besides his family, very little could bring a smile out of Commissaire Guy Aubret. A high-class red wine and goat's cheese combination perhaps; the gently rolling fields of central France almost certainly. But for a man who had eschewed the family farm and spent thirty years as a policeman working his way up through the ranks, he was still constantly disappointed by how far humanity could sink. He shook his head, chewing on yet another Gaviscon tablet, almost feeling the acid rise up through his body like mercury in a barometer.

'I don't like it,' he muttered to himself. He turned and looked about him, taking in the scene. He stood near the water's edge; behind him was a grass bank and above him were trees providing a canopy. In front was the River Loire and to the right the Pont Napoléon. The immediate vicinity was sealed off all the way back to the car park entrance but he sensed, even at this early stage, there would be little of use to find; instead they would be overwhelmed by evidence perhaps none of which would be related to the deceased. The usual car park detritus of take away food, discarded bottles and cans, packaging of various kinds, and – especially here in Parking Napoléon – condoms, discarded needles and other signs of a shady nocturnal society. Nothing out of the ordinary for this place, but little to go on. There was a sign that indicated the place was liable to flooding. *Which is the only time it gets cleaned*, he thought.

The trees hid this spot from the road and the windows of the buildings opposite, which at least kept the gathering onlookers at bay. In fact, it was the perfect place to dump a dead body, though he doubted very much that the dead body had been dumped here. It could have been tossed in the water at any point, even hundreds of kilometres away and from either bank, such is the swirling current of the River Loire. It just happened to snag here, he suspected, a final private resting place.

'Everything is sealed off, sir.' The tall figure of Officer Helder Texeira stood at the top of the grass bank. 'But there's no one to interview, no witnesses as such. No one who was here last night anyway. And if they were, they're not saying.' He already sounded frustrated and the body wasn't even out of the water yet. This reminded the *commissaire* of another problem he was about to encounter. Texeira was an excellent officer, a bit hot-headed yes, but he brought a lot to Aubret's team and it was a good team too, even the new kid just down from Paris. But his number two, whom he relied on heavily at the start of any investigation, was on annual leave. Commandant Lydie Pouget was his *dossier* creator, a thorough and exacting officer, a talented organiser and a woman who took no crap from anyone, and he needed her here. Getting the *dossier* right is the first step in any serious crime investigation in France. The on-site police team start creating a document detailing everything they do, find and suspect, adding forensics reports as they arrive. The *procureur* chooses a *juge d'instruction* who then takes the *dossier* and directs the investigation, before reaching a conclusion, an arrest hopefully and advising the court in any subsequent trial. It's a hierarchical system, everyone knows their place and that is exactly the way Commissaire Guy Aubret likes it. Straight lines, no fudging.

Only he had no number two to start the *dossier*. The *procureur* had left that morning for a conference in Lausanne, Juge Dampierre was in hospital having his gall bladder removed and Juge Matthieu Lombard, who definitely did not work in straight lines, had apparently walked out of his office within the last hour, told no one where he was going and had left his mobile phone behind.

'OK, sir, we're pulling him in.' Divers from the Brigade Fluviale based in Tours had spent some time in the river looking, without result, for anything more before disturbing the body. They were now ready to roll the corpse on to the bank. The bank had also been scoured revealing only stiletto heel holes at the water's edge and a few cigarette butts. A body bag, the zip wide open, was laid down and the bloated headless victim, a large man, was unceremoniously dragged out, still holding the 'drowning position', so that now it looked like it was kneeling for prayer, even kissing holy ground. If it had had a mouth to do so. It was a foul sight and an even worse smell.

'Right, my turn I think.' A heavyset man in his sixties wearing a cheap suit and holding a medical bag struggled down the bank towards the *commissaire*, literally falling into Aubret as he lost his footing. It was like hitting a wall, the man practically bouncing off the solid policeman.

'Who the hell are you?' growled Aubret.

Flustered, the man introduced himself without looking the policeman in the eye. 'Doctor Hugo Cloutier,' he said, announcing it as if everybody would know and thus surprised at Aubret's lack of warmth or recognition.

'Where's Doctor Sebourg?'

'She's at a conference in Lausanne,' he said quietly, avoiding eye contact. 'Sorry,' he then added oddly, which did nothing for his standing.

Aubret closed his eyes and took a very deep breath. 'Great,' he said quietly. 'Get on with it then, Doctor. Texeira!'

'Sir.' The younger policeman grinned down at him.

'Get the new kid, er...'

'Benbarek.'

'Right. Get Officer Benbarek to make a note of all the cars and their registration plates in the car park right now. Then get Lemery to run a check. Is there CCTV here?'

Texeira laughed. 'What do you think? You don't get CCTV in a free car park.'

'OK. How's that *dossier* coming along?' The smirk left Texeira's face immediately. 'I thought so,' Aubret muttered. 'Never mind, not your fault. Give me what you've got and I'll take it from here.'

'Yes, sir! And thanks.'

'OK. And Texeira. We both know what this place is used for. Start asking around your contacts. You never know, we might get lucky and they've offed one of their own.' Texeira disappeared from view and Aubret turned back to the doctor who was kneeling awkwardly by the headless body. 'Right, Doctor, talk to me.'

The doctor, now wearing rubber gloves and blue galoshes, didn't look up. 'There's not much I can give you yet, Commissaire, not much at all.'

'Try.'

This time the pathologist did look up, but even as he began to talk still could not manage eye contact. Some people don't, Aubret knew that, but if you can stare into the gaping neck hole of a rotting headless corpse, you should certainly have the stomach to look at who you're talking to.

'Well, it's a man, bloated from the river and he has lost his head.' He turned back to his cadaver.

'Thank God you turned up,' Aubret said sarcastically.

Chapter 4

Lombard got off the bus at Maison Blanche on the north bank of the Loire and barely recognised an inch of it. Surely it hadn't been that long since he had been by here? His wife Madeleine had been dead well over a year; she had been ill for a few months before that... maybe as long as three years then. He blew out his cheeks and then admonished himself for behaving like a man who is far older than one in his late forties. The truth was that Madeleine's death had aged him, the opposite to when her life had made him feel much younger. He walked along the pavement in the warm sunshine, his linen jacket hanging by a finger over his right shoulder before stopping at a wide gun-barrel grey electronic gate. This was definitely new; there were still plots available to buy according to the sign on the wall, though he genuinely couldn't imagine a worse place to live. In his experience these gated communities, designed to keep the riff-raff at bay, were just as much a hotbed of crime as any forlorn, institutionally ignored housing estate. Maybe less physical violence, but just as many drugs and certainly more economic crime. The kind of law-breaking which unfortunately didn't get the salacious public as vexed in their calls for more effective policing.

He couldn't remember what, if anything, had stood on this plot before, though he imagined that whatever it was would have been more appealing than this balconied ziggurat of sanctimony. He was at least beginning to get his bearings though. He had vague recollections of a bar further along the road, the Bar Rive Nord perhaps? It was run by a reformed armed robber, Gilles Fostan, and he used to go in quite often. Lombard himself had spoken at Fostan's hearing to obtain the alcohol licence, and he had been given a warm welcome ever since. Right then, Lombard decided, I'm thirsty.

A few minutes later he was standing outside what he now remembered used to be called the Bar Beronne, a play on words as the next stop on the number eleven bus route was Barberonne. The bar was no longer there, however, which was unfortunate as he had now talked himself into a genuine thirst and he sincerely doubted whether the replacement, the vainly named Le Gym des Dieux, would offer anything more than a protein shake. He stood outside wondering what to do next. It was tempting to just cross the road and catch the next bus back into the city centre, though the large number of people waiting at the stop put him off that idea. And not just the number of people either but their collective attitude, the way they puffed their cheeks, checked their watches, shook their heads; it all suggested they'd been waiting for some time and even if the bus were to arrive, he didn't fancy the idea of a packed-out ride.

He turned back to face the gym, its large tinted windows showing large tinted men straining to lift, pull or carry various monstrous looking pieces of gym equipment. Each wore a grim, sweaty determination that Lombard found fascinating. *I wonder what happened to Gilles Fostan* he thought, the joyless looks on the faces of the men in the gym reminding him that Fostan was of course an armed robber by trade, and that these muscular individuals didn't look too far removed from that. He decided to go in and find out, see how old Gilles was getting on.

Once again the blast of air-conditioning was overwhelming as he approached the reception desk. Behind it slouched a man in his early thirties with buzz-cut hair and millimetre perfect goatee beard. He was scrutinising his phone which guiltily reminded Lombard that he had left his own phone in his office. The man was wearing a grey T-shirt with the sleeves roughly cut off and he was managing to flex his biceps, or make them dance somehow, while he pressed the screen with his thumb. Maybe it was a muscle-building exercise.

'They really do have an app for everything these days, don't they?' Lombard said, smiling as he approached the desk.

The man grunted something in reply but didn't look away from his phone. Behind him were more windows and more beefed-up bodybuilders, but the tint also meant that Lombard was reflected back at himself, superimposed on the weight trainers beyond like a 'Before and After' advert. He couldn't have looked more out of place. His lean frame and floppy, lightly greying hair, the jacket still over his shoulder like an old-fashioned catalogue shoot. His deep, shadowed, sad eyes could match any of the exercisers for determination and doggedness, but there was something else in those eyes that none of the men behind the window had. They had acceptance, a certain level of peace. Lombard had been to the bottom of a personal hell, he may even go there again, but for now, a lack of decent employment aside, he was doing just fine and it would take a lot to knock him off his stride.

He couldn't help raising a faint smile at the behemoths sweating behind the reception window, and this time the receptionist noticed.

'Can I help?' the man asked, an attempt at a warm smile tried to break out as he eyed up Lombard professionally.

'I'm looking for an old friend,' Lombard replied.

'Well, we haven't been here long, maybe I know him.' The man seemed to relax a little sensing that Lombard wasn't looking for a place to work out.

'He owned this place when it was a bar. His name is…'

The man's demeanour changed immediately, and he practically growled his interruption. 'I know his name and, as you can see, this ain't no bar. Run along, yeah?'

Impishly intrigued, though not intimidated, Lombard slouched on the desk. 'You see, that would involve exercise, not really my thing.' Behind the window he noticed that all of the bodybuilders had suddenly stopped exercising and were turning their attention in his direction. They looked like cinematic zombies as they slowly started moving towards the window.

'Like I said, run along,' the man repeated coldly.

'You have a panic button?' Lombard couldn't help laughing at the man, who stood up at the perceived insult, practically filling the entire reception area. Still Lombard smirked.

A side door flew open and a muscular young woman emerged, one that Lombard recognised immediately.

'Papa!' she exclaimed. 'I thought you were going to wait outside?' And she kissed him on the cheeks, grabbed his arm and dragged him out.

Chapter 5

'How long has he been in the river, would you say?' Commissaire Aubret sighed heavily. This was not going well.

The doctor didn't look up. 'Difficult to say. Perhaps not long, a few days at most. Cold water slows down the putrefaction process but I'm going to have to open him up to really see what's going on.'

'What about the head?' Texeira asked, returning to the scene and immediately sensing his superior's frustration.

There was a pause. 'Well, it's not here.'

'I know it's not here!' Texeira's short temper wasn't what the situation needed. 'But can you tell how he might have lost it?'

'What my colleague means, Doctor, is this.' Aubret wasn't usually the one to step in to calm things down, but he felt he had no choice. 'Could this be an unreported boating accident, a rudder incident or something like that? Or...'

'Or is he a late eighteenth-century nobleman?' The doctor chuckled to himself before realising that Aubret was now somehow giving off thunderstorm vibes. 'Sliced clean through, I'd say,' he added hurriedly. 'I can confirm that later though. What's this?'

He plucked an object out of the heavy fibres of the sodden checked shirt and handed it to Aubret. The *commissaire* centred it delicately in his gloved palm. It was a circular medallion on a short, chunky silver chain. A deep red background highlighted, in raised silver, the fleur-de-lys held by an octopus. He turned it over, but there was nothing on the other side. Aubret showed it to Texeira who shrugged and put it in an envelope.

Aubret turned back to Cloutier. 'Can you turn him over? I'd just like to see the front.'

'Well, I'd rather not Commissaire, it's…'

'Give me a break, Doctor. I have a headless corpse. That means IDing the victim is going to be nigh on impossible as it is; all I've got so far is cheap jewellery. I just want something to go on, anything.'

The doctor moved the left arm of the body to look at the hands. 'Not good,' he said. 'He may have been in the water longer than I thought. There is sloughing of the skin on the hands, not sure there'll even be fingerprints. And of course, DNA only works if he's already on record.'

'Why are his knuckles so damaged, has he been in a fight do you think?' Texeira asked.

'Well, if he was, he lost!' Again the doctor mistakenly thought his joke would win over a tough crowd. 'No,' he said more seriously. 'His knuckles have scraped along the river bed. You can see it's the same with the knees.'

Aubret bent down, putting a shadow over the doctor. 'What's that?' he said, nodding towards the body's hip. 'There's something in his pocket.' He pointed directly at something poking out above the frayed denim seam.

The doctor peered even closer and reached into his bag, producing some tweezers. Carefully and, Aubret reluctantly acknowledged, skilfully he slowly pulled out a water-damaged laminated card, about the size of a bank card. It was a driving licence and on it was a passport-sized photo of a bald man with several chins, looking blankly into the lens. Beside it was a name, Thibaud Barbier, and a date of birth: June 16 1977.

'Gotcha!' Aubret exclaimed, using his phone to take pictures of the back and the front before passing his phone up to Texeira to take a look. 'Thank you, Doctor, anything else in the pockets?' he asked, then waiting for confirmation there wasn't before turning to Texeira. 'While you've got my phone, Officer, get Commandant Pouget on the line for me, will you? All leave is now cancelled.'

Chapter 6

'I appreciate the help obviously,' Lombard moaned as Commandant Lydie Pouget dragged him along to the car park. 'But am I really old enough to be your father?'

'It was all I could think of,' she replied impatiently. 'There are some pretty nasty types in there, I just thought I'd get you out.'

Lombard stopped walking and shook his head. 'Old enough to be your father!' he said with a mock parental authority. 'So why are you hanging around places like that then, young lady?' It was meant as a joke, but she blushed instead of laughing and he knew why. Commandant Pouget's dating failures had become the stuff of legend in the Brigade Anti-Criminalité of Tours. Attractive, intelligent and dedicated, she had absolutely no luck with romance partly, Lombard knew, because for a lot of men, good looks, intelligence and dedication were absolutely terrifying attributes in a woman. Most men preferred, thrived even, on low self-esteem and neediness. That he had learnt this insight from his late wife was an irony not lost on him either. And he'd been happy to learn.

'Seriously though,' he tried again. 'Why go to a place like that?'

She stood still finally as she opened her car door, sighing with heavy, muscular shoulders as she did so. 'I'm seeing a guy…' she said, hiding her eyes from the sun.

'Another policeman?' Lombard tried to make it sound like it made no difference to him at all, but he still couldn't control his natural curiosity.

She hesitated before replying. 'Let's just say we met through work.'

'Good for you.' He tried to sound as diffident as possible.

It didn't work. 'Look, I spend my entire working life surrounded by fake alpha males. Men too frightened of women to communicate. Too fake courteous, scared even. Completely empty with no idea what to say to a woman like me.'

'So why…'

'Why chase that on my time off?' There was a fire in her eyes now, as she wrapped her plaited pony-tail into a bun. 'This is my comfort zone, Lombard. Dealing with people like that is second nature, it's easy. I don't have to think.' Her eyes became momentarily less defiant. 'Everything away from that is bloody hard work.'

Lombard nodded and smiled impishly. 'I'm not judging you, Commandant. I don't do much judging at all at the moment. Do they know you're police?'

'Christ, no!' she laughed, and it brought on an awkward silence for a moment.

'So,' Lombard said eventually, determined to change the mood with the only way he knew how. 'Shall we go for a drink? That's why I came here after all. At least I think that's why I came here.'

'Haven't you got work to do?' she asked, raising her eyebrows, knowing, like everyone else, that work, of the mundane, day-to-day stuff anyway, was rarely his priority anymore.

'Probably.' His reply was deliberately diffident. 'And I have my grief counsellor at twelve. I was just gathering my thoughts,' he added, lying badly.

She smiled. 'In a gym?' She put the car in reverse and pulled out on to the road.

'Well, in my defence, it didn't used to be a gym. It was a bar, run by an ex-con, Gilles...'

'Fostan. I know. That was his cousin you just met. A thug by all accounts, but again, I know my way around blokes like that.' She belatedly put on her seat belt as the alarm warned her to do so.

'Not a close family by the looks of it,' Lombard said quietly as he took in this information.

She snorted in response. 'Gilles Fostan signed the bar over to his cousin, Victor, a few years ago. He also signed over a mountain of debts that he didn't tell Victor about. Then he disappeared. Nobody's seen him in three or four years.'

Lombard nodded slowly. 'So anybody sniffing around after Fostan gets a warm welcome?'

'You got it.'

'Fair enough,' he smiled. 'I'd be the same. Though I doubt he ran away, Gilles Fostan. His size meant he was out of breath just pouring a beer.'

'So the cousin sets up a gym.' Pouget's frown showed that, annual leave or not, her brain was still in work mode. 'From one extreme to another. It's a gym with a purpose too; he has a private security firm.'

'And all after he's paid off his cousin's debts? My, he must work hard.'

They drove back towards the centre of town, each struggling to think of conversation that wasn't just about work.

'So where do you want to go then?' Commandant Pouget asked eventually. She tried to make the question sound breezy, playful even, hiding the awkwardness of the situation.

Lombard watched two motorists argue at a traffic stop. 'I suppose you'd better return me to my office,' he said, regretting asking the younger woman for a drink. 'I can't be seen socialising with women young enough to be my daughter! Not when I have no work to be getting on with.'

Pouget changed gear but without her usual efficiency. 'Why do you stay?' she asked, trying to sound breezy, though it got lost over the crunching gears. A distracted Lombard didn't answer immediately. 'Sorry,' she said, cursing herself. 'It's really none of my business.'

Eventually Lombard tore his attention away from what was happening outside and furrowed his brow. He was aware that the previous low-key awkwardness was now at a much higher level, but he didn't quite know why, other than both of them could be a bit difficult. The old Lombard would have let the tension fester a bit, not to deliberately cause a deeper issue, but to try to work out for himself what the issue actually was. But old Lombard had caused trouble for himself by doing so, ruining his last few weeks with a dying Madeleine just for wont of a simple, straightforward question – honesty even.

'Sorry,' he said, aware that needless apology, the most English of traits sometimes got the better of him. 'But what's none of your business?'

She took her eyes off the road, looking at him to make certain for herself that he wasn't playing games with her.

'We all know the *procureur* wants you out,' she began nervously. 'So why do you stay?'

He smiled and made it clear he was giving it some thought. 'Partly I stay because my mother is here. Partly

I stay because Madeleine is still here.' He paused. 'I screwed up. I screwed up badly. So even though Madeleine's been dead nearly eighteen months, I'm only now starting to accept – is that the right word? Feel, miss, celebrate her. I don't know. All of those things.' He could sense the younger woman was squirming at the intimacy of a conversation she hadn't really asked for.

'Is that why you keep her antiques shop open? To give you something to fill your time?'

He breathed deeply. 'It's our home, we still live above it,' he said after a brief pause. 'Mine and the cat's that is. Not Madeleine obviously.' He could have added that he did feel her there occasionally, spoke to her even, but then realised he should probably keep something back for the damn grief counsellor, throw the man the occasional bone. 'And as for the *procureur*,' he added more lightly, 'I enjoy my job. I'm good at it, when I'm allowed. And if I can do that *and* annoy the hell out of Procureur René D'Archambeau, then that's not a bad life, is it?' She laughed nervously. The *procureur* was not a popular man, but she also knew that her immediate boss, Commissaire Aubret, would frown on any public show of disrespect. 'Why are you still in Tours anyway, Commandant?' Lombard asked. 'If you're on annual leave, that is. Aren't you going away?'

She sighed heavily, her shoulders slumping like a child's. 'It's my sister's wedding next week. My *younger* sister's wedding,' she added, the emphasis speaking volumes.

Lombard was about to offer some ineffective reply when Pouget's mobile reverberated through the car's audio system. The screen said 'Commissaire Aubret'.

'Sir?' she answered.

'Commandant?' Aubret's voice sounded harassed, and slightly out of breath. He was walking, clearly. 'Look. I know it's your annual leave, but I need you here. Dead body at the car park under Pont Napoléon.'

'Well, actually...'

'I know. I wish I didn't have to call you, but between you and me, Texeira can't write the *dossier*. He's just not organised enough.'

'I can get...'

Aubret continued to talk over her. 'The *procureur* is away at a conference. Juge Dampierre is in hospital and out of action and as for Juge Lombard...'

'Sir!' Lydie tried to interrupt, but Aubret was on a roll.

'...apparently he walked out of his office an hour ago, didn't say where he was going and left his phone on his desk. I wouldn't be surprised if he never came back!' There was silence in the car. 'Are you there, Pouget?'

'Yes. And she's not alone, Commissaire.' Lombard grinned.

'Is that you, Lombard?'

'Yes. Commandant Pouget and I were just going for a drink. She picked me up at the gym.' Pouget gave him an admonishing look, not appreciating his game-playing.

'Jesus Christ,' Aubret said at the other end, no longer walking around. 'I don't know which is worse. You two socialising or you, Lombard, going to a gym.'

Chapter 7

Pouget slammed on the brakes and parked the car at an angle to the pavement. It wasn't just her dedication to the job that had gripped her and was rushing her, it was horror at the thought of what Texeira might be doing with the precious *dossier*, something she regarded as her own. She trusted Helder Texeira as a colleague, she knew he would always have her back in any given situation, but she knew also he would be making an unholy mess of anything that required organisation, a linear thought process, and due care and attention. She ran from the car without closing the door, leaving a more sedate Lombard still buckled-up in the passenger seat.

He watched as she sprinted across the road, ducking deftly under the red-and-white police tape and he thought about his own sudden lack of urgency. He'd never been one to get too hyped up, there was adrenalin for sure, but it was always under control. This was different, however. He felt somehow disconnected from the scene, almost an impartial observer, which in some ways was a demand of the job, but was this impartiality or was it doubt? Because D'Archambeau rarely gave him anything meaty these days, he was, unexpectedly, quite unsure how to react. It piled on the pressure, a refinement of the torment.

Unclipping his seatbelt he eased languidly out of the car, buttoning up his jacket as he took a deep breath. Whatever it was, whatever this odd wavering of confidence was down to, he had a job to do. Lombard held back. Like an actor waiting in the wings for his cue. He knew his lines, he knew his role inside out; it was written specially for him. But as with an actor, the audience changed each show, their lives and moods would affect if not his performance, then its reception. He stepped forward into the limelight that, if he were honest, he suddenly didn't feel he missed.

He climbed carefully down the steep, moss-covered stone steps, from where he was able to take in the wider scene. An ants' army of forensic officers were digging about, while the body, wrapped in its carrier, was being loaded into an ambulance. The police diving squad were in the water, but it was largely too shallow to actually swim so they looked more like an invasion party instead. A gentle wind rustled the leaves of the large plane trees and the sunlight dappled its way through the branches. The contrast between the two scenes was stark as was the image of Commissaire Guy Aubret in a huddle with Commandant Pouget and Officer Texeira, a winning team having their pep talk. Lombard approached the group silently, looking about him as he did so. It was Aubret who noticed him first.

'You don't look like you've been to a gym?' His tone wasn't mocking, but nor was it warm. This was his patch, the crime scene his area of expertise and he was just letting Lombard, despite being his boss, know that. A working Aubret had no time for pleasantries and Lombard didn't expect any.

'No. Well, I didn't know it was a gym. I thought it was a bar.' Lombard half-smiled.

'Figures,' was the gruff reply.

Texeira and Pouget moved away discreetly.

'It strikes me you're lucky I was here, Guy.'

'Well, you're the last cab on the rank as it were.'

Lombard grinned and they shook hands warmly enough this time. Not as warmly as they once had maybe, but the respect was still there; the butterflies in Lombard's stomach stopped fluttering momentarily. Nobody else spoke to him the way Aubret did, that faux disrespect, the mockery. Madeleine had done obviously and in some ways the relationship with Commissaire Guy Aubret was similar to a marriage. A relationship built up over years of being alongside each other, in each other's pockets, sometimes with their backs against the wall, sometimes basking in the glory of a job well done. There was trust there too, or at least there had been. Just as Lombard had mistakenly doubted Madeleine's dishonesty, Aubret had questioned his honesty. The two were connected of course. Lombard's deep despair had caused what he realised was a cry for help; Aubret had unknowingly responded and what was an easily explainable confusion over evidence tampering had escalated. The difference was that Lombard was happy to let Aubret continue to doubt him, maybe even distrust him too, for the moment. It gave Lombard the distance he felt he needed from the world and leverage too. Something else that also underlined their working relationship as a marriage was that they bickered constantly and to Lombard that was a good sign. It was a silent, brooding Aubret you had to watch out for.

'Well, if I'm the last cab on the rank, Commissaire, the meter's running. What have we got?'

Aubret turned a few pages back on his notebook, a force of habit when he knew the facts, such as they were, by heart already. He took a deep breath.

'Headless corpse, reported this morning at 9.15…'

'By whom?'

'I'm coming to that!' Aubret's irritation was immediate, as was Lombard's smirk. Then relenting and sounding dubious, he added, 'Anonymous. Male. Said he was walking his dog.'

'Are there any dog prints?'

'No.'

Lombard shrugged. 'Lots of people don't like to get involved, but it's more likely he was here with something entirely different on his mind yesterday evening, then his conscience got the better of him this morning.'

'I've got Texeira asking around on that. This is just a guess at the moment, an educated one. Find the prostitute, find the anonymous informant.'

'So, we're assuming two people who won't want to be involved found a corpse with as yet no identity. Well, that's a good start.'

'I don't like loose ends. I sure as hell don't like anonymous tip-offs either. Also...' He turned to face Lombard, a look of victory on his face, a rare moment to be savoured as for once he was ahead of the *juge*.

'Also?' Lombard smiled back, allowing the moment.

'Also, we *do* have ID.' He held up a brown paper evidence bag, now used because plastic bags had been found to destroy the DNA on a piece of evidence. 'Thibaud Barbier,' he said. 'I have his driving licence and Lemery is on the case back at the office.'

He handed Lombard his phone to look at the picture of the licence.

'Thibaud Barbier, forty-six. He looks older than that.' Then he repeated the name, 'Thibaud Barbier.' Throwing the syllables and consonants around his mouth like boiled sweets and staring closely at the emotionless passport-style photo of the man. Eventually he shook his head. 'I don't recognise the name.'

'Me neither,' Aubret replied with a touch of relief that Lombard hadn't got one up on him this early. 'But it's a start. Lemery will have a full biog soon,' he added with pride.

Lombard handed the phone back. 'So we know who. We need a why, how and where. Bearing in mind we have about a thousand kilometres to play with, none of that is going to be easy.'

'Actually, the Loire is thirteen hundred kilometres long.'

Lombard smiled, and put his hands in his pockets, almost sheepishly. 'Yes, but what Lemery didn't take into account – I assume she gave you that information – is that at this point we are roughly two hundred and seventy kilometres from the estuary at Nantes, and surely Monsieur Barbier could not have travelled upstream. Unless he's part salmon, of course.'

Aubret flushed but was saved by a member of the diving team. 'Monsieur le Commissaire. I can't see what else we can do here, sir?'

Aubret moved off to talk further with the officer in the wetsuit who was standing incongruously in shallow water up to his shins, leaving Lombard pondering on the bank. The likelihood was that they had got lucky. The body had become snagged or it really could have gone as far as the Atlantic. But then why go to the trouble of dumping a body so it may not be found, removing the head in case it was, but leaving identity on the corpse itself? That didn't make sense.

'Did Dr Sebourg have any idea how long Barbier had been in the water?' he asked, as Aubret returned having reluctantly agreed with the diving squad that little more could be achieved for now.

Aubret puffed out his cheeks as only a man about to deliver bad news can. 'It wasn't Dr Sebourg,' he said, annoyed that he had a note of apology in his voice. He saw Lombard evidently tense up. It had become a feature of the 'new' Lombard, as Aubret often referred to him, the post-Madeleine Lombard, that any personnel change upset him greatly; he needed a regular cast around him.

'What's happened to Karine?' he asked, the worry and concern obvious.

'She's just away at a conference, that's all.'

Lombard took a deep breath and nodded. 'There's a lot of conferences these days, must be the school holidays. Who's the locum?'

'A Dr Hugo Cloutier,' Aubret said, unable to hide his opinion of the man.

'I don't know him. But you don't like him, that's obvious.'

'No. Not particularly. But neither do you and at least I've met him.' Lombard conceded a smile. 'Anyway, first he said two or three days at most, then changed it to more than a week.'

He called out to Pouget to take over, which she effectively had done already.

'Two or three days, a week... let's hope this Cloutier can narrow it down.' Lombard stared intently at the fast-flowing river, as if hypnotised by it before suddenly snapping out of his trance. 'Why don't we go and see what Lemery has found out about this Barbier then? There's nothing more here it seems.' He turned his back on Aubret and headed towards the stone steps.

The policeman bowed his head and allowed his chin to rest defeatedly on his chest. Damn Dampierre and his bloody gall bladder. Juge Lombard was the only *juge d'instruction* in France who insisted on being a hands-on investigator.

He knew this because all the other *commissaires* he ever met delighted in reminding him about it. Lombard had become famous for it, or infamous depending on whom you spoke to. As had Aubret in his way. Other police forces were free to get on with their work as police, as primary investigators, while their *juges* sat like Solomons waiting to pass judgement from behind antique leather desks and not, repeat not, ever get in the way. He trudged heavily up the steep stone steps where Lombard waited for him at the top.

'Hard work those steps, Guy,' Lombard said airily. 'I know a good gym if you're looking for one.'

This did not help Commissaire Aubret's mood.

Chapter 8

Lombard wasn't sure how, or why, the change could have happened, nor even aware that it had. Twenty minutes ago he was reluctantly on the fringes of an investigation, hauled in because no one else was available and had briefly, though seriously, wondered whether he was up to the task. There was something in the face of Thibaud Barbier that was nagging at him though, haunting him even.

'Can I see that photo again, please? Barbier.' He stopped to ask Aubret this as they were crossing the busy avenue Proudhon, much to the consternation of drivers who had miraculously stopped for them. One of them hooted their horn in frustration and was greeted with twin looks of confusion and a discernible slowing down of pace as Aubret even stopped on the zebra crossing to fish in his pockets ostentatiously for his phone. Finding it at the third attempt he handed it to Lombard who shaded the screen from the glare of the sun as they finally reached the pavement.

'What do you see?' Aubret asked. No *commissaire* wants their *juge* in as permanently close proximity as Lombard but he was willing to concede that his occasional flashes of insight, inspiration, however you want to describe them, had been a help in their long association together.

'I'm not sure,' Lombard replied without looking up. When they reached the bustle of the Wednesday *brocante* on the place de la Victoire he sat down on a bench, still scrutinising the screen. It took a moment for Aubret to realise that the *juge* was no longer at his side, but he turned back and sat heavily on the bench, a good metre from Lombard, and sighed like a parent with a wandering child. 'It's the eyes,' Lombard said simply, passing the phone back.

'I don't see anything there.'

'Exactly. There *is* nothing there.' He shook his head. 'There is nothing in the eyes at all,' he added sadly.

'So? It's a passport style photo. No smiling allowed.'

'Yes, I get that.' Lombard stared off into the distance. 'They rinse the subject of all personality, I know. But you can't hide what's in the eyes and, I repeat, Barbier has nothing there. No joy, but no sadness either. No hate, no warmth. Nothing. Nothing at all. The man was alive when that picture was taken obviously, but not really living, if you see what I mean?'

'Kind of,' Aubret grunted, humouring his boss.

Lombard took a deep breath and frowned. He didn't really know what he meant either, but it bothered him nonetheless. 'Did you take a picture of the back of the licence?' Aubret's response was a cold stare. 'Let me rephrase that.' Lombard smiled. 'Can I see the photo of the back of the licence please, Commissaire?'

Without saying anything, Aubret found the photo and passed the phone back to Lombard who zoomed in on the image, surprising Aubret that he knew how to do so. On the back of the licence, in table form, was a list of the vehicles allowed on French roads, from small-engine motorcycles through to heavy artic loads via cars, trailers, vans.

'I haven't looked at that yet. When did he get his licence?' He was annoyed with himself for not paying more attention. If he'd had Pouget with him from the start he would have had more time for the details.

'June 16 1995. So, on his eighteenth birthday, the first day he could legally drive. He didn't hang around.'

'Maybe he wanted to get away?'

Lombard nodded slowly. 'There might be something in that, Guy. Also, a few years later he had his HGV licence and a coach driving licence.'

'And based in Tours, as the licence was issued here at the *préfecture*.'

'Yes, though if he was a long-distance driver,' Lombard conceded, 'he could have been dumped from anywhere between here and the Cévennes Mountains in the Ardèche, if we're working on the course of the river. We haven't narrowed it down still.'

'Why the Cévennes?' Aubret asked automatically, immediately regretting doing so and expecting a lecture on height, rock formation, meteorology and population trends from the trivia-obsessed Lombard.

'Because that's where the Loire first rises…' Lombard looked like he might carry on, but with obvious effort, stopped himself. 'Anyway, why are we speculating the old-fashioned way when no doubt Juliet Lemery will have all we need to know, researched, printed out and bound for us already?' He stood up and looked yearningly at the busy bar behind them. 'I'm hungry,' he said. 'Are you hungry?'

'Hungry?' Aubret couldn't suppress his surprise. 'You're normally thirsty by this point!'

Lombard smiled warmly, letting the *commissaire* know that he took no offence at the remark. Besides, it was true, he just preferred to keep people on their toes for now. His reputation and his standing in the *magistrature* itself were still under question. D'Archambeau still held a file accusing Lombard of tampering with evidence and though he had the proof that he hadn't, he was nonetheless treading a fine line. It was a high-wire act that kept him keen and a reputation for duplicity, albeit bogus, he found, was an enjoyable cloak to wear.

He stood up. 'I'm both hungry and thirsty,' he said. 'I'll get something on the way to the station. Some fruit perhaps,' he added, vastly overplaying his hand but also enjoying the effect it had on his long-time colleague who was visibly struggling having to reassess everything he thought he knew about Juge Matthieu Lombard.

'Clearly we don't know a lot yet.' Lombard was thinking aloud as they weaved their way through the crowded streets.

'I almost forgot,' Aubret was annoyed with himself. 'That's not all we found.' He stopped and produced his phone again, flicking through to the photos. Lombard took the proffered phone and shaded the screen from the sun.

'This was on the corpse?'

'It was.'

Lombard snorted and handed the phone back. 'What a mess.'

'What is?' Aubret couldn't hide his impatience.

'That image on the medallion thing. It's like Masonic tourism, there's a bit of everything there.' He took the phone back. 'Look, the fleur-de-lys. Ancient heraldic symbol of monarchy, restoration of the throne and so on. The octopus, symbolic in some traditions as signifying the inconsistencies of man. It's all a bit childish really. Probably some new upstart – supposedly secret – society trading on the trend for conspiracy theories. Send us fifty euros and we'll send you a disc on a chain and a graphic explanation of why the earth is flat. Ask Lemery to check up on it.'

'Will do. And the red circle?'

'No idea.' Lombard said diffidently, pretending he didn't have some suggestions. Aubret gave him a look, one borne of experience and a little impatience and Lombard got the hint. 'OK, it could be a Blood Moon. That usually means "new information" in a spiritual sense. It might just be an orange though,' the *juge* added. 'Like I said, childish. The more important question is: why decapitate the victim if you're going to leave ID to be found? That doesn't make any sense.'

Happier to be on solid police ground himself, Aubret nodded thoughtfully. 'I thought that and I'm hoping it's just that whoever they are, they are just sloppy. It was a heat of the moment thing, a panic decision to dump the body...'

Lombard stopped at the doorway of Les Halles, the indoor market. 'You don't believe that though, do you?' he asked softly.

'No,' was the terse reply. 'Just wishful thinking. But you never know. Another thought occurred to me that the driver's licence was planted and whoever we pulled out of the river back there *isn't* Thibaud Barbier.'

'That's possible.' Lombard stopped at a fruit and vegetable stall that looked almost unreal with its vibrant colours and inch-perfect stacking. A light mizzle of water was spraying on the lettuces, bouncing into their faces and providing a welcome relief from the heat outside.

'I'll take two peaches, please,' Lombard said to the tall girl behind the fruit. She put them carefully into a paper bag and Lombard paid. Aubret, meanwhile, looked dumbfounded. One of the things that separated Lombard from the rest was that he wasn't French. It was a line between him and everyone else not just in the Palais de Justice but in the police force as well. It wasn't quite true of course; Lombard was French. He was born in Tours itself, but had lived in the west of England until his father died when Lombard was thirteen years old. His reluctant mother had brought him back. But to everyone in Tours, he was English. In the same way that to everyone in the west of England, on Lombard's rare visits 'home', he was French. And one of the clearest indications of his 'Englishness' was his food habits. He preferred tea to coffee, drank pints rather than a *demi*, regarded snails with suspicion, liked a sandwich on the go and rarely ate fruit. Aubret had never seen him eat fruit.

Lombard offered his colleague one of the peaches, which he declined as if it might be poisoned, and then bit hard into the fruit. The juice ran down his chin messily. Aubret relaxed a little. The reason, he suspected, that he'd never seen Lombard eat fruit, was because Lombard probably hadn't.

'I've got to be honest, Guy,' Lombard said after wiping his chin with an old tissue. 'I can't stand the stuff. It's too damned messy. But, I'm trying to break old habits.'

'Why?' was the typically no-nonsense comeback.

Lombard thought about this for a second. 'To see if I can, I suppose.' He put the remainder of the peach in the bag with its twin and threw them in the bin. 'I do need to buy a fish though.'

'Are you going to eat that here too?'

'It's for the cat, Commissaire. It has expensive tastes.'

This was another change in Lombard. This borderline obsession he had for a stray cat that had turned up on his doorstep and who he hadn't yet named, but fed it fresh fish off antique eighteenth-century dinner plates.

'I'll wait outside,' the policeman said.

Five minutes later Lombard re-emerged and they continued their walk to the station.

'Could it be a signal, do you think? A sign?' Lombard was swinging the bagged fish.

'What?'

'The decapitation, I mean. Could it be a message?'

'You mean gangland stuff, *le milieu*?'

'Yes, that's exactly what I mean. They leave ID on the body, they want Thibaud Barbier to be identified. But they remove the head as a message. Don't talk, they're saying. Barbier did and look what we did to him.'

Aubret practically growled in response. If Lombard's theory was correct then it meant an entirely different approach. The case would probably even be taken out of their hands and organised crime 'specialists' would be brought in. He didn't like the thought of that. Once he had started on a case, he liked to see it doggedly through to the end, and like any self-respecting dog, he didn't like his territory being invaded by outsiders.

'There's something you don't see every day,' Lombard announced with an almost childish delight. He pointed to a small group of tourists standing on the corner of rue Marceau, looking upwards into the sun and staring at a new block of apartments. 'A real camera,' he continued. 'Nearly everyone just uses their phones nowadays.'

Aubret remained silent as they reached the police station, the *commissariat de police*. He wasn't happy. What if Lombard had come up with this gangland theory so that he *could* bring in specialists? To wash his hands, not just of Barbier, but of the job itself, which he knew from other higher-ups, would suit them greatly. He was trying to change things, he'd said so himself. This was an honourable way out, but honourable or not, it would be a pretty shitty thing to do to him after all their years together.

'Listen, Juge…' a red-faced Aubret snarled.

'Before you say anything, Commissaire,' a stony-faced Lombard interrupted. 'What we just said about a gangland message, it's between us for now, right? I know what the form is, so do you, but I want this. We do it our way. Is that understood?'

'Yes, Monsieur le Juge. Understood.'

Chapter 9

Lombard and Aubret came silently up the stairs, approaching the glass double doors without attracting attention from inside the large open-plan office. Almost everyone was out anyway. Pouget and Texeira were finishing up at the crime scene, and the 'new kid', whose name Aubret hadn't managed to chisel into Lombard's memory bank, was with them. Officer Chrétien saw the two men arrive but too late as they had seen him first. He'd been sitting at his desk, feet up, flicking through a magazine, utter disinterest in anything going on around him or with the group. Slowly he put the magazine down as the doors opened and looked up in a deliberately unhurried manner, almost in challenge, but was ignored as the two investigating grandees went straight to the *commissaire*'s glass partitioned office. He picked up his magazine again.

Chrétien knew he wasn't popular and, as it was for most things in his life, he couldn't have cared less. He was tolerated because his father had been a famous cop in Tours, long-serving and well-respected. Chrétien junior wasn't even a very good policeman but he was good with witnesses, particularly female witnesses. When pushed he could exhibit a charm, warmth and interest that was frankly lost on the rest of the squad who reluctantly had to acknowledge his talent and its merits. Though as Texeira had once remarked, 'Chrétien should have been an actor.'

Aubret closed the door behind himself and Lombard and lowered the venetian blind, shutting them off from the office. A gesture that was more symbolic than necessary as Chrétien had his back to them and was in the far corner, surrounded by a bank of screens that would make NASA proud; Juliet Lemery was probably not even aware that they had turned up.

'It's a risky game though, isn't it?' Commissaire Aubret was a stickler for rules, hierarchy and protocol. His initial agreement in wanting to stay with this case until the end, and not pass it over to some fancy organised crime squad, was now fighting a battle with his own way of doing things.

'It needn't be.' Lombard went to the window. 'Can I see Barbier's driving licence again?'

Aubret nodded towards his in-tray where Lemery had already left blown-up, hi-resolution copies of the licence. Lombard smiled at her efficiency and picked up a copy, holding it up to the light coming through the window.

'What do you mean, it needn't be?'

'I know what you're thinking, Guy. You don't want to let this case go any more than I do, but those are the rules if you suspect the involvement of organised crime.' He turned and looked seriously at Aubret. 'Well, those suspicions have to be channelled through my office. I'm in charge of this investigation. I can choose to ignore them.'

The *commissaire* narrowed his eyes. 'Even if you think those suspicions are on the money?'

'If I don't ignore them, we lose control of our own investigation.'

Aubret took a box of Gaviscon out of his pocket, while Lombard returned to the photo of Thibaud Barbier. 'I get why I don't want to give it up, I'm a stubborn bastard,' he began. 'But what's your reason? I got the feeling you weren't that bothered when you showed up at the river.'

'I was bothered, I just had stage fright.' Then he said with a sudden passion, 'But it's these eyes, Guy, look at the eyes.'

Aubret looked again. 'I still can't see anything.'

'Exactly. Exactly that.'

There was a quiet knock on the door and a timid Juliet Lemery handed Aubret a sheaf of papers. She closed the door silently as she turned and went.

A paternal look of concern from Aubret as the door shut revealed all you needed to know about the working relationship between the two.

'Still nothing?' Lombard asked softly.

Aubret sighed. 'No. I'm not trying to force the issue with her. She seems happy enough, if happy is the right word.'

'But her place is secure now?'

Aubret bristled at the thought, standing ramrod straight, as if about to march into a fight. 'I told them if they force her retirement on trauma or whatever they engineer, they'll lose me too. She may not talk since that kid blew his brains out in front of her, but she's invaluable to this squad. And anyway, we have a duty to her.'

Lombard nodded and gave a half-smile. 'I'd offer to leave with you as a mark of solidarity but I'm not sure that would help your cause.' Aubret snorted in response. 'Anyway, what has she found?'

The policeman sat down and scanned the notes. 'We have an address, home and work. He worked for Fil-Bleu, here in Tours, as a bus driver.' He shot Lombard a quick glance to see if he was gloating. He wasn't. 'Home address is, oh shit. Home address is in the *quartier* Sanitas.'

'So he probably wasn't murdered for money then,' Lombard said sarcastically.

'Not unless he was a dealer.' Aubret shrugged, before screwing up his face in disgust. 'Can you put that fish outside of the office, please? I'm finding it hard to concentrate.'

It took Lombard a second or two to follow Aubret's meaning, and it was only then that he realised that the fish, despite being in a sealed bag, was beginning to give off a distinctly fishy odour. Opening the door to the outer office, he placed the bag on the floor just outside and reclosed the door.

'So, bus driver, rough estate. Family?'

'Nothing that Lemery can find, nothing on record anyway. No marriage licence, no dependants. Some medical history, anti-depressants mainly.'

Lombard walked to the window and looked down on the street below. It was busy with people coming out from offices to enjoy the sun, laughing and chatting in groups. There was life.

'Not much is it?' he asked rhetorically.

'It's nothing. Forty-six years of life and you die alone like that, leaving nothing and no one. What's the point?' Too late he realised his mistake and visibly grimaced while both of them had their backs to one another.

'How's your family, Guy?' Lombard asked, a forced note of cheerful bonhomie in his voice, though he didn't turn around. 'Fabienne and the children?'

'They're all well, thanks.' He didn't feel this was the time to elaborate.

'That's good to hear.' Lombard smiled and turned back to the room. But Aubret saw through the smile and he'd seen those eyes before.

There was a knock at the door and a face Lombard didn't recognise poked his head round.

'Monsieur le Juge?' the young man said confidently.

'Yes.'

Aubret interrupted and immediately regretted doing so. 'Oh, this is erm…' He wished Pouget was with him.

'The new kid?' Lombard smirked as Aubret flushed, not with embarrassment but irritation. 'Benbarek? Just call me Lombard, it saves a lot of time.'

'I have your phone for you, sir,' Benbarek said, not comfortable with Lombard's lack of formality and also smart enough to see that his immediate boss, Commissaire Aubret, most certainly didn't like it. 'Commandant Pouget suggested I go over to your office and pick it up for you.' He handed the phone over and Lombard stared at it with a look of dread.

'If I must,' he said quietly. 'Thank you.' Then his mood changed immediately. 'Benbarek. Any relation?'

'Unfortunately not, sir,' the young man answered with a grin. It was a question he was used to answering. 'Though I'd claim it if I could.'

Aubret interrupted with a quiet cough, indicating that that was quite enough small talk. 'Ask Chrétien to come in, will you?' he barked.

'Sir.' The officer closed the door behind him.

'Who's Benbarek then? The original I mean.'

As usual Lombard was slightly embarrassed by his vast knowledge of trivia, or more accurately embarrassed by his inability to keep these nuggets to himself.

He sighed, as though Aubret had dragged the information out of him after a rigorous cross examination. 'Larbi Benbarek, or Ben M'Barek or just simply Ben Barek, also known as the Black Pearl and one of the greatest footballers of his generation. He played for Morocco and for France.' He let Aubret digest this irrelevance or at least try to work out if it even was an irrelevance.

'Couldn't he make his mind up then?' Lombard gave a half-smile and chose to ignore Aubret's tactlessness on roots and origins. 'Well, our kid isn't from Morocco anyway, born and raised in a grim Paris suburb and a rising star by all accounts. *Laïcité*,' he said, stressing the French constitutional law of secularism.

Lombard knew Aubret wasn't a racist, but he knew also that his value system was outdated and was stuck in the old idea that racism and religious intolerance didn't officially exist in France because everyone was counted as French by the state and religion was separate. The reality, even in a far less vicious form, in Lombard's own experience, showed a very different version of events. Aubret's problem, if indeed it was one, was that he had never been an outsider and therefore lacked empathy for it. Rather than go down a rabbit hole of reality versus the letter of the law, Lombard sat down opposite the *commissaire* and turned his phone on. It pinged about a dozen times from missed calls and messages and he could feel Aubret's eyes boring into the top of his skull as he pretended to concentrate on the screen.

Their relationship had changed since his suspension; Aubret no longer quietly tolerated Lombard's unique, hands-on approach as an investigating magistrate. Instead he huffed and puffed at the injustice of his lot, hoping that Lombard would retreat back to his own desk out of a sense of shame and just let the actual police get on with their job. Just be on call when they needed a search warrant or a phone tap. Lombard may have changed in many respects, he was even unsure as to who exactly he was now, but he wasn't going to alter his way of working nor hide away because others thought he was guilty.

'I suppose you're going to want to get involved as usual,' Aubret said eventually. Lombard nodded, still without looking up. The policeman sighed heavily again, like a teenager who doesn't get their way. 'In that case, you take Barbier's apartment and I'll go to the bus depot and speak to colleagues.' Now Lombard looked up, and Aubret was slightly unnerved by the look on his face. 'Or you can take the bus depot and I'll take the apartment,' he added.

Lombard put his phone in his pocket. 'We'll both take the apartment,' he said with a steely edge. 'And then we'll both take the bus depot. I want to get a sense of Thibaud Barbier before others tell me what they think.' He stood up. 'Coming?'

Chapter 10

Aubret pressed stop on the ignition and stared out of the window as the intermittent wipers came to a halt. The windscreen was being slowly spattered with light rain drops as he stared through them at the small shopping precinct in front of him.

'This shower has come from nowhere,' Lombard said gravely from a slumped position in the passenger seat.

'The weather isn't my priority,' Aubret replied stiffly. Through the windscreen he watched intently as a group of young men gathered on the precinct concourse. They were standing in front of a run-down *épicerie* which also advertised mobile phone repair, money telegram facilities and a few hand-written sellotaped A4 sheets in Arabic.

'Shall we go?' Lombard asked, seeing, with some amusement, his colleague's reluctance.

'I may stay here,' Aubret replied. 'Make sure my car stays in one piece.'

'Put your armband on then.' Lombard was having a bit of fun while referring to the orange *police judiciaire* armband that was worn by plain clothes policemen.

Aubret turned to him slowly. 'If I do that I'm not sure *I'll* stay in one piece.'

They both stared out of the window. The group on the precinct – some in hoodies, some in traditional Moroccan thobes, all in overpriced trainers – were trying hard not to stare back, or even register the presence of two strangers, two middle-aged white strangers, in the car park, their car park. There was no aggression, just a wary curiosity. This meagre, depressing strip of land with its graffitied shutters, its packed out pharmacy and its kebab shop that also sold pizzas and tacos, a low-wattage sop to the trend for fusion food, no doubt. It was all just convenience. Everything was quick and disposable, Lombard thought, as disposable as the people who lived in this place, hidden away off the main avenue de Grammont. There were no pretty white tourist 'trains' doing a tour of Sanitas.

'The last time I was here,' Aubret began, his voice tinged with disappointment, 'was last year. A clean-up job after the riots. The Compagnies Républicaines de Sécurité...'

'Ah, the charming anti-riot forces of the CRS. I've seen their work.'

'Exactly. They'd bashed a few heads on behalf of the state, and got a few heads bashed themselves, on behalf of what though I've no idea.'

'For something to do, I suppose,' Lombard said quietly.

'They'd have more to do if they spent less time destroying things they *do* have!' Aubret flushed in his pugnacious way. 'Their own cars burnt. A new basketball/football piste torched. Windows smashed of the shops *they* use. What's the point? What have they gained?'

'A few bashed state heads?' Lombard replied and received a look of contempt for his facetiousness. 'Maybe they don't want hand-outs from one hand and a truncheon telling them to be grateful in the other. Just a thought.'

Aubret conceded the point with a reluctant cock of the head, before they both noticed that the group in front of them parted allowing a respectful corridor to emerge for someone to pass through. That someone was a very smartly dressed woman in what Lombard had once seen described as a ball-breaker suit. A blue skirt that came to just above the knee, a fitted buttoned-up jacket of the same colour with a white blouse underneath, also button-up, heeled shoes, not too high, and a hijab of exactly the same blue as her suit. She moved a large leather laptop case from one shoulder to another and walked towards the car. Aubret opened his window.

Before either spoke, Lombard watched as the group of young men dispersed, sloping off with just a few of them looking back over their shoulders as they did so.

'Commissaire Aubret?' the woman said loudly enough for a few of the stragglers to look back. It wasn't a surprise that the two men in the car turned out to be cops; that hadn't bothered them. The woman, though, clearly represented some sort of power or even threat that the cops didn't. 'Soraya Moujahid,' she said confidently, smiling as she did so, showing perfect white teeth, but with just a smudge of red lipstick visible on the front two.

'Madame,' Aubret nodded. 'This is my colleague Juge…'

'Juge d'Instruction Matthieu Lombard, we're honoured. We don't get many famous faces in the *quartier* Sanitas. Unless it's a politician wanting to clean the streets,' she added caustically. 'Are you going into politics, Monsieur le Juge?'

She stepped back from the car door allowing Aubret to get out. He rolled his eyes at Lombard before he did so, which amused him.

Lombard closed the door behind him and stretched. 'I can't imagine anything worse than going into politics, madame,' he said with a smile. 'There's far too much of that stuff about already.'

He was greeted with a warm smile again. 'Shall we go?' she said, in a hurried business-like manner. 'I have another appointment in thirty minutes.'

They walked swiftly across a small park towards a lowish four-storey tower block about which everything looked grim. Well, almost everything. Of the sixteen apartments in the block, with their uniform brown shutters, peeling exterior walls, broken furniture and bikes on tiny balconies, two apartments had glorious floral displays. A small point of beauty in an otherwise bleak view, but which in effect only highlighted just how run-down, forgotten and unloved the rest of it was.

'You must be well known around here, madame,' Aubret said, as they approached a heavy-duty door, the same colour as the shutters. 'I'm not sure I'd have walked through a group like that, certainly not with your confidence.'

Lombard had often thought how the *commissaire*'s lack of tact or political awareness was actually a help, more than a hindrance, in an investigation. He had an innate ability to make people very angry, very quickly. It caught them off-guard so any front they were attempting to hide behind could quickly fall apart. But despite a brief flash of something, perhaps anger, in the eyes, Soraya Moujahid did not lose her poise.

'We are very different, Commissaire,' she said, loading the short sentence with multiple meanings. 'You are the law and that frankly doesn't stand for much around here; you are too often the enemy.'

'And you are a friend, madame?' Aubret snarled.

Again, Madame Moujahid was unconcerned by his forthright approach. 'I own a lot of property around here,' she paused for effect. 'I can throw their mothers out on to the street. They leave me alone for that reason and that reason alone.'

'You personally own the property?' Lombard asked.

'Yes,' was the simple reply. 'Well, my company does.'

'And have you thrown mothers out on to the street?'

She met his eyes directly. 'Not yet. The threat has so far been enough.' Lombard nodded silently, unwilling to hide his distaste. 'Are you going to lecture me on compassionate capitalism, Monsieur le Juge?' This time she smirked, tapped a code into a panel by the door, waited for a click and pulled the door open.

'As I said, madame, I'm not all that interested in politics and even less so in slogan oxymorons. Shall we go in?'

The big grin she gave him in response was a pleasant surprise, and she waved them both in.

Inside was dark and damp and it smelt badly, more like the stairs of an underground car park than a place where people lived. If it bothered Madame Moujahid she didn't show it, though she made a vocal note about getting the lightbulb changed. She led the way up the stairs.

'Monsieur Barbier lives on the third floor. What's he done anyway? I was told nothing on the phone but it must be serious to bring out a *commissaire* and a *juge*.'

'What makes you think he's done anything, madame?' Aubret asked gruffly.

'Why are you two here if he hasn't?' she countered. Nobody spoke for a second or two. 'He's a good tenant, Monsieur Barbier, in that he pays on time, every time. But we have had complaints in the past.'

'About what?' Lombard seemed surprised.

'About his... well, his habits, I suppose you'd say. The walls are very thin. I didn't build the place, I just own it,' she added quickly. 'And he'd be up in the middle of the night cooking. Pans clattering, bottles smashing. I'm guessing he drank. Even the smell of food goes through the walls here. So, we had complaints about anti-social behaviour and so on.'

'Did you do anything about these complaints? Could you do anything about them even?' Lombard was a couple of steps behind the other two. It was noticeable, even in a run-down place like this, how much pride people took in their home. Not all of them, some doors had what looked like punched holes in them, but they were the minority. Others had doormats outside, a selection of sisal mats with 'Bienvenue' or even 'Hello' – English still being considered the byword in chic for home decoration.

'Of course I did something about them. I logged them.' Madame Moujahid turned and smiled. 'Seriously though, I don't know what people expect me to do. Tell the man to stop cooking at night? Cut down on the drink? I'm his landlord, not his mother.'

'Or his wife,' Aubret added.

'I think a mother would be more likely than a wife. Here we are.' She took a set of keys out of her bag and turned the lock, but didn't open the door immediately. Instead she turned to the other two. 'Now I'm guessing you two gentlemen have seen some horrors in your time,' she started sarcastically. 'But I must warn you before we go in. You won't tell me what Monsieur Barbier has done, but I can tell you what he's like. He's a... how can I put this? He's a slob, sorry. The place is filthy and it stinks. He takes no pride in himself and so none in his apartment. Just a warning.'

She swung the door open. Inside was bright; the rain outside had stopped and the sun was streaming through a large window which had no blinds. Everything was neat, tidy and clean. Almost show home clean, like Lombard and

Aubret were prospective tenants and the place had just been professionally cleaned.

'What has he done, gentlemen?' Madame Moujahid asked without taking her shocked eyes off the gleaming apartment.

Chapter 11

Soraya Moujahid led the way gingerly into the open-plan living room and kitchen. 'This place was like a Sunday morning outside McDonald's and Domino's the last time I was here.' She seemed almost awestruck.

'When would that have been exactly?' Aubret asked, before adding, 'Please don't touch anything, madame. We'll have to get forensics in.'

She looked at him, then at Lombard. 'Please tell me what's going on? I know as a landlord I should be pleased at seeing one of my properties so clean, but it's so different, it's almost disturbing.'

Aubret and Lombard looked at each other. 'I'm going to make some calls,' Aubret said, wandering back to the corridor. 'And please don't touch anything.'

'You already said that, Commissaire!'

'I wasn't talking to you, madame,' Aubret said without looking over his shoulder.

Lombard shrugged.

'Your colleague's a real charmer,' Soraya said.

'And his bite is worse than his bark unfortunately. He's a damn good policeman though.'

'He needs to be with a personality like that.'

Lombard walked around the living room, noting the view of the shopping precinct from the window, the sharp tidiness of every surface, where it looked like ornaments, though there were few, had been placed deliberately and with precision. A stack of old *Monster Truck* magazines were aligned perfectly under the television, next to a pile of neat DVDs, also of truck stunt shows. That seemed the only thing so far that seemed a hobby, an interest. Something wasn't quite right though and he sniffed the air. 'It's quite stale in here, don't you think?' he asked rhetorically. 'It smells clean but old clean if that makes sense. Sorry. Thinking aloud, I often do that these days. When did you last see your tenant, madame?'

She took a deep breath, trying to maintain her composure. 'Please tell me why.' There was a hint of desperation in her voice, but he didn't reply, just kept sniffing the air. After a few seconds in which she realised he wasn't going to tell her, or at least not yet, she put her bag on the ground and took out her phone. Her desperation had now turned to annoyance. 'According to my diary, Madame Bilal, she's in the flat downstairs, complained to me about the late-night noise on May 25, so what's that, five weeks ago? I visited here a couple of days after that.'

'And what did you say to Monsieur Barbier?'

'I told him what he got up to in his own place was his own business, but that he needed to show some respect to others in the building.'

'You didn't threaten to throw him out?'

'No! It was just a polite warning. I did say he might want to tidy up a bit though.'

Lombard turned back from the kitchen where he'd been opening drawers and cupboards, holding a handkerchief as he did so. 'How did he take it?'

'Look around.' Soraya gave a false laugh. 'It looks like he took it pretty well.'

'I mean at the time,' he asked gently.

She glanced down at her phone but only to avoid Lombard's grey eyes. 'I thought he was going to cry,' she replied.

'What did he say exactly?'

'He didn't *say* anything. He nodded and shrugged and just sort of, I don't know how to describe it, he just sort of blubbered. He's a very large man, fat I mean, obese. He always looks like he's shaking. And I think I frightened him. Not just that time, but whenever we met, which wasn't often.'

'Did he need references to rent the apartment?'

'Yes. I got them from his previous landlord. An apartment he rented in Lyon. He's been here three years.'

Aubret came back in. 'So,' he said, putting his phone in his back pocket. 'What do you think, madame?'

It was Lombard who interrupted. 'The body of Thibaud Barbier was found this morning, washed up on the banks of the Loire, near the Pont Napoléon.'

A range of emotions swept quickly over Soraya Moujahid's face, before settling on resigned sadness. 'Suicide.' It wasn't a question exactly, more of a statement of presumed fact.

'We don't know for sure the cause of death, yet,' Aubret said. 'But...'

Again Lombard spoke over him. 'What makes you think it was suicide, madame?'

She turned to him and shrugged. 'I don't know really. He always seemed so sad, so unhappy. I don't think I ever saw him talk to another person, not one. Are you saying it wasn't suicide then?'

Lombard and Aubret exchanged a quick glance. 'I'd ask you to sit down, but that would go against the rules before forensics get here.' Lombard took a deep breath. 'Monsieur Barbier's head had been cut off.'

She instinctively lifted a hand to her mouth, her eyes opening suddenly wide and darting in shock. They let her regain her composure, watching intently all the time. In the end she just said simply, 'That's horrible.'

'At the moment we don't know why, or when, or even where.' Aubret shuffled irritably, annoyed, feeling Lombard was revealing too much. 'You say you saw him last five weeks ago. We'll need to speak to Madame Bilal downstairs.' He turned to Aubret. 'She lives below and complained about the noise.'

'She might be in.' Soraya adjusted her hijab and put her diary back in her bag. 'She works nights at a care home. I can go and check for you. She won't like being woken up though.'

'Thank you, if you would.'

'I'll come with you, madame.' Aubret was already unhappy about what he saw as his investigation demarcation lines being trashed. They both left quietly, leaving Lombard to look around on his own. First he placed his handkerchief on a kitchen stool near a small breakfast bar and tried to take in what he saw. The place looked clean but not lived in, why? Had Barbier's murder taken place here and then been surgically sterilised? If so, then forensics would find something, he was almost certain of that. It wouldn't be possible to decapitate a victim in a small living space and escape modern scientific detection methods.

Had Barbier cleaned it himself? Surely a warning, if it had been just a warning, from his landlord wouldn't have frightened him into such clinical action? And if it had, why were there no signs of anyone living in the place since?

He stood up and went to check on the bedroom and bathroom. So what would provoke a 'slob', as Soraya Moujahid had indelicately put it, to clean up their act? That answer seemed obvious – what else causes a man to completely change his habits? Love, usually. Or at least the prospect of it, the merest hint of it. Of course, that could also work in the opposite direction. A previously fastidious individual could lose love, and become a Thibaud Barbier. An apparently friendless, obese man. A slob.

Subconsciously Lombard sucked his stomach in, reminded himself to tidy up his own apartment later, and opened the bedroom door. The bed was neatly made, though the sheets looked old, hospital grey rather than starchy white. The clothes were an odd mix. Work uniforms and triple-extra-large sweat-pants, cheap supermarket makes with tops to match. But there were also a few other bits, smaller and still with tags on that were completely out of place. There was a pair of slip-on shoes, recently polished, with worn-down soles. He opened a few drawers and, careful not to disturb anything, looked for signs of the man's personality. All he had so far were some old magazines, stacked up as though he were in a garage waiting for his car to be fixed. He bent down and looked under the bed, an area that had clearly been overlooked by some of the more rigorous cleaning. There was a book, which had been dropped on the floor. Rather than move it, Lombard got the torch on his phone and tried to read the spine. *L'humanité en péril* by Fred Vargas. Finally, a hint of something to go on maybe. He knew of Fred Vargas, a crime writer with a quirky *commissaire*. Madeleine had loved her books. He left it where it was and went to the bathroom.

The bathroom was like stepping back into the 1980s. A peach-coloured bath and sink, a rubber shower head attached to an ancient double tap. A tired shower curtain hanging from a rail that looked like it was staying up purely as a result of goodwill. He shook his head. It was all profoundly depressing. Leaving aside the recent cleaning-up operation of the place, the apartment seemed to reflect almost exactly what he knew of its tenant. Unloved, tired, just about holding it together as the rest of the world sped by. He snorted a sarcastic laugh at his own conclusions. He was clearly spending too much time around therapists; their pat conclusions were beginning to rub off on him. All the same, he had to admit, there may be something in it.

It was the sadness, the loneliness of the existence that got to him. It just didn't fit with the violence of its ending. He placed his handkerchief on the closed toilet seat and sat down, almost sliding off as the seat moved sideways under the pressure. He knew what his problem was. He'd known it the minute he had seen the eyes of the dead man on the driving licence. They weren't that dissimilar.

After all, who, outside of work, had Lombard spoken to that day? A kid wearing headphones on a bus, an angry weights junkie, his cat and Madeleine. Only the kid and the muscle-bound gym rat had replied. He stood up and opened the small glass cabinet on the wall. Toothpaste, toothbrush, disposable razors, cheap shaving foam but, next to them, three different brands of expensive men's aftershave. Very expensive men's aftershave and two of them were still in their cellophane wrapping. Along with the new clothes still tagged, they told a story.

Thibaud Barbier had found a glimmer of hope. And sometimes it really is the hope that kills you.

Chapter 12

Aubret drove them through the backstreets of the *quartier* Sanitas and via the slightly more genteel neighbourhood of Beaujardin out towards the Fil-Bleu bus depot in Saint-Pierre des Corps. If the centre of the old city of Tours dripped with history, beauty and pageantry, then Saint-Pierre des Corps with its enormous shopping malls, a permanently rammed IKEA, industrial estates, edge-of-town exhibition centre and stadium, was what kept the modern side going in the direction of bustling progress – very much the tool shed of Tours. Inevitably it was not to Aubret's taste, though Lombard liked the contrast.

'We're seeing some real tourist high spots with this one,' the *commissaire* grumbled as he turned into the expansive car park of the depot. 'Look, Sanitas on wheels.' He nodded towards the enormous Romany camp that was next door to the bus depot. Provided by the city, each spot had its own toilet facilities, electricity and concrete post washing lines.

'If Madame Bilal worked nights, why did she complain about the noise and smell coming from Barbier's apartment in the middle of the night?' Lombard asked instead, deciding to ignore the remark.

'Yeah, that struck me too. I checked, she complained on behalf of her kids. Two boys, thirteen and ten.'

'And they're left on their own at night?' Lombard's instinctive reaction made it sound like a criticism, which he hadn't intended.

'Yeah. Poor kids. There's an uncle lives nearby if anything happens, but it's the only job she could find.'

'No husband?'

'Ran off years ago according to Madame Moujahid.'

Lombard looked around at the comings and goings of the buses. 'You made sure they don't know we're coming like I asked?' The question was posed to Aubret's back as he got out of the car.

'I did. Excuse me.' Aubret stopped a scruffily dressed man, rushing with his head down and carrying a baguette and some supermarket pâté. 'Who's in charge around here?'

'Well, it ain't the workers that's for sure!' the man snorted and carried on without breaking stride. Lombard didn't bother to hide his amusement as Aubret shook his head and exhaled a defeated half-laugh.

'I've found the union rep at least,' he said. 'Let's try that office over there.'

The office, such as it was, was a Portakabin parked half in the bus hangar and half outside, as though nobody could make a positive decision either way and had compromised. Aubret knocked on the door.

'Yep?' came a harassed voice from within. Aubret opened the door and climbed the few steps, Lombard just behind him closing the door as they entered the cheap office. There was a strong smell of stale coffee, the carpet tiles were coming away from the floor, a broken blind, half shut, was like the Portakabin's position itself, indecisive, was it up or down? An empty water cooler looked like it was gasping for a drink itself. And behind a small desk, which housed an enormous computer monitor, sat a middle-aged woman, vaping on something that smelt like a sweet shop. The woman peeled her eyes away from the monitor and put her glasses on to the top of her head, showing dark roots under her too blonde hair as she did so.

'Well, this doesn't look like good news,' she said sardonically, releasing a dense cloud of sickly vape, which she waved away. 'What can I do for you, gentlemen?'

Aubret made the introductions. 'Are you in charge around here?' he then asked, with a note of wariness.

'This place is such chaos, Commissaire, that I don't like to admit it, but yes. I guess I'm the most senior you'll find on this site. I'm Rosalie Lavigne, coordinator. I forget my official title. What's up?'

'Thibaud Barbier,' Lombard said simply. Madame Lavigne just looked blankly back at him.

'Is he one of mine?' she asked, a hint of apology in her voice. 'I should know really.' Lombard showed her the photograph and she put her glasses back on to take a closer look. 'Ah.' She sat back in triumph and relief. 'Line eleven. I know him now. We all know him as Boudah.'

'Because of his size?' Lombard asked.

'Yep. But also because he never says anything. He turns up, drives a bus, goes home. But he's not here,' she added. 'He's on annual leave.' She tapped something on to the keyboard. 'Yep, he saved up all his holidays, now he's got a month off. Lucky sod.'

'Thanks, madame,' Aubret said, unsure of whether to tell her the news.

'You immediately recognised him as line eleven,' Lombard said quietly, still looking at the screen. 'Do you know all your drivers by their routes?'

She put her glasses back on her head. 'Some I do, certainly Boudah, sorry, whatsisname…'

'Thibaud Barbier.' Lombard's voice was steely and Aubret tensed, sensing the *juge* was getting angry. 'His name was Thibaud Barbier.'

'Well, Barbier always wanted line eleven. He would get quite upset if he didn't get it. I remember now one of the other drivers telling me he saw him crying once. Hang on, you said his name *was* Thibaud Barbier? What's happened?'

Lombard gave Aubret a look giving permission to go ahead. 'Monsieur Barbier was fished out of the Loire this morning,' he said simply.

Rosalie Lavigne took a long, long drag on her vape, leant back and blew the smoke out on to damp, stained polystyrene ceiling tiles. 'Well, don't I look like a stone-cold bitch now?' She leant forward on her desk and looked from one to the other. 'That wasn't very nice of you, you know?'

It was Lombard who answered. 'Sorry, madame, but you were very honest. These things can't be cleared up or explained if everybody prepares a false eulogy.'

'No, I guess not. Poor Monsieur Barbier,' she said, proving Lombard's point. 'I'll print out his employment record for you. But like I said, he worked his shifts, went home.'

'Any time off for sickness?' Aubret asked.

'No. None at all.' She went to say something else then stopped.

'What is it, madame?' Aubret asked.

She sighed. 'He had a toothache once, he got an appointment but it was during a shift.' She looked at them guiltily. 'I gave him a hard time, I shouldn't have but I did. He skipped the appointment.'

'Was he bullied then?' Lombard's voice was harsh.

'No!' she snapped back. 'It wasn't like that. He just always rolled over, hated the thought of any confrontation.' She sniffed and grabbed a tissue from a box by her keyboard.

'And he always wanted line eleven...' Aubret mulled it over.

'It goes from Justices east of here, over to Mareuil past Fondettes, west of Tours.'

Both Aubret and Rosalie looked at him the way people might look at a precocious seven-year-old who can recite pi to a hundred decimal places, a mixture of admiration and alarm. Lombard didn't return their looks. 'I was on that bus route this morning,' was all he said.

Rosalie gave him the printout of Barbier's record. 'Is there anyone else we can talk to?' Aubret asked. 'Might someone have known him better than you?'

She gave him a hard stare. 'You could try, there's a shift change in twenty minutes. Try the coffee room, there'll be some drivers there. Want me to come with you?'

'No thanks,' Lombard said softly.

'There's no way you can let them know we're coming, is there?' Aubret's question was deliberately belligerent.

'No,' was the firm response. 'And even if there was, I wouldn't,' Rosalie replied.

'And thank you,' Lombard said genuinely, and with a touch of guilt.

She tried to smile in response but it was clear that she felt pretty rotten. 'Was it suicide?' Her voice seemed on the verge of breaking.

'Now why does everyone keep asking that?' the *juge* replied, though he didn't wait for an answer.

'You know,' – Aubret smiled as he talked, catching up with Lombard in the hangar – 'there was a time you wouldn't have done it that way.'

'How do you mean?'

'You'd have been… softer, with her maybe? Held back.'

Lombard stopped walking, and put his hand firmly on the *commissaire*'s shoulder. 'No, Guy. I would have always *done it* like that, you're just reading into it what you want to see.' He looked his old colleague directly in the eye, but said no more. In response Aubret raised an eyebrow, but he knew also where he stood.

'If you say so, Monsieur le Juge,' he said. 'If you say so.' They walked across the concrete hangar floor, stepping over electric charging cables. Then a pair of doors opposite them smashed open and a man hunched up in anger stalked out. It was the man they'd met when they first arrived. 'Hey, Lenin,' Aubret growled, grabbing his arm. 'Just the man I wanted to see. I want to talk to you about Boudah and his union membership.'

The man looked down at Aubret's hand on his arm; the look in his eye was of someone deciding whether it was worth the fight. The look in Aubret's eyes told him it wasn't.

'My shift starts in five minutes,' was all he said.

'Your shift starts in fifteen minutes,' Lombard said, looking at his watch. 'We won't use it all.'

The three of them walked back through the door into a windowless badly lit room. There were tables and chairs left messily as they were by people who had vacated them earlier. Two large coffee dispensers hummed against the wall; another empty water cooler and a large fake cheese plant only added to the melancholy of the place. There were three other people already in there, all noticeably at separate tables.

'Can you introduce us to your friends?' Aubret asked sarcastically, as all eyes turned away from their phone screens and towards the newcomers at the door.

'That's Magali,' he said, pointing to a small, mousy woman who was smartly dressed in her pristine uniform. 'That's Patrice,' he nodded at an unshaven man who had also made an effort with his dress. 'And that's young Robert.' Robert barely bothered to look up, and if any effort had been made with his uniform, it was to make it not look like a uniform. The tie was tied into a tiny knot and tucked in just below the collar, the sleeves rolled up revealing a gallery of Gothic art tattoos.

'And you are?' Lombard asked with a warm smile.

'I'm Denis, Denis Petit. I'm the rep here for the union.' He puffed out his chest at that and Aubret threw a quick grin at Lombard. Young Robert snorted in derision but stayed glued to his phone.

'Right,' Aubret said to the room. 'Thibaud Barbier, what can you tell us about him?' Nobody said anything. 'Nothing? Come on, he's a colleague...'

'You haven't told us who you are yet?' Robert finally looked up from his screen and challengingly at Aubret.

'I'm Commissaire Guy Aubret, this is Juge Lombard, we are...'

'None of us have to say anything.' Robert returned to his phone.

'Yes, he's right!' the union man agreed. 'This is an infringement of our rights as workers.'

'Oh be quiet, Denis!' It was Magali in the corner giving the reprimand. 'He smells,' she added simply. 'Sorry, but it's the truth.'

Patrice looked stunned at her honesty, his head sinking into his shirt collar like a startled tortoise. But he nodded his agreement all the same.

'I don't think I ever even spoke to him,' Robert said. 'Maybe a hello, but never more.'

'I thought you didn't want to say anything?' Aubret growled.

Robert looked up, his face that of a student about to crush the teacher's logic. 'There's a difference between not wanting to say anything and having nothing to say, Commissaire.'

'He refused to join the union,' Denis offered, the affront obvious.

'Did he join this instead?' He held up the image of Barbier's medallion.

'What is that?'

'Probably nothing. Did he say why he didn't want to join the union?' Lombard asked.

'Just said it wasn't for him. But you see, what with you being here, we could have protected him.'

'From what?' Lombard's eyes locked in on the now nervous union man.

'From whatever it is that you're here for!'

'Monsieur Barbier was found dead this morning. His body was pulled out of the Loire.'

Lombard let the news sink in. They still stared mainly at their phones again, but that wasn't the real focus of their concentration. Denis found a chair and sat down. Robert put his phone down slowly, Patrice sank even further into himself and Magali sniffed a little, reaching in her pocket for a tissue.

'We just want to know a bit about him,' Aubret said, his tone softer than before.

Finally, it was Patrice who broke the ensuing silence. 'None of us really know each other at all,' he said, his voice surprisingly deep for a small man. A few more questions were asked, the answers serving only to prove the man's point.

After a few minutes, Lombard shrugged and angrily pulled the door open. He heard Aubret ask anyone to get in touch if they remembered anything and stood waiting in the hangar, where the *commissaire* presently joined him.

'If I hadn't seen his body this morning,' Aubret sighed, 'I'd be wondering if he even existed.'

They began making their way back to the car. 'Excuse me?' A flustered Magali rushed up to them. 'Sorry, erm. Look. He didn't always smell. Well, he did. What I mean is… the last time I saw him here, weeks ago now, he smelt nice.'

'You mean he was wearing aftershave?' Lombard asked.

'No. Not aftershave exactly. He just smelt clean, soap clean, you know. He'd had a haircut too. I said to him, "Get you, who are you trying to impress?"'

'And what did he say?'

She looked down at the floor, pulling at her tissue. 'He didn't say anything, but he did smile. I'd never seen him smile before.'

Chapter 13

'Are you getting in?' Aubret asked impatiently through the open car window, the engine already running. Lombard was leaning back on the rear passenger door, his hands deep in the pockets of his blue linen trousers. He didn't look like a *juge d'instruction* or, as Balzac had named them, one of 'the most powerful men in France'. He looked like a lost and truculent teenager.

'I'm going to walk back, I think,' he said eventually.

'From here? It'll take an hour at least.'

'I have the time. You go back to the office, see if there's news from Pouget and Texeira.' He paused. 'Sorry, like you need me to tell you your job!'

Aubret turned the engine off. 'Is everything okay?' he asked quietly.

'Of course!' Lombard's smile was as fake as a market-bought Rolex; even he wasn't fooled by it. 'I need some time to think, that's all. I just need to be alone for a bit.'

The moment for anything like their former comradeship was gone and Aubret restarted the engine. 'Don't bottle it all up and play the loner on this, Monsieur le Juge,' he said, almost angrily. 'You've seen what happens to the loners around here. I don't want to be fishing you out of the Loire.' He put the car into gear and drove off. As usual his jackhammer diplomacy had revealed more than he knew.

Lombard removed his jacket, loosened his tie and put his hands back in his pockets. Aubret was right. He saw signs of himself in the life of the unfortunate Thibaud Barbier and it hurt. And though Lombard wouldn't describe himself as a loner, he would say he was lonely and didn't that just amount to the same thing? People were struggling to say anything concrete about Barbier in death because, aside from complaints about him, he'd barely impacted them alive. Nobody mourned, and nobody even realised he wasn't around any longer.

He stopped at IKEA and bought a vile-looking hotdog and a bottle of water. There was almost a frenzy in the air, couples and young families pawing over flat-packed furniture like hyenas with the husk of a felled wildebeest. Couples and young families though. Planning a future, literally building their lives together one Swedish MDF bookcase at a time. It felt very alien to him, the emotions involved were no longer emotions he remembered or currently had, like a nerve ending that had been cauterised. You could be cynical about them, or you could have regrets and jealousy. Lombard had all three.

He threw the hot dog, uneaten, into a bin, getting a suspicious and angry look from a little girl. 'I forgot I'm vegetarian,' he smiled, getting a doubling down on suspicious and angry for his troubles.

He took a deep breath as he emerged back into the sunlight, hooked his jacket over his shoulder, took a big glug of water and restarted the walk back into town. He actually felt a bit better for having recognised the issue he had with the dead man. If Aubret had realised it before he had, and he'd certainly articulated it in his inimitable style, then Lombard needed to get his 'head out of the air' as the French would say. He wasn't going to be much use to Thibaud Barbier if he just mooned about feeling sorry for them both.

Thirty minutes later, with sweat clogging his shirt collar, he took another long drink. This time it was a cold beer from a bar outside the station and he'd ordered a *tartine Savoyarde* which would probably serve as dinner as well as an afternoon snack. The table was shaded and offered some respite from the sun. It also gave him a great vantage point to watch the hectic comings and goings of the Léonard da Vinci Garden. He couldn't imagine the great man would be all that impressed with what had been erected in his honour. There was so much architectural beauty in Tours and yet post-war town planners seemed hell-bent on contrasting it with brutalist structures that were more Eastern bloc than Loire Valley. The water fountain looked like a capsized boat, a plastic monstrosity that acted as a meeting point for the town's drunks and pickpockets. Not that he minded drunks and pickpockets. He firmly believed that to be a great city you needed a firm history, beauty, parks, a university to provide youth and, for the contrast, the kind of people you'd cross the street to avoid. *Les clodos*, as his mother would call them, bums, curling her lip while chucking them a few centimes if she thought Lombard wasn't looking.

'Oh shit!' he exclaimed, suddenly remembering something and pulling his phone from his pocket. The phone rang longer than usual, either because his mother hadn't yet woken from her late afternoon nap or, more likely, she saw it was him and was making him sweat. Rightly so, he realised, he'd been feeling sorry for himself and had completely forgotten about the family he actually had. If it was mourners he wanted, he knew that she would mourn him terribly.

Perhaps even finally show the love for him in his death that she was unable to show in his life. Eventually she picked up.

'Yes?' she said, and he had visions of her stamping her foot at the same time.

'Maman, lunch,' he gabbled. 'I completely forgot.'

'So did I,' she said simply. 'Never mind.' It was entirely possible that she was speaking the truth. Charlotte Lombard's social life had never let up. It had started some time around her teens in the early Sixties, and carried on since. She described herself as an activist and there had been no shortage of causes in her life, each and every one of them meaning more to her than any traditional familial ties. His father, an English policeman, had been a one-night stand. The result had been dumped with James and she had returned to France. When his father died, there was nowhere else for young Matthew Spence, as he was known then, to go, but the next thirty-odd years still felt like mother and son were working each other out.

'I was working,' he began.

'On a case!' For all her faults and her anti-state leanings, she was immensely proud of her son. 'That weasel D'Archambeau actually put you on a proper investigation then!'

Lombard laughed. 'The weasel D'Archambeau is away at a conference and there was no way to contact him. I happened to be around.'

'Well done you!' Any pretend indignation at the missed lunch date was dropped. 'You must tell me all the gory details,' she said salaciously.

'I'm taking you to lunch on Sunday. I'll tell you all about it then.'

'Where are you taking me? There's a new vegetarian restaurant in Saint-Cyr.' Lombard rolled his eyes, which if she'd seen him do would have created mixed feelings. Irritation at his unwillingness to try different things and pride that at least that was the Frenchness in him.

'Well, we'll see. It may be booked up.' He doubted it.

'Oh!' Charlotte said suddenly. 'I forgot! I can't make Sunday.' She tried to dampen her obvious enthusiasm, so as not to provoke his interest.

'What is it this time, Maman?' He feigned an interest, also not wishing to provoke her; theirs was an eggshell relationship, always so fragile.

'I'm not at liberty to say,' she replied, coquettishly. He didn't like the sound of that. He had more sympathy with her campaigns than she realised, but some of these protests – anti-government, anti-racist, pro-trans, environmental – they had become more violent in recent times. The genuine activist groups infiltrated by nihilists of both extremes, old enemies finding common ground in wanton destruction.

'Please be careful, Maman,' he said, gently. 'And behave yourself.'

'I will not!' she retorted, a playful edge to her voice. 'I can do what I like! I know the *juge d'instruction*!' The phone was turned off at her end, as he knew it would be. A parting shot from a woman who always had to have the last word. So much like Madeleine, he smiled, and the reason then that they never really got on.

His phone vibrated on the round table; this time it was Aubret.

'Which *gym* are you in this time?' he asked sarcastically, and Lombard could tell he was chewing on the inevitable Gaviscon.

'I'm just having a power juice after an afternoon's exercise,' he replied. 'What's up?'

'I thought I'd keep you up to date, save you from coming into my office.'

'I don't mind coming to the office.' Lombard felt slightly affronted.

'Yes, that's as maybe,' the *commissaire* took a deep breath, 'but you're not very popular around here at the moment.' The words hurt Lombard and he couldn't help it. Again this vulnerability, this sudden desire in light of the Barbier investigation not to feel alone or ignored.

'If you say so,' he replied.

'You left that damned fish rotting here, the place smells like a small port in Normandy!'

Lombard took a deep breath, admonishing his oversensibility. More work for his grief counsellor.

'So, any other news?' he asked. 'Apart from decaying marine life?'

'Not much. Texeira hasn't had much luck with the streetwalkers; he's saying it's their shift patterns though. They'll be out later and he'll go back.'

'Overtime or browsing?'

'I'll ignore that. Lemery hasn't uncovered much. As before, no family, no record. Born in the east near Strasbourg, left school at sixteen, apprentice mechanic. A succession of driving jobs around the country.'

'Why the nomad existence?'

'I don't know. Maybe he just pissed people off wherever he went and moved on.'

It sounded horribly plausible.

'There must be something else, Guy. Why has he suddenly smartened up, his apartment and himself? We need to know his habits.'

'Agreed. I'll let you know if anything else turns up.'

'What about the autopsy?'

'Tomorrow, late morning. Pouget's going. Do you want to go?'

'Not really.'

'No, me neither. She's got the stomach for it. Talking of strong stomachs, the new kid…'

'Benbarek.'

'Benbarek, right. He's delivered your fish to your door.'

'Oh thanks,' Lombard replied sarcastically. 'That'll please the neighbours.'

'Probably not is my guess.' His tone was getting friendlier. 'Anyway, I'll talk to you tomorrow. And Lombard…'

'Yes, Guy.'

'Don't have too many power juices, eh?'

In the end, the advice was ignored. Not massively so, but enough for Lombard to return to 'their' favourite place. The Parc Mirabeau, a short walk from home, and where he and Madeleine had lazed away the hours talking and reading. Over the last few months he'd got to know the council workers who locked the gate at night and if they found him asleep on a bench, they'd leave him there, knowing who he was. He'd climb the gate when it was time to go home, on his own, leaving Madeleine somewhere in the park.

He walked slowly home, enjoying the cooler night air. He felt lightened by his nap, and by being, he was convinced, in company with his wife. There was a time when she would talk to him there, while he wrestled with his demons and his mistakes. But he felt that they had made peace now.

He turned from the rue Emile Zola and into rue Buffon and immediately he smelt his own doorway. The fish, which had clearly been there for some hours, was screaming pungently for attention and there were a number of cats hanging around, none of which was his own. He made sure no one was about, grabbed the sealed bag and ran to the *préfecture* car park, just fifty metres or so away. If the stench of rotting fish carcass deserved a home, it was as near as he could get it to high political office.

Feeling guilty, childish and elated in equal measure, he went to his own front door at Madeleine's now seldom open antiques shop, opposite the Grand Théâtre de Tours. The moon, high in a cloudless night, gave the image a wonderfully Gothic feel. He pushed open the door and his cat immediately appeared, curling round his legs and no doubt wondering where the source of the lingering smell was to be found. 'Sorry, cat,' Lombard said. 'I don't think you'd have enjoyed that anyway.' The moon filtered through the shop windows, casting shadows that looked like a German expressionism exhibition, each projection a grotesque image of its real self.

Then he saw them. Two bare feet dangling off the end of the antique Louis XV giltwood divan. The feet were exposed by the moonlight, but the rest of the body was in darkness. He bent down to try and get a better look and fumbled for the torch on his phone. The hair was shaved and he couldn't tell if it was male or female; nothing in their dress gave any further clues, but the feet were small and delicate, dirty too. He sat back on his haunches wondering whether to wake whoever it was up, which obviously he should do, if they could be woken that is. The cat was less wary than he was, and after rubbing along his thighs briefly, it jumped on to the divan. The person gave a deep breath and a sigh and turned over, waking suddenly, blinded by Lombard's phone torch. A young woman put her hands over her eyes.

'Uncle Matt?' she asked, nervously.

Chapter 14

At first he had no idea what was going on. He hadn't heard that name in a few years and it threw him, literally, backwards in shock.

'Elise?' he asked in disbelief. Then he recognised her. The last time he'd seen her, she was a slightly geeky eighteen-year-old. Her parents had held a party to celebrate her *baccalauréat* results and he and Madeleine had travelled up to Rouen for the occasion. She looked very different. Gone were the sensible shoulder-length bob and knee-length dresses. Her shaved head made her look beautiful, but it also felt like a statement of anger. She wore baggy black canvas trousers and an equally baggy jumper.

She smiled and hugged him tightly. 'It's so nice to see you,' she said and squeezed him tighter. Much tighter than she had ever done before, setting off Lombard's alarm system. *She must be in trouble*, was his immediate thought.

'Where have you been?' He pulled back from the embrace. 'Your parents were absolutely distraught when you ran away.'

She pulled back too, a defensive look in her brown eyes. 'They know I'm all right. I text Mum every now and then to let her know I'm alive.'

'You know that's not enough,' Lombard admonished, while trying to remain an ally. 'Why did you go like that? Without telling them.'

She slumped back on the furniture, elements of the teenager she once was rising to the surface. 'Do we have to talk about this now?' It was a sulky response, one that he sensed might create a barrier if he pushed it.

He stood up. He had some sympathy with directionless travel, and he certainly sympathised with Elise who had been very close to her aunt until she'd left home.

'Have you eaten?' he asked, standing up. Then realising that even if she said no he had nothing in at all.

'I'm fine,' she said, yawning. 'When was the last time you saw them?' She tried to make it sound indifferent, but it didn't work.

'Your parents? At the funeral. Like I said, your mother was distraught.'

There was a long silence.

'What funeral?' The question was asked so quietly as to be barely audible and it was drenched in fear.

'Oh God.' Lombard's reaction was involuntary. 'You don't know, do you?'

An hour later they were sitting on a bench in the locked Parc Mirabeau under the moonlight eating greasy kebabs from polystyrene boxes with abrasive wooden forks.

Elise spoke quietly, her voice occasionally breaking with emotion, but she spoke with an emotional maturity that Lombard was grateful for, but which he knew he would have had to shut down if it had come from someone else. He didn't like to discuss Madeleine even with his grief counsellor, but he felt he owed it to Elise, who had been utterly rocked by the news. He talked about how swift Madeleine's physical decline had been, but that her spirit never sagged. She was still angry at the world and what was happening to it politically, ecologically, financially. She hadn't been angry at the cancer, she didn't consider her own position to be another injustice in an unjust world. It was never about her. At times Elise couldn't hold back the tears and at others she laughed, a roaring snorty laugh that was reminiscent of Madeleine herself. She also offered up memories that Lombard had long forgotten and was, surprisingly he found, grateful to hear.

What they didn't talk about was Lombard's own guilt-ridden role in Madeleine's last few weeks. The utter bitter conviction he'd had that she had been having an affair. She hadn't been, of course. His fevered imagination, fired by despair and loneliness, had sought even more hurt from the flimsiest of evidence. It had been a subconscious mental defence mechanism against the certainty of her death which he'd found, and still found, hard to reconcile. In his mind, the two of them had made peace since but he knew he would never forgive himself, he knew it was too late for that. He just hoped she'd never noticed his coldness when, on occasion, he could no longer cope with the idea. Even at the merest memory of those times, there was an involuntary physical movement of guilt, or he coughed from embarrassment. His nervous tic of shame.

'So you come here to this park to be with her?' Elise asked, wiping her mouth with a paper napkin.

'Yes. She's still here I think, she loved this place. Well, we both did.'

'And you talk to her? I like that.'

'She doesn't talk back anymore,' he said sadly, before adding in a forced, lighter tone. 'I finally get my say!' They fell silent for a moment. 'Where have you been, Elise? What have you been doing?'

The young woman sighed. 'Why do you need to know?' she asked defiantly. 'It's my life.'

'OK.' He stood up and put the meal detritus back into a small plastic bag. His tone suggested that was the end of the conversation, but he'd already gathered from how the evening had gone so far that Elise liked to talk, she wanted to share. She wasn't keen on empty silence at all, so his experience told him to wait and she'd need to fill it.

'I haven't done much,' she said as she slumped back on the bench and scratched the ground with a once-white trainer. 'I had no plan and I've pretty much stuck to that.' Lombard stayed silent. 'I've grown up a bit though. I feel free. I know what I like and I know what I don't like and it's me who's made those choices, they haven't been made for me. That's all I wanted.'

'That's good,' he said enthusiastically, offering encouragement. 'And I like your new look.'

'Really?' Her question was almost desperate.

'Yes. Is it squatter chic?'

She laughed. 'How did you know?'

'It's kind of obvious. Where was it?'

'Bordeaux.' She paused. 'What do you think my dad would think of my "new look"?' There was a bitter edge to her voice now.

'Well, I'd make sure there's a defibrillator to hand when you see him,' he joked. 'I don't know Bordeaux well, did you like it there?'

'Loved it! I made a lot of friends there. Some of them moved up here, so I followed. I wanted to see you two.'

He put his hands deep into his pockets and shrugged in needless apology. He didn't want to go over that ground again. 'Are you going to tell me why you left? I've told you my news.'

She smiled at him and threw her arms around him, crying gently again. 'It was like living in a prison,' she spoke quietly. 'Dad decided what I was studying, where I would study it, the path I would take after studying. It was mapped out for me like I am a SIMS game.'

'He's a very successful man, your father.' Her father, Edouard Battier, was Madeleine's brother, and Lombard was right, a very successful man indeed. A highly sought-after tax accountant for people who didn't want to pay tax. Lombard had also found him joyless and bombastic, and was glad the siblings weren't close enough to want regular familial contact.

'Yes, he is very successful.' Elise's tone was caustic. 'But he's also suffocating. I told him I didn't want to study finance, that it didn't interest me and you know what he said?' Lombard could guess. 'He said interests were for time away from work! What a dinosaur!'

'But to go without saying anything, especially to your mother, to Christiane.'

'She would have told Dad. I had to just go.' She leant forward urgently. 'I didn't want my life decided at eighteen. I'm still only twenty-one now! I still don't know what to do, but I know I want it to be my decision.'

'I'm sure he thought he was doing what was right for you.' Lombard's platitude was hollow, so he hugged her again to dig himself out of the hole. 'It's so lovely to see you though,' he said quietly.

'The world has changed, Uncle Matt, and they haven't.' Her hands were playing nervously in her lap. 'Will you tell them? My parents I mean. Will you tell them I'm here?'

He looked up at the moon. 'I honestly haven't thought that far ahead. When was the last time you let your mother know you were alive?'

She shrugged. 'A couple of weeks ago, I think.' Lombard didn't believe her. 'My aunt wouldn't have told them.'

'I'm not so sure about that. You'd like to think she wouldn't, maybe I would too, but you know what she was like when she thought people *expected* her to behave in a certain way.' He didn't sound very convincing, but he was buying himself some time while he worked out what to do. He knew very well that Madeleine would not have told her brother that Elise was with him, but his job made that decision less clear cut. 'Anyway, let's get back. You're probably still the last person to have slept in the spare room, so it should be all set up.'

'So can I stay for a few days? Probably until Sunday,' she asked, watching him as he demonstrated the easiest route over the gate. 'I don't know where my friends are staying yet.'

As she followed him he had the sense that she wasn't telling him everything, holding something back. Was that because he wasn't Madeleine or because he was a *juge*, and therefore the law. He hoped it was the former. She stumbled on the last drop down and he managed to break her fall as her bag hit the ground, spilling its contents.

Embarrassed she started shovelling her possessions back in. There was no need for unease, he could see nothing that he hadn't expected to see. A tobacco pouch, papers, a lighter, a packet of condoms, some tissues, a notebook that stood out a mile because of its bright pastel colours, a memento from the past maybe. He bent down to help her.

'You don't have to hide any of this from me.' His voice was gentle. 'I'm off-duty so I'm not judging tonight!'

She laughed. 'Thank you, Uncle Matt.'

He was going to have to get used to that. He picked up the last item, a reading book. 'Ah, Fred Vargas,' he noted for the second time that day. 'Your aunt was a big fan of hers.'

'Not you though?' She put the book away.

'I find crime hard to read. I have to deal with it all day.'

'This one's not about crime, it's not fiction. It's called *L'humanité en péril*, it's about climate change, consumption, how to save humanity.'

'I see,' he said distractedly, though processing the information. He would expect a newly politically aware young person to be reading something like that, it was their future that needed saving after all. But middle-aged, obese, lonely bus drivers?

Chapter 15

Lombard woke early the next morning after virtually no sleep. He'd got up on a couple of occasions, as was normal, but had had to remind himself that he wasn't alone. After the first time, he'd found some old shorts and felt more comfortable. He knew really that he should inform Elise's parents that she was safe and with him in Tours, but he knew also that, no matter what safeguards he promised, they would be on his doorstep by lunchtime. He could betray his loose friendship with them or betray the trust of Elise, and that wasn't much of a battle in his mind. She was more vulnerable than they were, was his decision – fragile and young.

Having convinced himself that he was acting in her best interests, he got up and fed the cat. Then he went through a rare early morning routine with perhaps greater care than usual. He shaved a bit closer, put a comb through his wavy hair, which inevitably fought back, then found the least creased of his shirts. If he was to act as a surrogate parent he had to convince Elise, and to an extent himself, that he wasn't gently sliding downhill, decaying through relentless grief and loneliness.

She hadn't surfaced by the time he left for the Palais de Justice, but he left a note with his mobile number on it and suggested meeting up later. He envied her freedom, but he wasn't keen on the idea of her searching for friends in a squat somewhere in town either. He rang Sergent Brosse at the *commissariat de police* and called in a favour he wasn't owed. Brosse was a seen-it-all policeman, weary and unsurprised, and who had, so far, managed to keep Lombard's mother out of serious trouble. Charlotte Lombard had caused many public scenes in her climate change, animal welfare and societal justice campaigns, and on more than one occasion had 'assaulted an officer of the law in the course of doing their duty', Brosse had recited. He was a good man though.

'Juge Lombard,' Brosse wheezed down the line. 'Now what can I do for you?'

'What are the major squats in town at the moment, Sergent, recent ones probably?' Lombard was talking as he walked along boulevard Heurteloup, his voice competing with the morning rush-hour traffic as the noise bounced around the five-storey Haussmann-style buildings of one of Tours' major thoroughfares.

'Interesting. We've had some activity in the last couple of weeks in that regard. Can I ask why?'

'It might be linked to a case,' he lied. 'I just want an idea of what I'm dealing with.'

'Madame Lombard isn't thinking of moving into one?' he joked.

'My mother? She's far too house-proud.'

'OK, Monsieur le Juge, leave it with me and I'll get a couple of addresses together for you.' Lombard heard him shout something away from the phone, presumably at a feisty drunk in reception, and then shut the phone off. Reaching the top floor of the Palais de Justice he made himself an espresso from the new machine he'd had installed and moved into his office. He couldn't remember the last time he was in as early as this, and even before the clerk of the *magistrature*, Muriel Fauvion. He was aware, however, that his rather absent-minded behaviour of recent months had had the endlessly patient Muriel concerned, but being behind his desk before she was even in the building would surely cause her the greatest alarm. He heard her arrive in the room next door and went out to greet her.

Muriel Fauvion, tall and elegant, was not easily surprised and, having worked in the *magistrature* for nearly ten years, had picked up some of the skills of investigation and couldn't help but notice the strong smell of coffee as she had arrived. Without turning round, she said, 'Is something wrong, Monsieur le Juge?'

Lombard smiled as she did eventually turn towards him, a perfect eyebrow raised archly in mock admonishment.

'I'll say there is, Madame Fauvion. You're late, I believe.'

'Ha!' she laughed and they kissed each other's cheeks in greeting. It was probably not done in the office to be that informal, but they were friends too and Muriel, though younger than Lombard, felt a strong maternal streak towards him. 'It's not like you, Lombard,' she began, putting her desk together for the day. 'Have I missed something in the diary?'

She never missed anything in the diary; in many ways she was Lombard's diary. The physical connection of his organised world without which he would be lost.

'No, you haven't missed anything.' He wasn't sure how to proceed. 'I just... maybe it's time I got more involved, you know, in...' He paused.

'In life?' She finished the sentence for him, adding a touch of hope to the question.

'Yes. Maybe.'

'Well,' she started busying herself with files, not wanting to add to his obvious discomfort. 'It's different for everyone, grief. There's no right or wrong way, is there? But if you feel it's time, then that's good.'

He smiled at her. 'Thank you,' was all he could manage, though it was enough. Muriel was about to say something else when Lombard's mobile phone started braying and vibrating from his office. He pulled himself away to retrieve it.

'Lombard.'

'Monsieur le Juge. You answering your phone is getting to be a habit.'

'Yes, yes, Guy. What is it?'

'Two things. First, I have the initial findings of the autopsy report. Nothing of any great surprise unfortunately, maybe a couple of leads. I'm going to email it to Madame Fauvion now, so you can have a read when you get to the office.'

Lombard went to his window and looked out on the early morning traffic, a tram glided past. 'I'm at the office, Guy, just give me the highlights.'

There was silence at the other end as Aubret recovered from the shock that Lombard was not only up, about and switched on, he was actually at work.

'OK,' he said eventually, before Lombard interrupted.

'Did you go early to the mortuary then? Or was this locum at your office?'

'Dr Cloutier's secretary rang this morning, said it was ready and that she was sending it over. Why?'

'No reason. I just prefer to talk to a pathologist, rather than just have conclusions. You know how it is, some of them tend to leave out their suspicions on paper.'

'I agree. But anyway, this is all we have at the moment. The secretary said the doctor was already on to the next one.'

'Fine, what have we got then?' Lombard sat down and Muriel placed a blank pad and pen in front of him, turned and left. Lombard watched her as she went.

'In basic terms Thibaud Barbier died of a heart attack brought on by oesophageal rupture after recent bariatric surgery. A gastric band in layman's terms.' Aubret left the statement hanging, knowing that Lombard would be mulling that over.

'You mean he ate himself to death?'

'That's the conclusion, yes.'

'So why remove the head?' Lombard wasn't expecting an answer; it was just a natural question to ask.

'I have no idea, neither does Cloutier. If he has then, like you say, it's not in the report. Only that the head was removed with skill and a very sharp implement.'

Lombard stayed silent for a moment. 'It doesn't make sense. Why have a band fitted and then eat through it. It's almost a form of suicide.' Aubret didn't reply. 'Does he say how long he'd been in the water?'

Aubret sighed at the other end. 'Again, nothing conclusive. He says no more than a week based on deterioration of the skin. The internal organs are more damaged because of the rupture and the water damage.'

'Well, it's a narrower timetable than we were working on I suppose. Anything else?'

'There's a tattoo across the shoulders, quite faded, but...'

'What's the tattoo of?'

'Nothing really. Just a wavy line. Looks like an ECG graph.'

'Well, that's ironic,' Lombard said derisively.

'Do you still think it might be a gangland message?' Aubret asked quietly.

'I don't know,' was the exasperated reply. 'Unfortunately there's nothing to rule that out. It might be literally heartbreak though; at least it would be if it wasn't for the missing head.'

'What do you mean?'

'Why does someone make the kind of changes in their life that Barbier made, Guy? Weight-loss treatment. He tidied up his apartment, he made himself presentable for the first time in years, he wore aftershave, he washed.'

'He fell in love?'

'That's what I think too. So why then effectively kill yourself? Because of heartbreak? Those changes meant nothing, they didn't work, he lost again.'

'But the head…'

'But the head. Exactly.' They both stayed on the line, but in silence. It all seemed too literal for Lombard's liking. What happens in love? In a relationship? You can have your heart broken. You can lose your head. The death of Barbier could be anything: organised crime, a warning, a message or just another grubby little domestic.

'We still haven't found whoever discovered the body.' Aubret broke into his thought pattern. 'Texeira's working on it and we're going back through ex-employers, but he didn't leave much of a mark. Nobody seems to remember him.' He heard Lombard slam the desk in frustration. 'I take it you aren't going to sit behind that desk of yours and wait for the results to come in?' The *commissaire* wasn't being facetious, he just knew how Lombard worked.

'I want to see this doctor. I want to talk to him about what's not in his report.'

'Fair enough,' was the *commissaire*'s reply. 'I'll send the new kid round with a car to take you out to Chambray later on.'

'The new kid being…'

'…being Adam Benbarek. Like the footballer, didn't you know?'

Lombard smiled. This was a frustrating investigation, one that made little sense as yet, but at least he and Aubret were getting back to some sort of normal. 'You said you had two things, what's the second?'

'A girl has gone missing.' Aubret's voice had tensed up.

'How long?' Lombard asked, while concentrating on the notes in front of him.

'Since last night, not long. Eighteen-year-old kid, the family reported it immediately. They think something's up.'

'Do you think so too?'

'I don't know either way, but I have to deal with it this morning. It's the Daucourt family.'

'The make-up billionaires out in Rochecorbon?'

'That's them.'

'OK, let me know how it goes. She's probably just gone out for a breath of fresh air, a bit of freedom. You know what these families are like, suffocating.'

There was an uncomfortable silence on the other end. 'They asked for you personally, Lombard.'

'I think I have other priorities, don't you?' Again Aubret stayed quiet. 'Yes, yes, Guy, I know.' Then he continued, adding a snide pomposity to his voice. 'May I remind you gentlemen how this department works. *My* department. I am in charge of the *magistrature*, I assign the *juge* to the case and you, Commissaire, do as you're told by the *juge*. You both do as you're told by me!'

'I'm glad you've had time to work on an impersonation of the *procureur*, really impressive.' Aubret sighed. 'But we both know that a missing billionaire heiress tops a friendless dead bus driver.'

'We don't know for sure he was friendless,' Lombard snapped back, holding up the medallion image again and looking at it. 'If that medallion thing is what it is supposed to look like, if it's real, then he had friends and possibly in high places. Lemery couldn't find anything on it, so whatever it is, it is secret.'

'He could have picked something like that up anywhere though.' Aubret's tone was dismissive.

'True. Or someone else might have dropped it?'

There was a lengthy pause at Aubret's end. 'You mean whoever found the body?'

'It's possible, Guy. I think we need to find these people.'

'Agreed. But first we have a missing heiress to check up on.'

Lombard sighed heavily, frustrated at what he regarded as an inconvenience, but also frustrated that he knew Aubret was right. They had no choice but to put Thibaud Barbier aside for a while and visit the Daucourt family.

Chapter 16

Aubret turned off the roundabout and drove slowly into Rochecorbon, the small town on his left and the Loire on his right. Lombard sat hunched in the passenger seat, watching the river. 'So. Rosa Daucourt. Eighteen years old, didn't come home last night. She went into Tours and just hasn't come back.' Lombard seemed unable to take his eyes off the great river, the sun shimmering on its surface like diamonds under lights. 'And you've seen them already?'

'Briefly, this morning, yes, but I wasn't who they were expecting. I don't know which worried them more, the missing youngest daughter or a *commissaire de police* not entering through the tradesman's entrance.'

'And are they genuinely worried for her?' It seemed a harsh question to ask, but Lombard had dealt with powerful, rich families before. Anything could befall them – genuine disaster, family tragedy – but usually what mattered most was the loss of face, embarrassment, or worse a public show of weakness.

'I don't know. They're an odd bunch for sure. Cold. I'd tell you more, but you make your own mind up, that's your way.'

He turned off the road and up a short, well-maintained drive. The plane trees on either side an exact mirror image of those opposite. Money and precision. There was no room for disorder here, it wouldn't be tolerated. Approaching a large grey gate, maybe twelve foot high, Aubret stopped at a security panel and pressed the buzzer. The lenses in the camera focussed and the gates opened smoothly allowing them entry.

Lombard watched the landscaped gardens slide by trying to hide that what he felt was a mix of awe and revulsion. This was serious money they were riding into. 'Anyway,' he sat up straight. 'The Daucourts, what do we know?'

'You mean you're asking me for once?'

'No, Commissaire, you concentrate on driving.' Lombard smiled, but his grey eyes, usually watery, hardened as he delved into his memory bank. 'The Daucourts,' he repeated. 'Or to give them their full title, the disgraced billionaire Daucourts, originally from Besançon on the Swiss border. Sold what was left of their cosmetics business and moved here in 2019.'

Aubret made some kind of throaty rasping noise, expressing his bitterness. 'They may be officially disgraced, but they're still a powerful family with influence. What have they lost really? It looks like they're doing all right to me.' He nodded towards the magnificent house that stood at the end of the drive.

'Disgraced maybe, but these places on the banks of the Loire were built hiding caves and largely paid for by smuggling anyway, so there's a certain symmetry, I suppose.'

'Symmetry, right.' Aubret wasn't convinced.

'A certain amount of plea-bargaining went into it as I recall,' Lombard continued. 'They owned Beau Visage, a multi-billion-euro cosmetics company.'

'I vaguely remember it.' Aubret was concentrating hard, keeping the wheels off the pristine verges.

'One night, the lone security guard gets a series of threats. Violent threats. You have five minutes to get out, leave the gates open and you won't be hurt. He calls the police; that was his first mistake. They descend on the place. Nothing happening. The family are there. Nothing to worry about, they say. Hoaxes. Happens all the time. Then a series of small explosions happen. The police investigate, despite the family saying it's nothing. And what do they find? A secret highly illegal animal-testing lab.'

'How do you know all this stuff?' Aubret was genuinely in awe. 'It's like sitting with the internet.'

'My mother,' Lombard said flatly. 'She likes to keep me informed of people she thinks shouldn't be roaming the streets.'

'But Daucourt senior, Charles, he did go to prison right?'

'He did. But it wasn't exactly a Siberian gulag. He was sentenced to five years in the *maison d'arrêt* here in Tours.'

Aubret crunched his gears at the top of the driveway. 'How long did he actually serve?'

The car came to a standstill next to a round water fountain, and Lombard, taking in the grand façade and not looking at the *commissaire*, said quietly, 'Eighteen months. He suffers from Alzheimer's disease and was given early release.' Now he turned his eyes to Aubret. 'There was, needless to say, quite the hoo-ha.'

'Faked it?'

'That was the claim. But the independent medical examiner and a high-ranking magistrate signed the release documents. No points for guessing who the high-ranking magistrate was.'

'Oh great.' Aubret's tone was fatalistic, as if he'd been expecting it all along. 'No wonder he's rushing back from Lausanne. He's a family friend probably.'

'Exactly.' Lombard's tone was the same, then he seemed to shake it off. 'On the other hand, Rosa Daucourt may have genuinely disappeared and not just run off to join the circus, so let's keep an open mind.'

They sat in silence for a moment taking in the view. The house, a nineteenth-century chateau, had been restored to the point that it looked almost brand new. Even the grey slate on the pitched roof seemed to shine and bring out the russet red of the bricks and the beige of the cornices. The many, many windows reflected the park in front of them and the river in the distance. The garden was landscaped at just the right angle to make it look like it banked directly on to the river, cutting out the view of the road that actually divided them. Immaculate stone steps led up to a large blue door, painted duck-egg blue, the same as the many shutters on the façade. On the left was a wrought iron orangerie housing trees that looked like they shouldn't be indoors, giving the impression that they had been locked up against their will, imprisoned. The whole thing was slightly unreal, like a fairy tale, a CGI creation for a film.

'It's good to see that criminals are punished,' Aubret muttered.

The large front door opened and a tall man in an expensive yet ill-fitting suit emerged and shielded his eyes from the sun, removing round spectacles as he did so. Lombard and Aubret looked at each other and then opened their car doors at the same time.

'Juge Lombard is it?' the man barked, still covering his eyes.

'And Commissaire Aubret,' Lombard replied.

'Yes, yes,' was the dismissive response. 'This way, please. We *have* been waiting some time.' He turned and went inside, leaving the door open behind him, not as an invitation, just saving him the bother of having to wait as they climbed the half a dozen or so steps to the entrance.

Inside was like stepping back in time. The blue theme from the shutters outside was continued on the carved furniture, dressers, buffets and secretaires, all covered in fine porcelain jugs and dishes, some gold edged. Lombard knew enough about antiques, it being mainly Madeleine's business, to know real quality when he saw it: originals. He picked up a blue *jardinière* and looked at it carefully, then caught Aubret's eye. 'A month's wages there, Commissaire.'

His eyes searched the high walls and the artwork hanging in ornate frames, almost all of them of the Realist school. He saw at least one Millet and a large Manet as the centre piece. It was impressive certainly, very tastefully done too, but it also felt if not ostentatious then designed to cow whoever was allowed through the door. We are power, it said. We are old money.

He put the *jardinière* carefully back on the desk he had picked it up from and immediately gloved hands appeared and unnecessarily straightened it. He hadn't seen a butler arrive, though he guessed that stealth and discretion were the minimum requirements in a domestic servant. 'If you'll follow me, *messieurs*,' he intoned deeply.

He led them both further down the hall, past closed white doors, before turning right and standing in front of a pair of double doors with round brass handles. The man, who was slightly stooped almost as an actor playing the put-upon faithful retainer, straightened his tie and his smart black suit and opened both doors simultaneously, pushing them wide.

'Juge d'Instruction Lombard and Commissaire Aubret,' he announced.

The two men followed him in, while he retreated behind them closing the same doors all in one fluid movement.

They were greeted with quite a sight. There were five other people in the room. Two – one presumably Madame Daucourt and the tall man who had, in a fashion, greeted them on arrival – stood at the mantelpiece in front of a large fire grate that housed a basket of lavender. A younger woman and a younger man sat formally, awkwardly even, on an expensive divan, while the last figure present was a thin old man, in a wheelchair, a blanket across his lap, staring out of the window into the gardens beyond. It was a perfect tableau for an old aristocracy, ill at ease with the modern world and its intrusions or even just itself. It looked like one of those photographs of the British royal family that were designed to make them look relaxed, approachable and warm. It inevitably did the exact opposite.

Chapter 17

The next few moments of awkward silence did nothing to change Lombard's mind, though he began to sense a new dimension too. This didn't feel like a family at all, it was more like the board meeting of a company with a power vacuum.

'Where is she?' the old man in the wheelchair gave out a desperate cry, still not taking his swollen eyes off whatever it was he saw in the garden, his gnarled, arthritic hands shaking with emotion or disease, or both. If it was an act it was a good one.

The tall man who had left them at the door stepped forward from the mantelpiece, walking towards Lombard and Aubret. 'I am Auguste Daucourt.' His tone was sharp and cold. 'I am the eldest son and the family's legal representative and I must start by saying how disappointed we are that it has taken this long for a *juge* to show any kind of interest in the disappearance of our dear Rosa. This family is not without influence and I think your lack of respect reflects badly on you and your department.'

There was a pause, which the volcanic Aubret was determined to fill. 'Finished, monsieur? Because you know you could have said that at the door when we arrived. I guess you needed the audience, right? Well, now you've shown your family you're at work, keep the complaints for another time. Unless that's your priority?' he added menacingly.

Daucourt flushed. Aubret was right. This was a performance of self-justification, but that works both ways and he clearly regretted 'going public'.

Lombard gave a smile that managed to be both warm and cold at the same time; it said 'don't push me'. 'I am sorry you feel disappointed, monsieur.' There was steel in his voice. 'I am *disappointed* that I woke up yesterday and had to deal with a murder. Still…' – he dropped the half-smile – 'it's how you deal with disappointment that counts, don't you think?'

Auguste Daucourt stood six foot two yet managed to have no discernible body shape. Right now though, he looked about four foot eleven and he stepped back. Lombard noticed a smirk on the face of the young woman sitting down and she didn't bother to hide it.

'We haven't got time for this nonsense.' The older woman left her position at the fireplace and stepped forward, her hand outstretched. 'I am sorry, Monsieur le Juge, we are all very concerned and on edge. I am Olivia Daucourt, Rosa's mother. Everything here is very tense as I am sure you will appreciate.'

Aubret had told him she was English but there was no trace of an accent. She was tall with long grey hair, beautifully layered, the grey looking almost false it was so perfectly patterned with the hairstyle. She wore a tight-fitting jumper that was designed to show her body at its best, a body that looked far younger than her sixty or seventy years; it was difficult to tell exactly and he was only guessing at sixty or seventy because of the age of the eldest son. Her trousers were olive green and flared, adding height to her tall frame. She looked like she'd stepped from the roaring twenties.

Lombard shook her wrinkle-free, heavily moisturised hand and bowed his head. 'Please call me Lombard, madame. My colleague Commissaire Aubret you already know. Perhaps you can introduce me to the rest of the family and we can take it from there?'

'Of course.' She walked through the centre of them all; none of them looked directly at her, but sat sulkily instead, avoiding attention. The old man still stared out of the window. 'Auguste you've already met.' She didn't bother looking at her still wounded son. 'He is our eldest son. He is now in charge of the family business…'

'What's left of it…' Auguste Daucourt said truculently, sitting on the opposite divan to the younger woman, his hands in his lap. If his mother looked younger than her years, he was the opposite. A thirty-year-old middle-aged man, with all the fears and disappointments that come with middle age but none of the experience to cope with them or to seek brief solace in. He looked a lot like his father too, which Lombard imagined must be quite hard on Auguste Daucourt. Watching a future version of yourself fall apart physically and mentally in front of you must be like sitting in front of your own Dorian Gray painting. He certainly didn't look like he was handling it too well, his downcast eyes flicked around the room without landing on anyone else's and despite a strong Roman jaw, he bit his fingernails. A man on the edge.

'This is his wife Nadine,' Olivia continued.

Nadine gave a cold almost sarcastic smile, but said nothing and didn't look at him. She was an attractive young woman and it was difficult to see how Auguste would even have the confidence to approach someone like that. Though maybe he hadn't had to, was Lombard's conclusion.

'And this is Jules, our youngest son,' Olivia continued her introductions.

Jules looked like he had wandered into the wrong family. Tall and muscular, deeply tanned and with shoulder-length blond hair, he stood athletically, holding out his hand. He didn't say anything, just nodded. And for once one of the Daucourts watched another of the family as Lombard saw Nadine's eyes follow the younger brother as he sat back down.

'Jules has just come back from the Amazon basin,' Olivia declared proudly. 'The company has gone in an entirely new direction and now produces cosmetics made only from natural products.' It felt like an awkward sales pitch and Olivia Daucourt's face showed that she regretted it, that it was out of place. 'And this is of course my husband, Charles Daucourt. He is, as you can see... quite unwell.' The old man didn't turn away from the window, he just stared out of it as though he were expecting someone to arrive, his eyes so watery it must have been hard to see anything.

'Apart from what you have told the *commissaire*, have you anything to add?' Lombard asked the question to the room, but couldn't immediately take his own eyes off the old man. No one said anything. 'So, on Monday afternoon Rosa went into Tours. Was she alone?'

Olivia sat on a cushioned window seat next to her husband, in his direct eyeline. 'Yes. I asked one of the staff to drive her in, but she wanted to go alone. You know how teenagers are?'

Rather than admit that the sum total of his experience, such as it was, had all come in the last twenty-four hours, he didn't answer the question.

'So she cycled, which we know as that has been confirmed by the *commissaire* and the bike found. You say she took no extra bags, nothing sentimental...' He let the inference hang in the air. 'And you were expecting her back at...'

'We hadn't arranged a time, we just assumed she would return for dinner. Why wouldn't she?' Olivia Daucourt's question was pleading, but as far as Lombard's sympathies lay, the answer to 'why wouldn't she?' was sitting all around him.

'Do you usually eat dinner all together as a family?' he added, trying to be kind.

'Oh yes,' Nadine said bitterly, causing her husband to stand up quickly, though if he had wanted to offer a riposte, he didn't do so.

Lombard walked around the room to silence. On a table by the door was a collection of silver-framed family portraits; none of them were of the relaxed 'family on holiday' type, nothing that wasn't posed or rehearsed. A selection of studio shots over the years. Put them together, flick-book style, and you'd have small growing big and the big withering with age. Except for Madame Daucourt, who never aged, not at all.

'You moved here in 2019,' he said eventually, not taking his eyes off the photos. 'And presumably you all live on site...' He paused. 'Is that for your safety?' Nobody replied, though the atmosphere had definitely changed; even Nadine no longer smirked. 'How long have you been receiving threats, madame, and why didn't you report them?'

It was her eldest son who spoke eventually. 'We have always had them, for as long as I can remember. Apart from the break-ins at the old laboratories in Besançon...'

'...Where your father was arrested and subsequently jailed.' Aubret added, prodding the mood with a heavy stick.

'Apart from that incident, nothing has ever happened. I'm afraid it comes with the territory,' he added grandly, adopting a pose of righteous burden at his lot in life.

'You don't think that Rosa's disappearance has anything to do with these threats then?' Lombard asked. 'Were there letters? Phone calls?'

'Mostly they were letters,' Jules intervened. 'Crank stuff. Cut and paste warnings. We just threw them away. At least we always used to. I assume we still do. I've just got back.'

It was a perfectly reasonable thing to add under the circumstances, but Lombard felt it wasn't offered to be helpful just as a way of distinguishing him from the other family members. Again, the *juge* had a sense of a brewing competition.

He picked up a photo from another table. It was the three Daucourt children. Rosa giving a gap-toothed, off-the-cuff grin, which didn't match her formal dress or the family pose. Jules towered above her and then the elder brother, who faked a smile badly, making it look like he had colic. There was something different about him. Was it his jaw? Lombard turned to look at the standing Auguste. It was his jaw. He shook his head. What do you get the heir to a pharmaceutical cosmetic company for his birthday? A new jaw, really? Again, he thought about Rosa and had every sympathy if she had just had enough and run away.

'You say mostly letters,' Aubret asked, sensing Lombard's mind had drifted.

The family seemed to descend into some telepathic conference deciding who should speak at that point. 'It's all very childish,' Olivia said after a lengthy gap.

'What is?' Aubret persisted.

'Children's toys,' she said obliquely, as if that covered everything.

'Madame…' The *commissaire* was losing patience.

'Mutilated stuffed toys, rabbits mainly. Childish, as Olivia says.' Auguste was dismissive, which was about the only emotion he seemed to have, even addressing his mother as though she were a colleague, rather than family.

'Heavy-handed, obvious imagery though.' Lombard put the photo of a jawless Auguste back on the table carefully. 'What with your family background. Again, why did you not report any of this?'

'We didn't want the attention, Monsieur le Juge. It began while we were campaigning for Charles's release on compassionate grounds and we felt it best not to add to the storm.'

'And it still goes on?'

'Every now and then.'

'And you've discarded all of this evidence, haven't you?' Lombard sighed deeply after being greeted with silence. 'I'd like you to give the *commissaire* as much information as you can on these threats, warnings, whatever they are.' He made for the door.

'Is that it? That is all the famed Juge Matthieu Lombard can do?' Auguste Daucourt had been waiting for an opportunity to re-establish his position, but he had chosen unwisely.

'I have been talking to the family, monsieur, as you are well aware, but you have destroyed potential evidence, which isn't enormously helpful. We will do all we can to search for your sister but I want to know anything else that happens here – a threat, a communication, anything. Immediately. Is that understood?'

'I must say...' the Daucourt son spluttered.

'Must you?' Lombard replied immediately. 'As a son, as a brother or as a legal representative? Because if it's the latter I'll speak to other more important members of staff first.'

Aubret coughed to cover an involuntary laugh. Even the frosty Nadine looked to be biting her tongue. Before finally turning his back on the Daucourt heir, Lombard paused and reached into his pocket. 'Do you recognise this?' he asked sharply, holding up a picture with the image of the medallion on it.

'No,' Auguste said, barely looking at it. 'Should I?'

'Not necessarily, monsieur, it just would have made my day, that's all.' He opened the doors himself and left the room angrily.

Chapter 18

Aubret had deposited an angry Lombard at the Palais de Justice, knowing the *juge* would nip around the corner before going in, and calm down with a coffee, or something stronger. Towards the end of the brief journey back, the *juge* had sat quietly, but the furrowed brow and tensing of his hands had betrayed a state of mind railing against privilege and obfuscation. In their short exchange, Aubret gathered that Lombard saw the Daucourt family as a distraction from more important work. Barbier had had very little and had lost it all, violently; the Daucourts had had everything, wanted more and, in the end, lost little. Their problems were home-made and he was convinced poor Rosa, stifled and lonely, had got out while she had an opportunity; probably before they bought her a new jawline for Christmas. He'd given Aubret no further investigative instructions on the girl's disappearance, there being no evidence of kidnapping and no remaining evidence, if it had ever existed, of any threats. Rosa was not a minor; there was little they could do other than hold the Daucourts' hand, and Lombard had other things to do.

Some time later, Officer Benbarek pulled up neatly at the kerb in almost the exact same spot as the number eleven bus had the day before, opposite the Palais de Justice. It seemed much longer ago than twenty-four hours and Lombard felt he'd been derailed somewhat, as much as he ever was on rails that is.

'Turn left here,' he said to the young driver. 'Double back on to avenue Grammont.'

'You mean, follow the signs to the hospital?' Benbarek replied smartly.

Lombard nodded, raised his eyebrows and gave a half-smile without looking at his colleague. 'You know, you don't need your Parisian smart arse shield down here. We're friendlier people, for the most part.'

'Sorry, sir,' was Benbarek's contrite reply.

'And certainly do not call me sir. Lombard will do.'

They drove in silence out to the suburb of Chambray-les-Tours where the largest of the Tours hospitals was situated, l'hôpital Trousseau. It was another enormous brutalist structure that, on the outside at least, they had tried to soften with peace gardens, benches dedicated to those who presumably didn't make it out on their own two feet and even a small vineyard right opposite the entrance to the A&E department. If it made a difference it didn't seem to be having an immediate effect on the small groups of smokers huddled where they shouldn't be, some even connected to IV apparatus.

Nothing could be done to make the inside warmer though; it had been in decline for years, a decline that looked terminal. Did it even ever look new? The walls were a sickly green, a mustard yellow or even a muddy brown, sometimes a striped concoction of all three. When these various colours – which to Lombard's mind screamed visibly of bodily fluids – weren't in use, there were whole walls dedicated, for some inexplicable reason, to tropical scenes. White sandy beaches, swaying palms and turquoise surf on badly faded wall-size stickers that were inevitably peeling off, having long since given up clinging to their charade. He was just grateful Madeleine hadn't had to come here in her final months. The hospital had a fine reputation, despite its appearance, but you just couldn't get past its tired, jaded look. It looked like death. The oncology department which Madeleine had attended was in a shiny new building near the botanical gardens, gleaming with confidence. We can cure this, the newer l'hôpital Bretonneau screamed, though they hadn't.

Benbarek's phone rang as they walked towards the wide lift doors, breaking the low hum of the reception area. 'It's the *commissaire*,' he said apologetically. 'I should take this.'

'Of course.' Lombard walked into the open lift door. 'I won't be long anyway, you can wait at the car for me.'

The second floor where the Institut Medico-Légal was housed was slightly less grim. Even in France the health budget was being squeezed and the money went less on communal areas, which looked as sick as the patients, and more into research and prevention. And in pathology, the dead finally get to tell their own story, with the more modern pathologists practising some form of thanatology, that death might not just be the result of a physical act or a medical failure but a product of many things: spiritual, ethical, sociological or psychological. Dr Karine Sebourg, the usual pathologist, was certainly of that mind and though it blurred police lines at times, which of course Lombard was a fan of anyway, it used everyone's expertise and got results. Dr Hugo Cloutier, however, judging from his rather basic autopsy report, was not given to thanatological thought processes. Lombard was here to give him a push in that direction. Either way, he was going to give him a push.

A tired-looking nurse showed him into a small office and told him that the doctor wouldn't be too long. Lombard had been in Dr Sebourg's office before and it was always immaculate. Well-ordered shelves with dated journals and files, reference books and wall charts. There were no personal mementos of a life outside the hospital; not that she was a private person, she just wasn't sentimental. Dr Cloutier, in the brief time he had been there, had left his mark though and the desk was a shambles on which stood a picture of a young boy – an old picture, slightly drained in colour in a battered wooden frame.

The door opened and a harassed-looking Cloutier bustled in, closing the door behind him.

'Dr Cloutier?' Lombard stood and offered his hand. 'Juge Lombard.'

Rather than take Lombard's hand, the doctor removed his glasses and cleaned them on his white tunic. It was an odd gesture, possibly even unfriendly, though he didn't look like he was being antagonistic. He had a round, open face, a couple of days of prematurely grey stubble and a thinning hairline. He motioned for Lombard to resume his seat and took his own, rifling through the paperwork on his desk. Lombard wasn't convinced he was looking for anything specific.

'I'm not sure why you're here, Monsieur le Juge.' Cloutier's voice was short of breath as he spoke without looking at Lombard. 'I sent my report to Commissaire Aubret late last night. I presume he's seen it.'

Lombard was silent for a moment, long enough for it to be uncomfortable, forcing Cloutier to finally look him in the eye. 'Forgive my methods, Monsieur le Docteur.' His tone was apologetic. 'The results of your autopsy were passed on to me. I just wanted to know a little more about what you *thought*.'

'What I *thought*?' Cloutier sounded derisive. 'What does that matter? I gave you the facts, Monsieur le...'

'Just Lombard.'

'It's your job to do the thinking.'

Lombard stood up. He was perfectly calm, but he intended to give the impression that he wasn't.

'What makes you conclude the body had been in the water for no more than a week, Doctor?' Lombard pretended to read a wallchart.

Cloutier cleaned his glasses again. 'There was no putrefaction... the PMSI is a notoriously... that's the post mortem...'

'...submerged interval. I know that.' Lombard still did not look at him. 'Why no more than a week?'

'It was an educated guess, Lombard!' The doctor was angry and frustrated.

Lombard turned to him and smiled. 'Good. I prefer educated guesses to unexplained conclusions. Go on.'

'There were signs of maceration on the digits, some separation of the skin, but not much detachment. Detachment usually occurs in the second week. But, and this is where the guesswork comes in.' Cloutier wiped his hands on his tunic and Lombard could see sweat forming on his brow. 'The Loire has a fast current and is shallow in many places. Damage to exposed digits, and there was a fair amount, was likely caused by dragging on the river bed.'

'So it may only have been a couple of days, even less?'

Cloutier shrugged. 'The internal organs suffered significant water damage because the head had been removed, the body filled with water more quickly. Accurate timing is impossible.' He paused, trying to regain a little composure. 'There is a new method involving bacteria on the teeth, but that is not open to us, obviously. And bone protein methods are still in their infancy...'

Lombard sat back down. 'You say that oesophageal rupture led to a heart attack because of the pressure on the gastric band.'

'The stomach was full, Lombard, so obviously he didn't drown. He'd have vomited most of it back up. So he was killed, or died, out of the water, and then his head was removed. The spinal cord was a very clean cut, suggesting a surgical implement. There are signs of scavenging on the open neckline tissue, again pointing to not a great deal of time in the water, but enough. I said all this at the crime scene. Except that the head may have been removed some time after death.'

'How can you tell?'

'The internal organs aren't pale, no signs of bleeding out.'

'In your opinion, Doctor, why would a man have a gastric band and then eat himself to death? That's what your report is suggesting I think.'

Cloutier shrugged. 'How do I know? Maybe he changed his mind, maybe he wasn't taking the necessary vitamins or calories after the bariatric surgery so that he still had hunger pangs.'

'And what was in the stomach?'

'That's all in the report!' he shouted. He slumped into his chair. 'Every type of fast food you can name: burgers, pizza, tacos, oh, and,' – he chuckled – 'he obviously had fine tastes as well, *foie gras*.'

'Was that in the report?' The doctor didn't answer.

Lombard rapped his knuckles on the arm of his desk chair. 'Why?' he asked simply.

'It should have been. I'm sorry. I know you wanted a report quickly. I missed that.'

'Why do you think *foie gras*?' Lombard was thinking aloud, but Cloutier's reaction was immediate.

'Why?' the doctor shouted. 'It's your job, the whys. Not mine.' The anger dissipated as quickly as it had surfaced and Lombard watched him for a moment or two, the man wringing his hands and avoiding eye contact again.

'Just one more thing, Monsieur le Docteur,' he said affably, reaching for a pen and paper. 'This tattoo on the victim's back, can you draw it?'

For a second Cloutier stared at the piece of paper then eventually and carefully picked up the pen. His hand shook a little, not drastically but enough if you were looking for it, which Lombard was. It was exactly as Aubret had described, like an ECG graph, or a mountain range, starting low and getting progressively higher, perhaps as it reached the coast.

Lombard took the piece of paper. 'Thank you, Doctor,' he said quietly. 'It's lucky I didn't ask you to draw a straight line, isn't it?'

Striding out of the building Lombard sent a text to Dr Sebourg. 'Urgent. Lombard,' it read simply. Then he took a few minutes to gather himself. He got back in the car.

'To the office?' Benbarek asked, turning on the engine.

Chapter 19

'You want to take another look at the guy's apartment then?' Benbarek was concentrating on the red light, his foot hovering above the accelerator. Lombard, slumped in the passenger seat, was a picture of sulky concentration.

'There's something we're missing,' he said eventually, as the lights turned green. 'Nobody knows much about him, yet he completely changed his life about a month ago. Smartened himself up. He made an effort when he hadn't before. Why and who for? And then he changed his mind.' He paused. 'I know who he is, Thibaud Barbier, but I don't know *who* he is.'

'Some people are like that, I guess. They hide.' Benbarek indicated to turn off to the right.

'Yes, I suppose. But can you these days? Really? It seems unlikely.'

They parked up at the same shopping precinct in Sanitas and again the groups were there hanging around aggressively taking a long look at the outsiders.

Benbarek stared aggressively back through the windscreen, while Lombard tapped in the number for Soraya Moujahid from a business card that she'd given him.

'I've heard of Sanitas.' Benbarek wasn't dropping the stare. 'Is this why you wanted me to come?'

They could both hear the phone ringing at the other end. 'To hold my hand, you mean?' Lombard didn't look up. 'You can drop me here if you like.' He turned the phone off when the answer machine cut in. 'You know, I'm actually quite flattered you've heard of Sanitas!' He chuckled. 'How ridiculous is that? Our own little concrete nest of hell up there with the *banlieues* of the big city.'

'They're all connected – same gangs, different estates.'

'I guessed that.' Lombard tried the phone again. 'Did you grow up in a place like this?' he asked, pretending he was just making conversation.

'Yep,' was the terse reply.

'That can't have been easy.'

'Even less so when I became a cop and had to start warning off brothers and cousins.'

Again, Lombard let the phone ring. 'And are they all still there? Christmas must be awkward.'

Benbarek laughed. 'We don't…'

'I know, it was a joke. Why the police then?'

Benbarek unhooked his seat belt, opened the door but then turned back to Lombard. 'It was a choice, one side or the other. My brother was shot dead in a turf war. I chose this.'

The young policeman stepped out of the car as Lombard again turned the unanswered phone off. 'Glad I asked,' he muttered to himself.

With eyes following them they walked across the park to Barbier's tatty apartment block, where Lombard punched in a code on the heavy scratched front door. He wasn't entirely sure if he had the correct four digits having only watched over Madame Moujahid's shoulder previously, memorising what he thought he saw. He allowed himself a pat on the back when the door lock clicked open. The same musty, sweaty smell lingered on the damp walls but the lightbulb had been changed; Madame Moujahid was certainly efficient.

The two men climbed the stairs slowly. 'It's just a thought,' Benbarek said quietly. 'But back where I grew up, if there was a white guy on the estate, he was generally the mule or the messenger. White guys get stopped and searched less.'

Lombard nodded. 'Their choice?'

'Mostly, yeah. It meant they were protected, they didn't get any hassle.'

Lombard thought again about the feelings he'd voiced to Aubret at the beginning, that this might be organised crime and so would technically be under the jurisdiction of a specialist unit. Especially, as Benbarek had pointed out, all these estates, from Paris to Lyon to Marseilles to Rouen, they were all connected; low-level foot soldiers on concrete battle-grounds controlled by generals well away from the danger of the conflict, protected from the grime by distance and wealth.

They reached Barbier's apartment; the 'Do Not Cross' crime-scene tape was hanging limply from the door jambs – as if anyone was remotely interested anyway, Lombard thought bleakly. He tried Madame Moujahid's number again, but there was still no answer.

'You don't have keys, do you?' Benbarek asked the question politely, but with a touch of smiling confidence. 'Do you want me to open it?'

'You'll need permission from a *juge d'instruction* who's not keen on paperwork.' Lombard returned the smile.

'Yes, the *commissaire* warned me about that.' Within seconds Benbarek had the door silently swinging back on its hinges, the job done. '*Voilà*,' he said, waving Lombard inside.

'Handy skills. I'm glad you made the choice to join us,' Lombard said, ducking under the tape and stepping across the threshold. Benbarek did the same and just held Lombard's arm, handing him a pair of vinyl gloves before closing the door behind them.

'What are we looking for?' Benbarek was shielding his eyes as they adjusted to the bright apartment after the dingy corridor. Lombard hung back in the shadow as his eyes got used to the light too.

'I don't know. Something that tells us who and why, I guess.' He stopped and took a deep breath. 'To be honest, not only do I not know what I'm looking for, I don't know if I'd know if I even found it.' Benbarek gave him a look to say that wasn't much help. 'I know, I know,' Lombard apologised with a shrug. 'Aubret probably warned you about that too.'

Benbarek smiled back at him. 'I'll start in the kitchen then,' he said, and walked through to the open-plan kitchenette.

Lombard made his way to the bedroom. All the furniture, what there was of it, was covered in a fine powder left by the forensic team but it was obvious that there weren't a lot of prints to be found. Barbier had done an excellent job of wiping away his old life, or at least his old self, leaving few traces behind. The book was there on the bedside table, put there after a dusting by forensics, *L'humanité en péril*, its stark orange-and-blue cover easily standing out against the dull grey, presumably once white, of the walls and of the bedside table itself. It just didn't fit, he still believed. Literally, it stood out in Barbier's known life as its blue-and-orange colours stood out against the bland furniture of his square, featureless bedroom.

The book also had a fine film of powder on it and Lombard blew the dust off as he picked it up. It was obvious that the book had not been read. The spine wasn't creased at all, there were no dog-eared pages; it looked brand new except for a little age colouration on the fore edges. He sat on the end of the bed and immediately sank into the tired mattress. Looking around the dull little room, he wondered again about the man's change of attitude. He could understand the need for it, everybody goes through something like that at some point. The desire, sometimes the last chance necessity, to be something completely different, to run away from the person you are. Barbier had done more than that though; this wasn't a gradual change, this was an entirely new life and any remnant of the old was gone. New clothes, unworn, hung in the wardrobe, but they wouldn't have fitted the outsized body of the man; it was aspirational clothing. *What I will be.* Lombard remembered a ninth birthday present that his English grandparents had bought for him. What was it called? An Etch-a-Sketch. An early tablet for children of the 1970s. Two dials, one horizontal and one vertical scraped a stylus in powder to draw images, and once you'd finished, you'd shake the thing and everything was gone. Barbier had shaken his life, erasing what had gone before. Or, the thought occurred to him, somebody else had done it on his behalf.

He wandered back to the open-plan salon where Benbarek was going through a bag of rubbish to be recycled. He didn't look up. 'There's nothing in here with a best before date older than ten days,' he said. 'I don't really know what that tells us though, I'm just trying to narrow it down.'

Lombard nodded. 'And presumably at the bottom of the bag was take-away stuff, polystyrene packing, plastic forks, pizza boxes. Nearer the top cardboard salad boxes and so on.'

Benbarek looked up impressed. 'Exactly that, though he still has some of the menus for his favourite pizza place. Pizzeria Napoli, place des Halles.' He handed the flyer to Lombard who absentmindedly put it in his pocket.

'Do you know this book?' He held the book up and shook it at his young colleague like an old-school fire and brimstone Bible preacher. Something fell out as he did so and he bent down to pick it up.

'What is it?' Benbarek asked, joining him in the salon.

'It's a ticket of some kind. Cascadeurs Monster Truck at the parking de la Salle de Boule de Fort, April 3. Two thousand and twenty-three. That's in Saint-Cyr, just north of the Loire.' He turned it over and read the penned message on the back. *'Bon anniversaire, mon fils, et bon courage.'* It was a woman's handwriting, neat and old-fashioned. 'Happy birthday, my son, and good luck.'

Benbarek shook his head. 'Why would you read a book about saving the world and go to a gas-guzzling stuntman truck rally? That is messed up.'

Lombard took his phone out and texted Juliet Lemery back at the police headquarters. 'When did Barbier's mother die?' he typed simply. As soon as he'd sent the message, the front door swung open loudly and a tense Soraya Moujahid stood in the doorway, partially obscured by the police tape but holding a telescopic baton.

'Oh thank God,' she breathed. 'It's you.' She retracted the baton and put it in her bag. 'Madame Bilal rang, said she heard people upstairs...'

'She has the ears of a bat that woman. Come in. This is my colleague, Officer Benbarek.' They nodded curtly at each other.

'When was the last time this Madame Bilal heard noises up here?' the young man asked, his habitual slouch disappearing as he stood to his full height.

'Everybody hears stuff all the time,' Madame Moujahid replied, stepping into the salon. 'As I've said, the walls and ceilings are paper thin.'

'So it might be rats, then?'

Madame Moujahid's jaw tensed and she looked at him squarely in the eye. 'I don't think Monsieur Barbier could get away with sounding like a rat, do you?'

'I didn't mean it like that…'

'Never mind. She hears stuff all the time. But word gets around when there's an empty apartment.'

Whatever tension had immediately surfaced between the two, Lombard wasn't interested. His phone beeped indicating a message and he expected it to be from Lemery.

It wasn't.

'I'll leave you two to lock up,' he said airily and wandered out looking at his phone.

'If you want to know about the headless man. Cinema on rue Blaise Pascal. Screen 6, back row, right. Three o'clock showing. Come alone.'

He shook his head. This latest twist was actually quite unsurprising, because nothing was making sense anyway. Then his phone beeped again and this time it was Lemery.

'1998,' the text said simply.

'Of course she did,' he muttered to himself, and wandered off to the cinema. 'So why did she write him a note just a few weeks ago, then?' he asked himself.

Chapter 20

With time to kill before his mysterious rendezvous, Lombard had a choice. Go back to the office and catch up on the growing mountain of paperwork, the inevitable bureaucratic, signed and sealed proof of existence that is the bane of French administrations; or, and it wasn't really much of a competition, wander slowly back into town and gather his thoughts along the way.

The ticket in the book and the message scrawled on it nagged at him. It was obviously a breakthrough of some kind, but he couldn't think how. Just when he thought he was getting to know Barbier even a little, something would blow in on the wind, offering up a contradictory presence – a different person entirely. His death and even his recent life were contradictory. Slobbish, tidy, weight loss, weight gain. And why was there so little history of the man? Obviously if his mother had died in 1998, it was unlikely they had attended a stunt car show together this spring. A mother *figure*, then? There was nothing in Barbier's apartment or effects, such as they were, to indicate anyone with even a minor role in his life, let alone someone close enough to call him son. There was so little in the man's life, now or in the past, and what there was didn't much hang together.

He felt his phone ringing in his pocket and checked the caller ID before answering it, hoping it wasn't Aubret with news of the missing, or absconded, Rosa Daucourt. It was a number he didn't recognise, but neither was it hidden and he answered cautiously.

'Uncle Matt?' Elise sounded breezy and happy, and it was good to hear her voice. 'Are you at work? I can hear traffic.'

'I'm on my way back to my office,' he lied. 'What have you been up to today?'

She filled him in on her day's events. A lie-in, a coffee and a wander around the city centre and, she said, unable to hide the excitement in her voice, 'I bumped into a friend!' He was pleased for her, but nervous too. *Is this how parents are all the time?* he thought. *Pride and fear, mixing like water and oil?* Maybe Olivia Daucourt had got to him despite himself. He and Madeleine had never had a family; they'd have been far too selfish to give up their space. He was relieved though.

'That's great news,' he said, pleased he didn't have to hide the relief face to face.

'We're going for a drink,' she breathed, as if it were an illicit thing to do. 'Do you want to join us?'

He most certainly did not want to join them, but he was also aware of his responsibilities as a surrogate guardian. That, in keeping her appearance in Tours a secret from her parents, he had a duty to at least make sure she didn't fall in with the wrong crowd. He admonished himself for the rather pompous introspection. His duties, if he had any, were nothing of the kind. Elise was twenty-two years old, old enough to make her own mistakes and enjoy them. Set against all that, however, was the fact that he really could do with a drink. He decided to hop on a bus and meet Elise and her companion on the rue des Halles.

The doors on the bus sighed open and the driver ignored him as he got on. It was the union man Denis Petit who stared blankly ahead, not registering any of the half a dozen passengers waiting and who robotically registered their travel cards on the reader as they ascended. It was only Lombard who didn't automatically find a seat and sit down, preferring instead to try and provoke Petit into at least acknowledging his presence. Eventually Petit did indeed look up, challengingly, a hint of confrontation in his bored eyes. Then it registered who was standing over him and he tried to row back on the aggression without losing face.

'Expecting trouble, Monsieur Petit?' Lombard half-smiled as he asked the question.

'Got to be prepared for anything in Sanitas,' was the sullen reply. He pushed a button to close the doors and the bus pulled away into the traffic, heading north.

'Why has the world become such an angry place, do you think, Monsieur Petit?'

If the non sequitur had taken the bus driver by surprise, he didn't show it. He merely took a pen from behind his ear and tapped a sign on the protective glass around his seat. 'Do Not Talk to the Driver when the Bus is Moving,' it read.

'That's as good an answer as any.' Lombard grinned. 'We're all locked in our plastic cabins, not listening to each other. Very philosophical.'

He would have liked to have stayed on the bus longer, quietly enjoying the discomfort his sheer presence had on the taciturn driver, but he exited halfway up rue Nationale and headed down the busy rue des Halles to the agreed meeting place. The scene was a glorious one. The chic clothes boutiques and expensive jewellers gave way to old Tours. In the bright summer sky the Tour Charlemagne stood opposite the Basilique Saint-Martin, two stout reminders of the medieval prestige of Tours. Beneath them, old timbered buildings had been converted into modern bars and restaurants and all the tables, teeming out on to the pavements were full of tourists, students and proud locals who could sit here knowing this was their town. *It is*, Lombard thought, *the best of Tours.*

The bar they had agreed to meet at was at the slightly less salubrious end. It was no less busy, but the bars were chrome rather than timber; the clientele less well to do than further back up the street. The Revolution Bar, painted black, stood opposite a Carrefour mini-supermarket, and its use of red starred Soviet symbols was a depressing reminder that anything was commercial fair game in the bright new world. Lombard, his values some way from communism as a rule, nevertheless felt a little sympathy for Lenin and Stalin. That their ideals – brutal and selfish as he regarded them – had been reduced to tap room paraphernalia and a cocktail menu selling Molotov Mojitos and the bizarrely titled Bolshevik Cosmopolitan. Elise waved from a corner table and stood up to greet him, kissing him on both cheeks.

'This is my friend Louis Aguirre. Louis, this is my Uncle Matt.'

Lombard held out his hand and struggled into what he hoped was a warm, welcoming smile. The young man had a confident, firm grip but the returning smile was watery, barely noticeable between a pencil-thin moustache and a soul patch beard that looked oddly old-fashioned on a young, handsome face. He had Mediterranean skin, which matched the Basque surname, but the most striking thing about Louis Aguirre was the eyes. They were brown and intense but it was the enormous pupils that were difficult to avoid and they lent the face an almost animalistic presence.

'Uncle Matt?' he queried with good humour. 'Elise, you didn't tell me Uncle Matt was the renowned Juge d'Instruction Matthieu Lombard.'

'Renowned makes me feel old,' Lombard joked back, noticing that Elise looked uncomfortable. He ordered a glass of rosé from a passing waitress, the other two not yet needing another drink.

'I didn't realise you were famous!' Elise tried to break the silence that had descended, before it reached an unpleasant level of tension.

'It's the law, Elise.' Louis sounded like an adult talking to a child or, given their faux-Russian surroundings, a mesmerising Rasputin figure. 'That's how we are suppressed. The law is might and might is power, and the more it is seen as a "famous" ubiquitous presence, the more successful that suppression becomes.'

Lombard was grateful for the swift arrival of his drink as he tried to pick through the anti-establishment buzzwords of the young man.

'Not a fan then?' he said, winking at his aghast niece. 'Is this why we're meeting in a sham-revolutionary bar? It was the closest you could find that doesn't have the bourgeois trappings of subjugation and control?'

Louis Aguirre threw his head back and laughed loudly and perhaps a little ostentatiously. 'I deserved that,' he said eventually. Elise joined in nervously with the laughter, while Lombard took a sip of wine and faked a smile. Again, he had to remind himself that he was not Elise's father and it was not his role to approve or disapprove of her friends. He couldn't help himself, however; he didn't like the man.

'What is it you do, Louis?' he asked idly.

Aguirre leant forward, a look of extreme intensity on his face. 'I work for charities,' his voice almost a whisper.

125

Lombard couldn't work out if the man thought that what he did was edgy or shameful. The look on his face suggested it was a passion though. 'Animal charities, ecological interests.'

'We need a more just world,' Elise interrupted.

'I couldn't agree more,' Lombard replied seriously, before adding with a twinkle in his eye. 'And my mother would certainly agree.'

'Ah yes, Charlotte Lombard. She's a big help in our work.'

Lombard didn't like the way Louis held his gaze after saying that, almost like it was a threat of some kind, or that at the very least the activist had something over the judge. It certainly felt like a challenge, though he couldn't see why. Unless Louis Aguirre genuinely saw Lombard as an old-fashioned male barrier to his relationship with Elise, in which case he had no idea how to get the message across that that was very far from being the case. At least, he wouldn't admit to it not being.

Lombard, not in the mood for confrontation, tried to turn the conversation to less controversial subjects, social platitudes that none of them were really interested in, but even the weather – or in fact, especially the weather – had Aguirre enervated. There seemed no off-switch on the man at all, and he was almost entirely humourless with it. It was a relief when his phone rang and he moved away to talk in private, his tall thin body gliding easily through the tables.

'He's very dedicated.' Elise spoke quietly, proud and disappointed at the same time. 'He thinks the time is right for a revolution.'

Lombard nodded in response. 'I'm not sure we've got over the last one.' He was trying to lighten the mood, but he was serious too.

'He's probably a bit nervous about meeting the famous Juge Lombard.' Elise giggled nervously. 'We've had such fun today. There was a fair on the Île Aucard and he won this for me.' Like a magician she pulled a plush toy rabbit from her bag.

'He won that, did he?' Lombard recognised it, remembering the threats to the Daucourt family. 'Where did you say this fair is?'

Before she could answer, Aguirre returned and picked up his rucksack from the back of his chair. 'I have to go,' he said, a touch of eye-dodging evasion on his face. Then he left abruptly, without ceremony or even the French social niceties of a kiss for Elise or a handshake for Lombard.

'Off to save the world, is he?' Lombard couldn't help himself.

Chapter 21

The cinema was located down a side street behind the train station. The posters on the walls outside advertised forthcoming and current attractions and almost every film had a number after it, signalling to Lombard a distinct lack of originality but also the upcoming school holidays. Also, almost every film had some caped or lycra-clad figure, bustling with photo-shopped muscle or cleavage, a stern look on their face – that is, if they weren't wearing a mask and as if to say, 'What me, again? Can't the world save itself this time?'

Madeleine had had strong views about the state of modern cinema and in particular the tsunami of comic book heroes. Her argument was that they weren't for kids, they were for adults that hadn't grown up yet: teenagers in their thirties, fetishistic mother-fixated little boys stuck in a lingering puberty. She had written numerous pieces about it for magazines, and become a darling of the defenders of French over US culture. At least she had until she then described French cinema as one of the main reasons French society was so toxically patriarchal. Madeleine liked making enemies, it fired her up. She would have laughed at her husband now in the foyer of a cinema super-chain surrounded by a mixture of young families, nervous dating teens and comic book geeks.

He approached the desk. 'One adult for screen six,' he said, receiving a disbelieving look from the young lady serving him. 'And a Sprite.'

'Screen six, are you sure?' He nodded, and wished that he had checked what the film was going to be. 'It's already started.'

'So I've missed the adverts then?' he replied more tartly than he'd intended.

He opened the first set of double doors and heard muffled noises from within the screening room, then opened the second set of doors and was almost knocked off his feet by the noise. Lombard made no secret of the fact that he liked peace and quiet; he wasn't a shouter, rarely raising his voice even. He had learnt early on that he didn't need to and that if you spoke quietly, but with authority, people would, albeit sometimes against their will, want to listen.

He turned left up the steps to find the seat he'd been told to find and a figure bumped into him, before offering a muffled apology and exiting through the doors, his ears presumably bleeding. Then Lombard realised that the seat the figure had left was top right, back row. He thought about going after whoever it was, but decided to do as he was told instead.

He pulled the cushion of the seat down and sat, checking first if there was a message on the chair itself, or underneath. There wasn't. He checked the cup holder for the same, before putting his Sprite in the empty space. Then he sat back, trying to gather his thoughts amid the aural carnage all around him; the ear-splitting rancour and the violently flashing images made him feel nauseous. It was so loud and the screen so large that he couldn't make out what the on-screen characters were actually shouting about, their American voices competing with the explosions and violently twisting metal. Sometimes he sought out English speakers, just to hear them, depending on how French or English he felt on that particular day. But this was horrendous, though at least dark enough so that no one could see him wince, as though he had a toothache.

After twenty minutes he was seriously wondering if he could take much more. There were reasons sound was used as a torture technique and he hoped that whatever message or sign was to be delivered wasn't going to require a long wait because he genuinely couldn't put up with this onslaught for long. The characters, whose faces were gravely serious despite the nonsense of their CGI surroundings, didn't have dialogue as such, just disconnected slogans that they roared at each other, each a competing escalation of blandness. He made a decision and reached into his jacket pocket, hoping to find a tissue he could tear in half and use as makeshift ear plugs. He found no tissue; what he did find was a folded piece of paper that he knew he hadn't put there. Immediately he stood up and took the steps down two at a time, racing out through both sets of double doors and leaving the Armageddon gibberish thankfully behind him.

He took a moment to gather himself, his ears still ringing from the assault. Opening the note, there was a simple message written in pencil.

Impasse rue d'Entraigues

Red NISSAN MICRA

20.15

ALONE!

'More games?' Lombard muttered to himself, though conceding that the impasse, the dead end, next door to his old lycée would clearly be a much quieter spot than the cinema. Something else that appeared obvious was that, whoever his secret messenger was, that person knew Tours well and knew how to avoid being followed. What did that mean exactly? Someone in the police even? Nobody that they had seen so far seemed to fit the bill at all. Also, the news that Barbier had been decapitated hadn't been officially released yet but this person knew.

With time to kill before his secretive rendezvous he decided he had time for a shower and to feed the cat and walked slowly towards home. As he did so, in his mind he ran through the list of Barbier's colleagues and acquaintances that he'd seen. All colleagues and acquaintances, no friends. The distinction was clear, but finally somebody other than him was taking an interest in the man. His phone rang in his jacket pocket and he fumbled to retrieve it; it was the *commissaire*.

'Where've you been?' he asked angrily and without preamble. 'I've been ringing your phone for the last half-hour.'

He looked down at the screen and noticed there were three missed calls from Aubret. Maybe that's why cinemas had got so loud? It was an endless race to outdo each other's volume, the phone versus the film.

'Yes, sorry,' he replied, vainly stopping to straighten his jacket and collar in a shop window. 'I was watching the demise of twenty-first-century culture.'

There was a pause. 'What?'

'Nothing, never mind. What's up?'

Relieved to be on safer ground, Aubret heaved a big sigh and got on with it. 'Benbarek tells me you went back to Barbier's apartment.' Lombard wasn't surprised that

Benbarek had told his immediate boss; also that said boss would take a dim view of breaking into the place, even if the interloper was an investigating magistrate. 'He said Madame Moujahid let you in because she had some news…'

Lombard smiled. '*Good for Benbarek*,' he thought.

'…says the neighbour heard Barbier in the flat just last week. That narrows our time frame down.'

'Maybe, Guy, she heard someone but we don't know it was Barbier. She didn't actually see him.' He was only guessing the last bit, but felt on safe enough ground.

Aubret paused. 'You don't think it was him then?'

'No. I can't be sure obviously. But no. There is no trace of the man in that place. A place he lived in for three years.'

'No. Forensics found nothing. Even his books and magazines had nothing…'

'I think someone else may have come along and cleaned it out afterwards.'

'I think you misheard me, Juge.' Aubret's voice hardened slightly as he mulled this over. 'I was talking about his books,' he said eventually. 'There wasn't a ticket signed by his mother? You know, little details like that that could be helpful.'

'Benbarek?' This time Lombard asked the obvious question.

'Yep. Doing his job.'

Lombard remembered he had, he would say, absentmindedly put the book and ticket in his pocket. He was aware that Aubret was trying to sound like a disappointed parent so as to cover up his genuine anger. He was failing badly and it spoke volumes that he continued to feel that Lombard wasn't to be trusted. Of course, the whole mix-up before he was suspended was just that, a mix-up that Lombard was too tired, too unhappy to protest. He had been accused of throwing away evidence but the truth was that it was nothing to do with the case they were on but everything to do with a mental disintegration at the impending loss of Madeleine. He could easily explain this to the *commissaire*, even produce the supposed evidence, but he wasn't inclined to do so – he felt ashamed. Anyway, he liked the distance and, in a sense, he liked not to be trusted. He didn't want anyone, even Aubret, getting that close again.

'Please, Commissaire,' he said soothingly. 'The book and ticket are currently sitting on my desk. I'll bring them over tomorrow, bright and early.'

He turned his phone off before Aubret could respond and quickened his step. The cat was waiting for him; the dust hung, glimmering in the light like a hologram galaxy of stars; everything was as it should be and it gave him a sense of comfort during an investigation where so far nothing made sense or was as it seemed. He threw the book on to a divan but removed the ticket carefully. Stuck as it had been in the folds, it's possible that forensics had missed it, so he placed it separately into the empty envelope of an unpaid bill and slid it into a drawer.

Showered and refreshed, he fed the cat – who seemed to crave company rather than food – and looked at his watch. He would be an hour early if he went to the Impasse rue d'Entraigues, and that might not be a bad idea. He might even regain some control in this chase, if indeed that's what it was.

Nevertheless, he hung back a little in the lengthening shadows as he approached his rendezvous. The streets were well chosen. No bars, no shops and a long time after the lycée had closed for the day, houses had their shutters largely closed, keeping the cold from their air-conditioning where they needed it, indoors. He stopped at the corner of the dead end and saw a red Nissan Micra parked at the very end. There was a figure in the driver's seat, the back of their head showing above the headrest. He approached with caution, looking around him at all times and regretted slightly not telling Aubret where he was going. But then, he'd been told to go alone and that's exactly how he felt, alone.

He made a mental note of the registration and continued to walk slowly towards the small, quite dirty vehicle. He really had no idea what to do from here – was this friend or foe? Making his way to the driver's door he pulled it open suddenly.

A man flopped out and landed face up at his feet, deep red blood oozing from a wide gash in his throat spilling on to Lombard's shoes and on to the pavement. He jumped back automatically with the shock and then felt a hammer blow as something hit him on the back of the head. He fell to his knees as though in penitence before a second blow knocked him down, unconscious and sprawled across the dead man in what looked like a violent embrace.

Chapter 22

Lombard didn't know if he was awake or not, only that he was horizontal and that his eyelids felt far too heavy to open. He worked on his other senses hoping to figure out where he was, possibly who was with him and whether or not he was safe. Those senses, however, weren't at their best as the inside of his head alternately throbbed and screamed. It was as if someone had decided to install the cinema actually inside his skull. The memory of the cinema brought even more pain, his recent memory fighting with the present to see which could cause the most discomfort.

The last thing he remembered wasn't going to improve things either. A man had fallen from the car, his throat cut wide open, a bloody gash revealing the grizzly material within. An image he would never forget, even though it was brief. Then he'd felt a painful blow, maybe two, to the back of his head and everything had gone dark.

So where was he now?

He couldn't hear anything other than the discordant maelstrom of his brain, a large talentless orchestra warming up in a tiny metal shed. Slowly and with some difficulty he opened his right eye, just slightly, but he had no focus. He could just about make out shapes moving around and he thought he heard voices as well, but they were too muffled to hear properly. He made a decision. He wasn't just going to lie here and let them finish the job, so he shot bolt upright to take whoever it was by surprise. He did so, and immediately blacked out again.

He had no idea how long he'd been out, but at least now he could feel that he was on a mattress somewhere. The explosion of drums and cymbals between his ears hadn't abated and he had a sharp pain in the back of his right hand, but his throat, though dry as gunpowder, felt intact, so that was something.

'I think he's stirring again,' he just barely heard a woman's voice say.

'OK,' a gruff male voice replied. 'Hold him down this time, stop him trying to get out.'

Lombard felt a panic. He was still in danger and he had to move quickly before it was too late. But he *was* too late. Powerful hands held him by the upper arms and he felt the shadow cross his closed eyelids. He made a vain attempt to struggle but knew it was futile, he could even smell the breath of his captor, minty fresh, like chewing gum.

'Yeah, you can tell he hasn't been going to the gym for all that long,' the gruff male said sarcastically and with a touch of relief. 'Welcome back, Monsieur le Juge, have a good rest?'

'Aubret?' Lombard's voice was weak, and he relaxed back into the bed knowing he was safe.

'You can leave us now, nurse.' Lombard heard Aubret give polite, but firm instructions.

'Don't overtire him please, Monsieur le Commissaire, he needs rest.'

'I promise,' was Aubret's insincere response.

'He'll have a terrible headache and likely problems with his vision, you must…'

'He's used to that,' Aubret interrupted, shepherding the nurse out of the room. He took a deep breath and turned back to the bed, where Lombard still had his eyes closed. 'You know Juge Dampierre is going to be very pissed off with you. He was hoping for the sympathy vote when he gets out but there's not much competition between his gall bladder and you being thumped with a wheel wrench.'

'Is that what it was? It felt heavier.'

'It was left at the scene so maybe the man who smacked you with it was a big fella.' He paused, and even in his weakened state Lombard could sense him gearing up for a showdown. 'With all due respect, Juge, Lombard... what the fuck were you doing? I have two murders now, an attack on an investigating magistrate, no *procureur*, a stand-in coroner and a missing young woman.' Lombard opened his eyes in panic. 'Do you think you could cut me in on my investigation?'

'A missing young woman?' he asked weakly.

'One Rosa Daucourt. Ring any bells?'

Lombard tried to concentrate and hide his relief. In his confusion for a moment suspecting that it was Elise who had been reported missing. 'Oh, right, yes.'

'I don't have to tell you what effect a distraught billionaire, politically well-connected family would have on our beloved *procureur*. I have to split my resources between that and one and a half decapitations.'

'Who was he? The man in the car?'

Aubret gave him a quick look before needlessly looking at his notes. Lombard had the feeling he was avoiding eye contact. 'Edmund Brunel,' he said simply.

'Journalist, investigative journalist.' Lombard winced as he shifted position. 'Had his nose broken more times than a boxer because he kept putting it where it wasn't wanted. He usually took down his target though.'

'You know a lot about him.' Aubret knew why.

'One of Madeleine's former colleagues.' He took a deep breath. 'Funny. She always said this would happen to him.'

They stayed silent for a moment.

'The question is, of course,' Lombard continued eventually, 'why's a world-class journalistic bruiser like Edmund Brunel investigating the death of a nobody like Thibaud Barbier?'

'And who would kill to stop him?'

They looked at each other, hoping that their worst fears of organised crime weren't being realised.

'We're obviously still missing something with Barbier.' Lombard spat the words in frustration.

'Take it easy, please.' Aubret did his best to soothe the anger in his colleague. 'I don't want the nurses telling me off. Now, what happened exactly? Why were you there?'

Lombard told him about the text, and then the note left in his pocket at the cinema.

'The next thing I know for sure is I'm in here,' he concluded.

'There's no proof it was Brunel who led you the dance, of course.' Aubret sat in a chair at the side of the bed. 'That's exactly the kind of thing that would get you following and not thinking.'

Lombard had no argument against that. 'We need to know what exactly Brunel was working on,' he said instead. 'I'll speak to a couple of Madeleine's friends, they might know something.'

'Lombard,' Aubret's voice was soft, but there was a granite edge to it as well. 'I want this as much as you do, but not at the expense of my job or my pension, understood? If it needs to be kicked up to someone else, so be it. I'm not like you. I have a family and kids to put through university...'

Lombard smiled. 'I understand completely, Guy. I really do. And I have my cat to think of.'

Aubret couldn't help himself from laughing while, with some difficulty, Lombard tried to sit upright. The *commissaire* arranged the pillows.

'Let's get Pouget over here,' Lombard said, trying to hide his discomfort. 'We'll go back to the start and see if we've missed anything.'

Aubret nodded his head. 'Commandant!' he shouted, causing Lombard to wince.

The door opened and Commandant Lydie Pouget strode in quietly.

'I'm flattered you'd arrange such strong protection, Guy.' Lombard forced a smile.

'Don't be. It was to stop you escaping.'

Pouget pulled up a chair and, in a brief moment that was out of character for her, shook her head at Lombard with a half-smile. 'OK,' she said. 'Where are we at?'

It was Aubret who began, pacing the room as he did so, each time screwing up his eyes as he turned into the shuttered sunlight. 'Thibaud Barbier, forty-six years old. Unmarried, bus driver for Fil-Bleu in Tours.'

'Line eleven,' Lombard interrupted. 'Almost an obsession that seems to be the only constant in his life, line eleven.'

'Line eleven, right.'

'Also, if he worked and lived here in Tours, can we not assume that his body was dumped not that far away?'

'It's not conclusive, Commandant, but all we have to go on.'

'No friends or family that we know of for certain.' Lombard was gingerly touching the back of his head. 'His mother died in 1998, but thoughtfully still sends him messages.'

'We have no proof that that was for him,' Aubret suggested.

'No proof, no. But it fits his interests.'

'OK.'

'Neighbours complained about late-night noise and cooking smells. His colleagues avoided him, he avoided them.'

'Except they noticed a change, just before his annual leave. Combed hair, a nicer smell. We have to assume he met someone.'

'Where though?' Pouget asked.

'It has to be on line eleven. It has to be,' Lombard spoke quickly.

Aubret nodded. 'Or the stunt trucks thing? Anyway, he completely changes his way of life. Cleans himself up, changes his dietary habits, throws out his old ways, literally. Then, within a fortnight, maybe less, he effectively eats himself to death, oesophageal rupture leading to heart attack.'

'So she's dumped him.'

'And then takes his head?' Aubret shook his own. 'It makes some sort of sense up until then.'

'Maybe he attacked her?' Pouget threw it into the mix. 'He was a lonely, desperate guy. She may have been a lonely, desperate woman but it went too far, too quickly.'

'That's a possibility,' Lombard admitted sadly. Though somehow he still felt this wasn't a domestic or sexual crime.

'What else about Barbier specifically?'

'There's the tattoo?' Pouget offered. Both men looked at each other – *where do you start with that?* was the conclusion. 'Described as like an ECG graph?' She held up a picture.

There was a knock at the door, followed by a nurse fussily stepping into the room. 'I told you to rest,' she said humourlessly. 'You have severe concussion. Lying around chatting isn't going to help now, is it? It's lunchtime soon, I want your friends gone by then.'

'I think I'll be out by lunch,' Lombard tried to make his voice sound stronger than it was.

'Oh really, and why's that then?' The nurse didn't look him in the eye, just straightened his sheets and checked his temperature.

'I've eaten here before,' Lombard muttered, and received a scolding look in return.

'Madame,' Pouget interrupted. 'This drawing here, would you say that's the image of an electrocardiogram?'

The nurse took a closer, suspicious look. 'I'm no cardiologist, but I'd say no.' She leant in closer. 'There's no baseline for a start, no hint of regularity. Now, that's enough. I want you two out in the next ten minutes.'

She left in the same fussy manner in which she'd entered, and the three of them gave it a few seconds before continuing.

Lombard flung the covers off his legs and stood, none too steadily by the side of the bed.

'What the hell are you doing, Lombard?' Aubret's frustration was bordering on anger; even Pouget looked annoyed with the *juge*, who was, with some expertise, removing the intravenous cannula from the back of his bruised hand.

'You heard the woman.' He looked from one to the other. 'We have to be out of here in ten minutes.'

Chapter 23

Aubret was making it pretty clear that, first, he wasn't happy a still groggy Lombard had discharged himself from the hospital, and second, having done so, it wasn't either the Palais de Justice nor the *commissariat de police* where they were continuing their ad hoc case review, but Lombard's antiques shop instead. He huffed and puffed, moving carefully through the furniture, nervous about touching anything while looking for somewhere to sit. Commandant Pouget was already seated awkwardly at a Louis XV secretaire while perched nervously on an Art Deco bar stool. Lombard's cat was sitting on the 300-year-old desk in front of her and craving her attention but Pouget, starkly aware of the spinster cat-lady stereotype, was having nothing to do with it.

Eventually Aubret found a sturdy-looking enough divan and guardedly sat down, immediately taking the attention of the cat away from a relieved Pouget. It wasn't comfortable though; there was something harder under the cushion that was causing an issue and he rummaged underneath and pulled out a book. *L'humanité en péril* by Fred Vargas. If he'd felt inclined, Aubret would have run up the stairs and confronted Lombard straight away. Not only had he not handed in the evidence, he had lied to him about it. He didn't doubt for one second that he was keen on solving Barbier's murder, just as much as he was, but why this almost pathological need to go it alone, to pointlessly break the rules. It served no purpose other than to destroy trust; and to Aubret trust was everything.

Lombard descended slowly down the stairs; he'd changed his clothes, almost exactly the same favoured linen trousers, shirt and jacket but without the bloodstains. His hair was wet and he still looked pale. In truth, he still looked like a man who had been beaten up.

'I know it's not quite regulation to have this conference here, but I do feel much better for having changed...'

'What the hell is this?' Aubret held up the book. Shaking with anger he had had every intention of playing it cooler than that, trapping the *juge* if he could, but the red mist had descended and he wanted answers now.

'I can explain that...' Lombard began.

'That is mine.' Elise appeared at the foot of the stairs behind her uncle, walked smartly through the scattered furniture and grabbed the book from a shocked *commissaire*.

'Commissaire, Commandant, this is Elise Battier, my niece. She's staying with me for... for now.'

Elise rounded on a still speechless Aubret. 'My uncle has just told me what happened. What the hell were you thinking?' she asked angrily. 'Letting him discharge himself in that state?' She looked fiercely into his eyes and though Aubret had only met Madeleine on a few occasions, he saw very clearly the family resemblance, and it wasn't just physical.

'You know your uncle,' Pouget said, trying to smooth the confrontation. 'He didn't exactly give us a choice.'

Elise let go of a deep breath and put the book in her bag. Then she shook her head, still angrily, though this time at Lombard. 'Yes, that sounds about right.'

Lombard smiled but it was more of a guilty grimace. 'I shouldn't be too long here.' His voice was forced, still strained. 'We should go out for dinner tonight, there's a new...'

'We are not!' Elise quickly shut him down and went over to kiss him on the cheeks. 'I'm going to do some shopping and we'll eat here,' she said, brooking no argument, 'and then you'll have an early night.'

'If you say so.' He felt embarrassed. 'Here.' He reached into his pocket and gave her a few bank notes.

She grinned at him and turned smartly on her heels to leave. 'No doubt I'll see you again, Commissaire,' she added smartly, before closing the door behind her; the jarring bell above the lintel sounded more like the signal to mark the end of a round of boxing.

Lombard picked up a bottle of water from the desk at the foot of the stairs, and took a large swig.

'Right then,' he said, still looking at the closed door. 'Where were we?'

A relieved Pouget looked at her notes while Aubret sat back down, still speechless. 'The nurse told us she didn't think Barbier's tattoo was an ECG. That was the last thing we talked about.'

'So what is it then?' Lombard asked, keen on the distraction. 'The ECG idea fitted. A worrying one, a result that had persuaded him to change his ways, perhaps. Pity. Is there a way you can date a tattoo? Find out if it's recent or not?' he mused.

Aubret stood by the window. 'We could ask Doctor Cloutier?' he said, though his voice suggested he wasn't dripping in optimism at the thought.

'Honestly, Commissaire, I don't think there's much point. If we carry your euphemism further, I think he goes to the same gyms that I do.'

'A drinker? Great. I wish Doctor Sebourg would get back,' Aubret remarked sullenly.

'Hang on, I sent her a text yesterday. Do I still have my phone?'

Pouget held up the clear bag of his belongings. 'Dead battery, I'd say.'

'Can either of you two get hold of her? I'm aware of the ethics but I want a second opinion on Barbier. I'm sure there's something missing.'

'Oh, they're already on their way back, well, the *procureur* is at least. My guess is he'll be more concerned with the Daucourt girl.'

Lombard decided to sit down and it was obvious to the others that he badly needed to rest. 'In a sense that gives us a bit of breathing space. He won't care about a dead bus driver or, even less, a dead journalist, not while he has Rosa Daucourt to occupy him. Girls run off. They get tired of being bullied by their own families,' he added.

'You have a great deal of experience in all that, right?' Aubret, having a daughter of the same age, couldn't dismiss it so lightly.

'Absolutely none at all until Elise turned up here two nights ago.'

Pouget decided it was time to step in again. 'Texeira has a lead on who might have found the body; whether it matters all that much I don't know.'

'Go on,' Lombard encouraged.

'There's a girl, well, woman, who works the Pont Napoléon beat every now and then and she's not been seen for a few days. She's known as Elaine, not her real name obviously, and she only has the one client apparently. She has a daughter. Travels in from the north of Tours.'

Lombard drummed his fingers on the desk. 'Get on to social services, maybe they're aware of a young girl with that kind of home life at one of the schools up there. Like you say, I don't know where it gets us but it's something.' He stood again, too quickly and grabbed the corner of his desk for support.

'We really should be doing this another time.' Aubret stood decisively.

'No, Commissaire.' Lombard felt himself losing control. 'It was your natural assumption that I'd taken that book, wasn't it? Hidden it behind a cushion…'

'You have previous, Lombard,' the *commissaire* snarled.

'Maybe.' Lombard was angry. 'And maybe sometimes I do things the way you wouldn't, but we might get further, quicker, if you'd stop investigating *me*. Christ, you're like some old-fashioned cuckold, who no longer trusts…' Lombard sat down again, spent. 'I'm sorry, Guy. Commandant.'

Aubret walked slowly over to the *juge* who sat with his eyes closed. 'So am I,' he said, putting a hand on his shoulder. 'But talk to me.' His voice was quiet, but firm.

Lombard didn't open his eyes. 'He could be me.' His voice wasn't sad, it was almost without emotion, just stating a plain fact like an answer in a quiz. 'We have too much in common; something changed in his life. He decided he had to cope with something new and in a different way. He had no family, no friends. A new life completely on his own. Someone kills him and cuts his head off and still no one mourns.'

There was an awkward silence while Aubret and Pouget exchanged worried glances.

'He must have had something. That kind of violence must have a reason.' Aubret took the decision to ignore Lombard's statement.

'But what if it doesn't? What if it's random? He's the perfect random target. Resources will move elsewhere after a while because no one is that interested in a result, there's no one to clamour for it.'

'You have family, and friends.' It was Pouget who intervened. 'So did Barbier, if not a mother like yours, then a mother figure. Someone must be mourning somewhere. At least according to that ticket.'

'Something else that doesn't make sense.' Aubret shook his head, though grateful to be back on more solid ground.

Lombard remained silent for a moment. 'You know what I think,' he stood slowly, carefully. 'I think I've had a massive whack on the head, and I should go and lie down for a bit. I may be able to think more clearly after a rest.'

'We haven't really got anywhere, have we?' Aubret was frustrated.

'I don't know about that.' Lombard smiled at him warmly. 'Maybe we cleared the air a bit. That book is on my desk by the way, at the Palais de Justice, if you want to go and pick it up.' He knew that wasn't the case but in his concussive fog, he couldn't remember exactly where he'd put it. 'I'll speak to some of Madeleine's contacts,' he covered, 'see if I can find out what Brunel was working on, though, as I remember, he didn't give a lot away. Anything in his apartment?'

'No, not much. It really looked like he just slept there, and ate.' Pouget was looking at her notes again. 'There was no laptop, no phone. We're checking all his records. But according to recent bank statements, about the only place he called in regularly was some pizza place. Pizzeria Napoli on...'

'...on the place des Halles.' Lombard went to his desk and pulled from his blood-soaked jacket the flyer he and Benbarek had found at Barbier's apartment. Sheepishly he gave it to Aubret, who raised an eyebrow in a sort of bored admonishment.

'Interesting,' was all he said.

'Indeed.' Lombard seemed rejuvenated. 'I think Elise and I will be dining out tonight after all.'

Chapter 24

In the end Elise had slipped back in while he had a sleep, leaving behind some random groceries and a note. 'Bumped into some friends. You should have an early night.' He couldn't really argue with that, but that didn't take into account that there was a no doubt steaming D'Archambeau heading back from Lausanne on a late train, so he had to get things in order first. He was, after all, currently the highest-ranking figure in the *magistrature* with Dampierre incapacitated and the *procureur* himself away. He would not be happy about being called back, he would not be happy to find Lombard at the helm and he would certainly not be happy to have two gruesome murders and a missing billionaire's daughter. Though the knowledge that Lombard had been attacked would no doubt cheer him somewhat.

Lombard still felt he was missing something. Perhaps he'd become too fixated on who Barbier was and not why he would have been killed; one led from the other naturally, but he felt he needed a change of focus. His friend, the journalist Louis Maichin, a useful and discreet sounding board, might help; he was also a safety net that could be used against D'Archambeau. The *procureur* was a smooth and dangerous political operator, but was too guided by his own vanity.

Having a friend in the media, the highly visible local press, meant Lombard could plump the man's ego like a soft pillow from time to time and protect himself in the process. It was a potentially dangerous game to play; the *magistrature* and the media never mixed and his position would finally become untenable if his 'collaboration' was discovered. All of those political manoeuvrings aside, Maichin was also an ex-colleague of Madeleine's and would certainly know more about the secretive, now dead, Edmund Brunel.

'Christ, you look terrible!' Maichin leant back showing a beige shirt bulging at the waist, his loosened tie pushed to one side. A waiter arrived, placing two beers on the table between them, and Lombard waited for him to depart.

'Good,' he said simply. 'I'd hate to feel this rough and not show it.' The waiter having gone, he filled him in on the background of the investigation so far.

'So where does Brunel fit in?' Maichin leant forward, his alert eyes catching the dull glow from the tea-light candle floating in a bowl on the table between them. He wasn't one to hang around or skirt the issue.

Lombard shrugged. 'He said he had information on Barbier, our headless corpse. Told me where and when to meet him. I went there, his throat had been cut and I got hit. I wish I knew more.'

'He *told* you he had information?'

'First there was a text, then a note left in my jacket pocket at the cinema. All very Cold War.'

'Yep. That's our Edmund. A good journalist, really good. But paranoid as hell.'

'Looks like he was right to be.'

They both stared out of the window. Across the street was the Pizzeria Napoli, its bright window throwing a light on to the delivery riders gathered out the front. 'What a job,'

Maichin sighed. 'Low wages, the chance of getting beaten up on delivery and all the time dodging immigration while you're doing it.'

'Do you know the place?' Lombard's question sounded innocent, but he wasn't fooling his friend.

'I wondered why you'd asked me here. Don't get me wrong, I'm as big a fan of...' He picked up the menu card. '...of vegetarian mocktails as the next man, but I knew you had a reason. Talk to me.'

Lombard smiled. 'The usual terms apply?'

'You scratch mine, etc. Yes.'

'Well, it's thin.' Lombard told him about the only concrete connection between Barbier and Brunel: the pizza place. They'd found the flyer in Barbier's apartment and Brunel's bank statements showed he ate there regularly.

'Lombard, I've been a journalist for thirty years and if there's one thing us journos know about, it's fast food, but that just sounds like a coincidence to me.'

They both turned to watch the restaurant across the street again, just as a group of about a dozen women came out of a door two units down and made their way into the pizza place. They were greeted warmly by a large man wearing an apron, who stood behind the counter and who showed them to a group of tables out of sight.

'It doesn't look very promising, does it?' Lombard rapped his knuckles on the table. 'What was Brunel working on, do you know?'

Maichin shook his head. 'No. I'd tell you if I did, but as you can see, he had to keep things pretty tight because he upset a lot of people. He'd disappear for a few months then come back with some VIP's head on a spike. He was really bloody good,' he added with mixture of awe and sadness. 'But it was probably always going to end this way.'

'That's what Madeleine always said. So, nothing at all? No hint?'

The journalist puffed out his cheeks. 'Look at who he targeted is your best bet. Bankers, organised crime, which, let's be honest, is much the same thing. He definitely had a thing for big business but also…' Maichin leant in again, more animated this time. 'Terrorism. I remember him saying once that the government and the wider media were riding the anti-Muslim wave; complacency he said, and that the Muslims weren't the main threat anymore; it was domestic terrorism. Political causes, nihilism… he probably had a file on your mum somewhere!'

Lombard laughed. 'I don't think she killed him though.' Then he winced as his head hurt.

'I know he spent a lot of time looking into climate change activism, but it got him into strife.'

'How do you mean?'

Maichin lowered his voice, moved the tea-light out of the way and leant in closer. 'A few years ago, he started researching a whole thing on this rich anarchist…'

'A rich anarchist?'

'Yeah, I know right? Some posh kid, doesn't have to work, gets bored, jumps on a bandwagon.'

'He might actually believe what he stands for too,' Lombard mused.

'He might,' Maichin nodded. 'But it's easy to have time for causes when mummy and daddy are footing the bill.'

Lombard conceded the point. 'So where was the strife? That sounds more like a Sunday supplement story.'

'This kid had connections up to the hilt, put an injunction on Brunel, a serious one and he was forced to leave it.' Lombard raised his eyebrows and Maichin caught the hint. 'Officially put it to one side at least.'

'So who was this rich kid?'

'He goes by the name of Clovis…'

'Ha! Of course he does. The first king of the Franks, died in 511.'

'Right. His father is actually some rich industrialist from the south-west. Lots of money, lots of influence, you know the story. Brunel was shut down and Clovis went "underground", or more likely got a position on the board of daddy's company and put childish things away.' Lombard closed his eyes and rubbed his temples hard. 'Go home, Lombard. Sleep on whatever it is.'

The *juge* ignored him and caught the eye of the waiter. 'Two more beers, please.' The waiter looked offended by the order and removed the mocktail menu with a theatrical flounce. 'But that was a few years ago… anything more recent?'

Machin leant back. 'If there was, he was keeping it quiet. And for good reason too, by the looks of things.'

'He wasn't one to sit around though, was he?'

'No, there is that. We'd normally get a sniff, but there was nothing new in recent times.'

Lombard nodded thoughtfully. 'Maybe he wasn't working on anything new at all.'

'Meaning?'

'Meaning he wasn't the kind to let things drop, was he? Especially if he was actually *told* to drop it. A red rag to a bull.'

'But how does Clovis, or whatever he's called, connect with Brunel and your bus driver?'

Lombard guardedly told him about the book, guardedly because it was an even thinner connection than the pizza flyer, but he realised he had precious little else other than these vague connections. If they even were connections.

The journalist shrugged in response. 'I've seen stronger evidence than that, but I've also seen worse. This book does suggest some common ground at least and there can't be too much of that between a wealthy nihilistic environmental terrorist and a friendless bus driver from the *quartier* Sanitas.'

'One lost his head enough to bomb his own inheritance and one literally lost his head.' Lombard snorted in frustration.

'That's it, that's the connection. God I'm an idiot!'

'Go on.' Lombard leant in again,

Chapter 25

Officer Texeira deftly carried three drinks back from the busy bar and put them down on the table.

'What is wrong with people?' He shook his head as if dealing with a great injustice. 'You wait ten minutes in a queue, get to the front and you still haven't decided what you want? Man, that annoys me!'

'Everything annoys you,' Pouget said flatly, taking her open can of Sprite, and handing the same to Benbarek. 'By the way, is this why you invited us along? Because you're the only one on duty and yet the only one who's drinking.'

'Cheers,' Texeira replied with a grin, lifting his plastic beer glass and taking a celebratory sip.

'I didn't think this place would get so busy,' Benbarek noted, taking the straw out of his can and laying it to one side.

'You Parisiens always think anyone outside of the *périphérique* is in bed by eight in the evening,' Texeira teased.

'And anyone outside of the *périphérique* has a chip on their shoulder about what goes on inside of it,' Benbarek replied testily, but was greeted with another Texeira grin which he then matched with his own.

'It is really busy here though since they opened this outdoor bar.' Pouget was scanning the crowd intently.

'I don't think you're ever off-duty, Commandant.'

Benbarek meant it as a compliment but, again, Texeira was in impish mood and said simply, 'She's looking for eligible men!'

Pouget gave him a filthy look which was met with a wink. Benbarek then said something which was drowned out by the band that were restarting after an interval.

'Oh good,' Benbarek said more loudly. 'More thrash metal. My favourite.'

A large crowd gathered in front of the stage dancing and cheering the band on, as the heavily made-up front man snarled and screamed his way through a song. The three officers all caught each other's eyes and smiled, a mutual acknowledgement that they all felt out of place and hoped the noise would soon be over.

'Why are we here anyway?' Pouget managed to make herself heard over the din.

'We're waiting for things to get busier in the car park back there.' Texeira hooked a thumb over his shoulder, indicating the Parking Napoléon in the dark beyond the stage.

'It's not as quiet around here as it used to be,' Pouget said. 'Maybe the prostitutes have found a new spot.'

Texeira shrugged. 'Maybe. But they were here on Sunday.'

'She must be scared,' Benbarek offered.

'Or worse.' Pouget shook her head sadly.

'I don't get it,' Texeira said, able to lower his voice at a break in songs. 'She must have told someone about it, one of the other prostitutes, she must have. The others who work here say they know nothing about it. Normally they stick together, you know? Swap numbers and so on, just in case.'

'Did you speak to the pimp? They usually know if there's someone new on their patch.' Benbarek's face dropped as a new song started as Texeira nodded in response rather than fight the noise.

'Sometimes you get amateurs, just doing it for the thrill.'

'Thanks, Commandant,' Texeira rolled his eyes. 'That means we're looking for the proverbial needle in a heroin rehab centre.'

Both Pouget and Benbarek looked confused, trying to work out if Texeira's metaphor was genius or nonsense. But fortunately a commotion at the bar meant they were saved the trouble.

A tall, thin man in a suit was being shouted at by customers in the queue for the bar, while another man, more athletic and blond, was trying to pull him away.

'Isn't that the Daucourt brothers?' Benbarek asked.

The altercation was becoming more heated as a large man in the queue took particular offence at something being said.

'I'm looking for her!' Auguste Daucourt shouted, slurring his words as he did so. 'I know she came this way.'

'If he's talking about his sister, we better get involved,' Pouget said, standing up as she did so. Benbarek and Texeira did the same, and all three got to the bar just as Auguste Daucourt threw a wild punch at a security guard who had come to intervene. The punch missed by some distance, but was reason enough for the security guard, who had a face suggesting that reasons weren't that necessary anyway, to throw one back. Auguste Daucourt fell to the ground while his younger brother shook his head in annoyance.

'Did you need to do that?' Texeira addressed the square-like security man, while pulling on his orange 'Police' armband and showing his ID. The man just shrugged and pointed at his own ID, which was strapped to his own bulging bicep. Pouget stepped in and took note of the security company, Fostan Sécurité, and told the man to go back to his position at the door, which he only reluctantly agreed to do.

Benbarek took Jules Daucourt aside. He was slightly inebriated, though not as much as his brother who was now sitting up and carefully moving his prominent jaw. 'I heard your brother. He said Rosa came this way. How long ago?'

Momentarily confused, the younger Daucourt brother was slow to answer. 'Not Rosa,' he said, trying to sound more sober than he was. 'Nadine, his wife. He's looking for his wife.'

'She's missing too?'

Jules Daucourt shrugged. 'Sort of. Not really. He just wanted to know where she went, that's all. We're supposed to be celebrating...'

Pouget joined in the impromptu interrogation. 'Celebrating? Celebrating what?'

The younger man realised that he had struck the wrong note. 'Well, not celebrating. Not really. I'm going back to the Amazon tomorrow.' He leant in towards Pouget. 'Can't wait to be honest,' he shook his head. 'This place is too dangerous!' He chuckled to himself.

'So you're not sticking around waiting for your sister to be found then?' Benbarek was having trouble hiding what he really thought.

Jules waved a hand and shrugged again. 'She'll turn up!'

Commandant Pouget and Benbarek took the brothers up to the taxi rank at the bridge to send them home, leaving Texeira with a 'Happy hunting!' salutation, which did nothing to fire his optimism.

He wandered out past the bar area and the band and back to the shadowy Parking Napoléon.

'Back again, love? No luck?' The familiar face of one of his contacts grinned at him from the half-light falling from a street lamp. 'Are you sure you didn't just dream her?' The cackle followed him into the darkness. 'Seriously though,' the hard-faced woman said, trotting up to his side on her high heels. 'You're bad for business, mate. I know all the girls who are here, someone would have said something about a body.'

Texeira shrugged and thought about what Pouget had said. 'Maybe she's not a working girl,' he said quietly.

'A tourist you mean? We get plenty of them.'

'And you tolerate that?'

It was her turn to shrug. 'It's a free country. You know, couples wanting to play games. It's quite sweet when you think about it. Though it often ends badly.'

'How do you mean?'

She laughed again. 'Think about it! It all seems fun when you're planning it in your comfy home, I guess. But then you're out here on the streets, it's cold, it's dark. He, and it usually is, looks more experienced at this than her... it happens.'

'Happen recently?'

'All the time. Just this week. Poor cow. I'd seen her before; sometimes her bloke would turn up, sometimes he wouldn't. He probably got off on that.' She drew on her cigarette.

'She's lucky you were around.'

The woman snorted. 'Yeah, I am an angel. I made her give me her number though, and a name. Elaine, though I doubt that's real. I told her that she'd put us all in danger and if she wants to hang around, fine, do what you want. But you play by our rules here. She said she knew the rules, that she wasn't a complete amateur anyway.'

'I don't understand.'

'I didn't pry, you don't, but my guess is she got lucky. She used to be a working girl, and she got a sugar daddy client.'

'And she was back this week?' Texeira asked, trying to hide his excitement.

'Sunday. This time he must have shown up. I saw her run out of the car park, a right look on her face. Christ knows what he asked her to do for him!'

Chapter 26

Louis Maichin undid his slightly old-fashioned striped tie and rolled it up slowly around his left hand. 'Most of this is going to be off the top of my head, so you'll have to dig around a bit.' He tapped something into his phone. 'Have you people got the resources, or do you want help with that?' Lombard nodded in good humour, but he was also getting impatient. 'Like I say,' Maichin continued, 'it's almost as vague a connection as your pizza flyer and book are between our Clovis and your Barbier, and you're not going to like the end.' He kept searching on his phone while subtly making sure that they weren't being overheard and that the waiter especially was off elsewhere. 'Gotcha!' he said, and sat up straight looking Lombard hard in the eye. The message was to concentrate. The *juge* moved his beer glass slightly to the side and laid his own hands flat on the table in front of him. If he'd closed his eyes, he'd have given the impression of being at a séance.

'This Clovis character, and by the way, from what Brunel hinted to me, they're not always the same person.' Maichin's voice sounded hurried; Lombard didn't believe the journalist was a man given to nerves but as a colleague had just been murdered, he was rightly on edge. 'This Clovis is more of a title bestowed on whoever leads the group. It's like an old mafia trick, use a title, not a name.' Lombard nodded. 'Well, this particular Clovis wasn't averse to violence. "By any means necessary" and all of that.'

'You still haven't given me a name.' Lombard couldn't help but be impatient.

'I'm a journalist, Lombard, let me set the scene.'

The *juge* didn't smile and Maichin got the not-so-subtle hint.

'Delaunay,' he said slowly, again looking around him. 'Lucien Delaunay. Ring a bell?'

Lombard currently felt like a cathedral bell had whacked him in the forehead, but concussion aside the name meant nothing to him.

'His family are petrochemical billionaires,' Maichin continued. 'Do you remember the bombing of an oil refinery in the south-west a few years ago? Three people dead.' Lombard didn't. 'That was Lucien Delaunay.' Maichin looked very pleased with himself while Lombard let the information sink in.

'What are you saying?' he asked, eventually. 'That this Delaunay bombed his own family's business?'

The journalist nodded. 'Covered up to make it look like an accident. According to Brunel. That's why you've not heard of it.'

'I still think I should have.' He couldn't help but feel affronted.

'This isn't Balzac's nineteenth century, Juge, the judiciary doesn't have the power or the access that the media have these days.' Lombard was still shaking his head when Maichin continued. 'He resented the fact that the family business was angling for Arctic gas drilling apparently, threw a tantrum. Families, eh? It's all relative.' He smiled at his own joke. 'The family had been trying to hide him for years, apparently – not the brightest, even reading and stuff.'

'I still don't see the connection to my victim though.'

'This is the ending you're not going to like.' Maichin placed his beer bottle down carefully. 'He's dead.'

'Brilliant. Well, thanks for that!'

'His body was found washed up on the banks of the Garonne, head removed. His family identified what was left of him from a tattoo on his shoulders. He'd gone into the mountains with a friend. Delaunay came back a headless, rotted corpse.'

'What kind of tattoo?'

'I don't know, is it important?'

'It could be very important. And the friend?'

'Who knows? He may just not have been found.'

Lombard leant back, drumming his fingers on the table, his legs twitching with excitement. 'Edmund Brunel didn't think this Delaunay was the corpse, did he?'

Maichin shrugged. 'Edmund could be a crackpot, don't get me wrong, a brilliant crackpot, but he loved a conspiracy too. It's up to you now.'

'Thanks a lot,' Lombard said quietly, hoping his genuine sincerity actually showed.

Maichin bowed his head in acknowledgement 'You're dealing with a lot of money here, a lot. Protected rich kids. If Clovis – ridiculous name – is responsible for Barbier, though Christ knows why, you'll never get him. Barbier was a nothing.'

'And Brunel?'

Maichin paused, shrugged. 'He was a journalist.' He grinned. 'Even lower.'

They both took a drink.

'Anyway, what about the girl, Rosa Daucourt?' Maichin asked after a few moments' silence. 'You know that'll be your boss's priority, right? The family is beginning to get restless, which is how I know about it.'

Lombard sighed. 'Of course, another rich family, only this one using the press.' He shook his head angrily. 'Damn it, kids run off. Just because it's some rich family doesn't mean I drop everything else. She's eighteen, for Christ's sakes. She's probably in a... in a squat somewhere, smoking weed. Living for the first time. Good on her. I've met the family; the only surprise is she didn't get out sooner.'

Maichin snorted in contempt. 'It's probably not even a squat she's in. This Clovis didn't squat, he recruited from them, but he bought nice properties and decorated them in squat chic; proper old money does that...'

'They can afford to.'

'So you reckon that's where this Rosa Daucourt has gone? Roughing it in a squat with the other millionaire activist kids?'

Lombard shrugged. 'It's a possibility. There's nothing to show she's been abducted, no ransom demand, nothing. The family's been threatened a few times.'

'Well, like I said, it'll be D'Archambeau's priority and he'll insist it's yours too. Billionaire family, you know what René D'Archambeau is like. It's all about the power.'

Lombard brooded for a moment and then got out his phone. 'Talking of power, do you know what this is?'

Maichin took the phone from him, his face lighting up from the electronic glow. 'It looks like a child won a competition to design a new logo for the masons.' He handed the phone back.

'I know what you mean. It doesn't seem real.'

'To be fair, those organisations rarely do. Where's it from?'

'It was on a medallion, found on Barbier's body.'

'I reckon he sent off for it,' Maichin joked. 'An ad at the back of a magazine.'

'The kind you write for?' Lombard joked.

'That'll do!' They fell into a friendly silence. 'Seriously, Lombard, D'Archambeau. He'll be gunning for you.'

'I know. As if I haven't got enough headaches.' He took a sip of his beer. 'He's going to be on my back from the start, isn't he?'

'Like an angry rash, yes. He won't like having been recalled from Lausanne. Your *procureur* likes his social life, a girl in every port as they say.'

'Really?' he replied, sounding unimpressed.

Maichin shook his head and smiled. 'You know you can be very naive at times. Just because you and Madeleine had the perfect marriage, doesn't mean everybody else has. The happy, shiny D'Archambeaus are a cynical, political union. They come together at weekends for social events only. She has lovers, he has lovers. It's a marriage all for show, made in the kind of magazine you find at a hairdressing salon.' Lombard went to interrupt. 'No! Not the kind I write for.'

They chatted for another thirty minutes or so and then the throbbing in Lombard's head became too much. Maichin was wrong about his supposed naivety. He was well aware of René's wanderings; they just didn't interest him that was all.

Maichin had offered to get him a taxi but he felt he needed the air instead. He was also starving so took himself across the street to the bright lights of the Pizzeria Napoli and ordered a ham and cheese calzone from the large man behind the counter. His greeting was definitely not as warm as for the group of women who he could hear still chattering and laughing away in the seated area at the back.

'Take a seat,' the man said without looking at him. 'I'll tell you when it's ready.'

Lombard did so but after a few minutes went back to the counter and took a sheet of paper from his inside pocket. 'Recognise this man?' he asked, holding up the picture of Barbier with authority and no preamble. Now he had the man's attention.

'Lots of people come in here, pal,' he snarled back.

'That's not answering my question, is it?' Lombard wasn't letting go. He wasn't one to throw his weight around if he could avoid it, outright aggression wasn't his nature. But he'd had a bad day, his head hurt and tomorrow wasn't looking much better.

'Trouble, Enzo?'

Lombard turned slowly and the enormous figure of Victor Fostan, the gym monkey, towered above him, cutting out the light. He looked even more imposing dressed in bike leathers and carrying a black crash helmet. He looked like The Terminator.

'Are you part of the delivery team?' Lombard didn't take his eyes off the other man's, but nodded towards his crash helmet.

'I own this place.'

With the stereotypical aggression of someone who pumped weights for a hobby, Fostan didn't take kindly to the insult but as he'd already been beaten up once in the last twenty-four hours, Lombard wondered how much worse a second one could be? There seemed to be a low rumble emanating somewhere in his opponent's capacious chest, preparing to unleash some physical hell, no doubt.

'Maybe you recognise him.' He held up the picture for Fostan to look at, but he didn't take his eyes off Lombard. 'Though I don't think he was a gym regular. He had the same physique as your cousin. What happened to Gilles, anyway?'

Suddenly their private confrontation, a silent world, was sent spinning into another realm entirely as the group of women he had seen enter earlier, surrounded them, still chattering and giggling.

'Fancy meeting you here,' Muriel Fauvion said, leaning into his ear, smelling of wine and putting an arm through his. 'Looks like you've found my secret single ladies' club.'

'Muriel!' Lombard, surprised and relieved, kissed her on both cheeks, while the women and Fostan stared at him, a wild mixture of emotions on their faces: anger, jealousy, fear. All except for one blonde woman, who averted her eyes, trying to hide her face and therefore standing out all the more. 'How lovely to see you,' the confident *juge* said loudly, though not taking his eyes off the disguised Nadine Daucourt as he did so. 'Singles night, eh? Let me walk you home.'

He left as part of the babbling group, without his pizza, and still thought he heard the low rumble of aggression behind him as he did so, or maybe that was his own stomach.

Chapter 27

Just as he had forty-eight hours earlier, Lombard held a cup of coffee and stared out of his office window. It was quieter on the place Jean-Jaurès than it had been the other day, because, to be accurate, that had been forty-six hours previously. Today he was even earlier and his mood very different to then. The literal headache was still there, like distant, rumbling thunder and the metaphorical headaches were piling up too.

Elise had not returned the night before and he was angry and concerned – concerned for her welfare and angry with himself because he felt responsible. She hadn't replied to his messages either and as far as he could tell, hadn't even seen them. He had convinced himself that she had come from Bordeaux following this Clovis character, either a new incarnation or the original, Lucien Delaunay, as Edmund Brunel had believed. Clovis: an early Middle Ages ruler who sought unity through warfare. This modern Clovis espoused the same, but for the cause of the environment, to save the world. You're either with us or against us and enemies must be destroyed.

He regretted deeply not going with his first instinct, which had been to contact Elise's parents, and instead going with what he thought Madeleine would have done. Then another thought hit him. Who was he kidding? His first instinct hadn't been to contact Elise's parents at all nor was it to do what Madeleine would have done either. His first instinct was to be needed. A middle-aged vanity, driven by loneliness and which had now put Elise in added danger. But then there was a flipside: what if Elise was simply having a good time? Living her best life, and Louis Aguirre, charmless and intense to Lombard's mind, was nothing to do with Lucien Delaunay or this Clovis? He admonished himself. *Is this what parenting is?* he thought. *Random, paranoid leaps of logic, filling in the space between exhaustion.* It's her life, he repeated to himself. These are her choices. I am not her father. And thank Christ for that.

There was a knock at the door and Muriel brought him in another coffee. 'You got home OK then?' she asked warmly. 'You did promise to walk me home, but then you could barely walk yourself.' She sat on the edge of the large desk. 'Can you please get some rest?'

'Yes, I will,' he smiled. 'And, sorry about that, thanks for putting me in the taxi.'

'I'd have come with you, made sure you got home safely, but we have a rule in our little club. We stick together on our nights out.'

'That's probably a good thing.' He sat down. 'I didn't know you were in a singles club,' he said, awkwardly.

'Well, I am single!' she laughed.

'Do you know all the other women well?'

'Well enough.' Her smile dropped. 'Why?'

'There was a woman there I'm particularly interested in.' It was clumsy to say the least and Muriel immediately stood up from the desk, a hurt look on her face. 'I didn't mean it like that,' he backtracked. 'There was a blonde woman. I think I know her, that's all. Smaller than you.'

'Lucille? She's pretty, isn't she?' Lombard made no comment as Muriel sat back down. 'She disguises herself because of a previous relationship, abuse. She's scared to be recognised.'

'That makes sense.' Lombard wasn't entirely convinced. 'Does she talk about it?'

'Never. She doesn't have much luck by all accounts, but she has a weird taste in men for someone so pretty, always going for odd little weirdos. Lonely middle-aged men.' She blushed, realising that she might just have described Lombard himself, but carried on hurriedly.

'Was she seeing anyone recently?'

'I think she was seeing someone.'

He showed her a picture of Thibaud Barbier.

She shrugged. 'That's not the person I met. He just disappeared anyway. Probably got what he wanted and just went.'

Lombard sensed her anger. 'Maybe, I've probably got the wrong person. I wasn't on the best of form! But thanks about the taxi, I mean it. I owe you. *Again.*'

'Well now, in that case, are you free on Friday?' Muriel purred, smiling at the sudden fear on Lombard's face. 'You can take me out for dinner. I'll borrow a blonde wig if you like?'

She wasn't naturally flirty, certainly not with Lombard, but she enjoyed putting him on the back foot, especially where 'they' were concerned.

His phone rang and he snatched it up off his desk. 'Lombard?' The raspy voice of Dr Karine Sebourg bled through the small speaker. 'I honestly didn't think you'd answer your phone!' she snorted down the line. 'What's up? Your message was somewhat lacking in detail.'

Lombard shrugged a 'what can I do?' at Muriel, who smiled back and wrote a message on the notepad in front of him, before leaving the room. 'FRIDAY – IT'S A DATE.'

Lombard briefly explained the death of Barbier and what they currently knew to Dr Sebourg, trying not to reveal too strongly his doubts about her locum, Dr Cloutier.

'OK,' she said, drawing out the short phrase suggesting that actually she knew why he was ringing. 'What's the issue though? Cloutier is a good man.'

Lombard paused. 'I'm not saying he isn't, but is he a good doctor? I just trust your judgement more and I need a break on this, just to see if we've missed anything.'

She gave a heavy sigh. 'Why would you think he's missed something?' It wasn't confrontational, she wasn't linking arms with the forensic pathologists' union; it was a question offered up in a way as to suggest that she needed confirmation of something she already knew.

'I think he drinks,' Lombard said simply.

'So do you,' she retorted.

'I don't have to wield a scalpel. And sorry, I don't trust his judgement.'

She sighed again. 'I know. Look, he's had some problems...' Lombard remembered the faded photograph of a boy placed prominently on the doctor's desk and belatedly made the connection. 'I won't be back for a few days,' Sebourg continued, 'but I'll just check on how he's doing, discreet enquiries. I'm not all that happy to do that though.' She paused. 'You know why you don't trust him, don't you?' It was a question delivered in as delicate a way as was possible for Dr Karine Sebourg, that is, not very.

'Go on.' Lombard didn't want her to go on at all.

'You're both very alike,' she said flatly. 'Hiding your troubles badly. Oh, and Lombard,' she hurried on, not giving him the chance to answer or get angry, 'D'Archambeau was not happy, not happy at all at being called back. He was having rather a good time there, I think.' The line went dead.

It was a double warning that Lombard didn't actually need. He was expecting a whirlwind when D'Archambeau returned, so ideally he'd like something a little more concrete in the way of evidence and even theory before that showdown took place, but also the flag about Cloutier and his behaviour. Maybe she had a point.

There was a knock at his door and he spun round in surprise. 'You're becoming disturbingly conscientious, Lombard.' Commissaire Aubret filled the door frame, though shielding his eyes from the sun pouring in through the window.

'How did you know I was here?' He pushed the Vargas book, which he'd eventually found, and the stunt park ticket towards the *commissaire* who picked them up and walked to the window. He put the book and ticket in his pocket, muttered, 'Never in doubt,' and then turned around, putting the sun behind him and scratching the top of his balding head. 'Your niece said you weren't there, and after I checked some of your favourite bars, I thought I'd try here. Imagine my surprise.'

'My niece? Elise was at home?'

There was a hint of desperation and relief in his voice that wasn't lost on Aubret. 'Yes. Is everything all right?'

'It is now.' Lombard gave a huge sigh, letting go of some of the tension that had gripped his chest since the previous evening. 'Kids, eh?' he joked.

Aubret laughed. 'Yeah, kids. And you've only been at it for a couple of days! Try twenty years.' Lombard couldn't suppress a yawn, holding up a hand by way of apology. 'You may have to smooth the waters when you get home, by the way.'

'Oh?'

'I just happened to ask her where she was when you were hit. She didn't like the suggestion.' There was no hint of apology.

'I'll bet.' Lombard tried to shrug it off. 'And?'

'Out with her boyfriend. Louis Aguirre, is that him?' Lombard nodded. 'She wasn't happy about needing an alibi, but someone has to ask these things.'

'You didn't really think she'd be involved though?' Lombard faked a laugh.

'No. But I have to check. You getting a beating reflects on me and I don't like that.' He slumped into the chair on the other side of Lombard's desk.

'I nearly had another one last night.' Lombard tried to laugh it off, but his colleague's tone changed immediately.

'Talk to me,' Aubret said, leaning forward over the desk.

Lombard felt slightly embarrassed, like a big brother had offered to sort out a bully for him, and he stood nervously, pacing the office. 'Do you remember Gilles Fostan?' he asked eventually.

'Fostan?' Aubret looked confused. 'The armed robber Fostan?'

'That's him.'

'But he disappeared a few years ago.'

'I know that. Well, I know it now. Did you know he had a cousin?'

'Yes. Victor,' the *commissaire* replied simply, but the one word conveyed so much. Not only did he know Fostan had a cousin, he was well aware of what he got up to.

'How have I not heard of him before?' Lombard asked.

Aubret sat down. 'This all kicked off when you were…' He couldn't find the words.

'On leave?'

'On leave, that's it. He has a gym out past Saint-Cyr, but he has a few sidelines too. Security officially. Thugs for hire in practice. A couple of fast food places.'

'I see.'

'He's done well for himself.' Aubret's voice was heavy with sarcasm. 'He's vicious though. There was a big squat out over Fondettes way. The owners, some rich family from Paris, couldn't be bothered with the courts so they hired Fostan and his army of goons. One kid nearly died, took a ferocious beating.'

'And what happened?'

Aubret looked at him, a cold glint in his eye. 'Your esteemed colleague Juge Dampierre felt there was insufficient evidence to push for a conviction. In my opinion though, that was bollocks. Dampierre lives near the squat and he didn't like it. Didn't like it at all.'

'I see.'

'What has Fostan got to do with this, if anything?'

Lombard went to the window. 'It might be another coincidence,' he spoke slowly, running things through in his head. 'But hear me out.'

'I'm all ears.'

'Line eleven.'

'Line eleven?'

'I said hear me out,' Lombard snapped. 'Line eleven. Barbier's line. Also has Fostan's gym on the north end of it. And in the middle? The Pizzeria Napoli. Both Barbier and Brunel frequented that pizza place and last night, so did Victor Fostan.'

Aubret thought about this for a moment. 'Well, it's something. I don't know what, but it's something.'

Lombard continued. 'Brunel upset people. Just suppose that whatever he was working on upset the wrong people and they hired Fostan to get him off their backs? That would explain how Fostan paid off his cousin's debts too.'

Aubret's eyes squinted, a sure sign he was interested. 'What was he working on, Brunel, do you know?'

'You're not going to like it.'

'No kidding?'

'Something about domestic terrorism.'

'Oh Christ.'

'Eco warriors, as the press likes to call them.'

'Psychopaths with a cause, you mean?'

Lombard nodded. 'Have I ruined your day already, Commissaire?'

Aubret didn't look at him, just stared off into the distance. 'Nothing new there,' he said eventually.

They sat in silence for a few moments. 'Why were you looking for me anyway?' Lombard asked after a while.

Aubret brightened. 'You know what, I almost forgot,' he beamed. 'Texeira has found the elusive Elaine and she'll only talk to our top man.'

Chapter 28

In truth Lombard had become less interested in what the elusive Elaine might have to say. Unless she, and whoever her mark had been, had actually killed Barbier or seen who had, both of which he dismissed out of hand, there seemed little that she could offer. It was a matter of dotting the i's and crossing the t's of the investigation. Admin work, nothing more.

At least those had been his initial thoughts when Aubret said that she had been located. His mind changed very quickly, however, as the *commissaire* explained the circumstances of her discovery and the descriptions of those involved. And even more so when he relayed the complicated, paranoid instructions and conditions under which she would agree to be met. Something wasn't right, something didn't ring true. This woman was frightened, very frightened. And so Lombard found himself sat on the backseat of a tram heading from Vaucanson at the end of the line near the airport in north Tours, back towards the city and waiting for Elaine to get on at Tranchée, just before the Pont Wilson. She would sit at the front and he was to sit on the seat behind her. He would have as long as it took to get to the station, absolute maximum fifteen minutes, to ask what he needed to ask and then she would alight and he would stay where he was.

For the second time in just a few days it felt he was being made to act out someone else's Cold War fantasies and the last time hadn't ended too well. He was certainly intrigued though, hooked even; he just hoped that this time he wasn't in for another headache.

It was mid-morning and it wasn't very busy. The early morning rush hour was over and the sedate, quiet pace of the tram fitted well with the few people on it. Half-asleep students, late-running shopworkers, the elderly who may or may not have somewhere to go, but just liked to be out in the sunshine before it got too hot. Texeira had done well to find Elaine and had done so by good, solid police work, which made Commissaire Aubret inordinately proud.

The tram glided along and despite what he considered to be the absurdity of these arrangements, they gave him a rush of excitement, his leg shaking with the adrenalin. This, he realised, was living. Two stops before Tranchée at Trois-Rivières, a youngish woman got on, pushing a pram. She looked thin and pale, her bleach blonde hair sitting messily on top of her head like a smashed meringue. The dark under her eyes told a story of exhaustion and constant battles, but also gratitude that the child, which looked too big for the buggy, was asleep. It occurred to him that Elaine might get on early, as he had, to see how the ground lay, but she didn't look wary, she looked weary.

Though she did sit at the front.

Lombard's pulse raced and having waited until after the next stop, he slowly made his way towards the empty seat behind her, trying to make it look as if to exit. He sat down again just before the tram came to a rest at Tranchée and was about to speak, when she stood, clumsily manoeuvred the buggy in the direction of the doors and got off. Was he meant to follow? He froze, and before he could get up a smart-looking woman in her thirties sat next to him blocking his exit. He sat back in frustration as the doors silently closed.

Commissaire Aubret would not be impressed, and he could imagine the gleeful admonishment, '*Stop playing at being a policeman, Lombard, you're a judge, go back to your desk.*'

He leant against the window and looked out as his quarry, the woman with the pram, crossed over the road.

'You are not the top man,' the woman now sitting beside him said quietly, but with no hint of fear.

She kept her eyes looking straight forward, and he doubted for a second whether it had been her who spoke, but no one else was sat close enough. Then she looked at him with cold eyes.

'What do you want from me?'

Lombard, rarely for him, had prejudged and wasn't prepared for the elegant, straight-backed and well-dressed person who sat beside him, a handbag and a thick black document portfolio sitting neatly on her lap. Her hair was in a tight bun and no longer blonde as in the pictures, but auburn and shiny. Her eyebrows were plucked neatly, framing her green eyes. There was a small stud in her elegant Grecian nose. In all, she looked like a lawyer and she regarded Lombard like a prospective client who she assumed was guilty.

'I'm Juge d'Instruction Matthieu Lombard,' he said, buying some time. 'The *top man* is out of town, I'm afraid.'

'I know who you are,' she replied, facing the front again. 'What I want to know is why you want to see me.'

The doors opened again and more people got on as the tram reached the rue Nationale. He had less than ten minutes left and no real idea of why he was there either, other than curiosity and maybe instinct.

'Why did you not report the discovery of the body immediately?' he asked.

He expected a sarcastic response along the lines of, '*Yeah, right, I should have the people swarming all over me!*' but it didn't come.

'I was told not to "become embroiled", that's what he said, "don't become embroiled",' she said quietly, for the first time her composure slipping a little.

'By your client?' he asked sympathetically.

'If that's what you want to call him.' Her voice hardened and he thought he heard the trace of an accent in her tone, Eastern European maybe.

'Is he a regular?'

'You haven't found *him* then? Just me.'

'Can you help us find him then?' She laughed bitterly, ignoring the question. 'Are you afraid of him?' He certainly had that impression as she knotted her fingers tightly on her lap. 'If you are, we can protect you.' Again, that laugh.

She turned to him. 'Look, Lombard. We just found the body. We had nothing to do with it.' Her familiarity struck him. He always insisted that people call him by his surname but rarely did they do so without prompting, and certainly not during what passed for an interrogation. It was like she knew him personally.

'So why not report it immediately then?'

'He told me not to. He told me to leave immediately and that he would deal with it.'

'Had you arranged to meet in this specific place? Is that where you always meet?'

'It wasn't the first time.'

'And the last?'

She didn't answer.

'Why does he frighten you so much? Do you think he had something to do with the body?'

'To use me as a witness?' It was obvious that the thought hadn't occurred to her. Then she shook her head. 'I wouldn't put it past him. But he told me to go.'

'That was very gallant of him.'

She missed his sarcasm and this time anger flashed in her eyes. 'You think that, do you? He wasn't protecting me, Lombard. He was protecting himself, his reputation.'

'Whoever it is scares you.'

The anger left her eyes and now he saw the fear. 'Yes, he does. It's OK for you and the police, but he really runs this town and he can hurt people.' He made to reply, to offer some form of comfort. 'Please, whatever you do, leave me out of it. Please, that's why I agreed to meet you. I have a child. His child.'

The tram drew to a stop at the train station and Lombard hastily wrote his number on to a piece of paper. 'Here, take this. Call me whenever you need to. We're going after these people and I promise to keep you out of it. There's such a thing as witness protection now in France, we can take care of you. We can set you up with a new life.' He knew he was overreaching himself with that claim. Witness protection in France was a very recent thing since the Bataclan massacres in Paris in 2017, and really only at this stage for terrorism.

She took his card. 'Thank you,' she said, but her voice told him that she wouldn't.

'One more thing.' He pulled out his phone and showed her the medallion image. 'Do you recognise this? It may be important.'

She looked at it, then at him. 'Where did you find that?' Her voice was cold.

'It was found on the body. Barbier's body.'

She looked him in the eye and her mouth hardened, partly in fear, partly in frustration. 'You see how lucky he is?' She stood up as the tram came to a stop.

Lombard grabbed her wrist. 'Call me, please. I mean it.'

She smiled at him now, shaking her wrist free. A weak almost condescending smile came to her thin lips. 'You are very sweet,' she said quietly. 'But will you always have your phone with you? No.'

She stood and walked out of the open doors, without looking back. This was what he and Aubret had dreaded, the organised crime link and the investigation being taken entirely out of their hands. He watched her sadly as she walked purposefully towards the station, then he nodded to Officer Chrétien, standing anonymously near the tram stop, to follow her.

Chapter 29

Lombard was tempted to stay on the tram all the way through to the end, and buy himself some thinking time. He was irritatingly aware, however, that his eccentric, at times bordering on whimsical, persona was by now becoming a little too predictable. He didn't regard it as an affectation, he genuinely liked to get lost; movement helped his thought processes, but to a certain extent he was playing up to it and the last thing he wanted was people he knew to expect it. He was acutely aware that, post-Madeleine, he really didn't have much idea of who he was, or even what he stood for, but he didn't want others to decide for him or for himself to become a parody.

He was mulling this over as he pulled at a *brioche*, staring glassily into the middle distance and beginning to attract the nervous attention of late-morning alcoholics gathered outside the station who hadn't yet refilled enough to quieten their demons. He had walked back from the next tram stop on the line and was wondering what he should do next. He had just boxed himself into a corner by promising the plainly scared Elaine protection. Protection from whom though? Elaine's fear, that life-threatening, child-threatening fear, usually came from ruthless criminal gangs who had no fear of their own, certainly not from the law. Trafficking in drugs and people meant that life was cheapened to nothing, and it may even be that Elaine, with her hint of a foreign accent, was here because of them, and therefore tied to them. He had promised her a new life; she may have already had to start one.

What did she mean? he wondered. *You see how lucky he is?* It inferred that the medallion didn't belong to Thibaud Barbier after all, but to whoever had found the body. And whoever that was had got close enough to drop the piece of jewellery, maybe even tampering with the body, with evidence at least. Had they taken the wallet and missed the driving licence? He wanted to find whoever scared Elaine now more than ever. It nagged at him that whoever she had been with was a criminal yet had reported the body. The two facts didn't fit. Why get involved at all?

Lombard didn't like to think of Tours being in the grip of some criminal dark shadow. At heart he was a romantic; even years in the judiciary hadn't trampled on that, despite some of the vile things he had had to deal with. Nor was it that he had a naive view of the world and certainly not of humanity and its endless capacity for cruelty and self-harm; but savagery and wickedness still had the ability to surprise him. With Madeleine's help he had built himself a shell, one that he realised was a little too safe, too complacent. He had made a promise to Elaine, one that he knew, realistically, couldn't be kept.

The gangs, if they could still be called that – it was like calling a multibillion petrochemical behemoth a corner shop – weren't the same as they had been. The families that had traditionally run the majority of illegal, sometimes legal activities had been brutally pushed aside. It was like the French Revolution for the underworld. The bourgeois aristocracy with their 'rules', such as they were, had been decapitated by ruthless interlopers – Turkish, Albanian, Russian – who had no such qualms about so-called tradition. He had talked with a senior English policeman who had been a junior copper when London had gone through the same violent transition. 'These people aren't even nice to their mothers,' he'd said. 'And they certainly don't only kill their own either.' He was almost misty-eyed for a time that, he admitted later after a few too many late night whiskies, had probably never actually existed outside of the folklore. And that was part of the problem in Lombard's opinion. The veneration of old-style supposedly philanthropic criminal elites; there was a myth that these violent thugs took care of their neighbourhoods, kept a sort of order like feudal kings, but it was just that, a myth. A powerful one though, bordering on fairy tale.

Cities weren't run that way now, at least Tours wasn't. As Benbarek had said, Tours is a satellite town, easily connected. A franchise like any other, ostensibly autonomous like a locally run fast food chain, but under the umbrella of the bigger 'partner'. Organised crime then was more difficult to pin down, virtually impossible to stop. Even if Elaine's connection was likely a local, he would be a Paris appointed regional representative – junior management with a gun.

Lombard had a choice to make. Deep down he still didn't believe this was about organised crime, *le milieu* as the French called it. He believed it was something else; the book, the deaths of Barbier, Brunel and, historically, Lucien Delaunay, pointed another way. That being said, he also knew that domestic terrorists – anarchists, call them what you will – despite their aims, were as brutally well-organised as any crime syndicate.

He could tell Aubret all of this and the *commissaire* would, quite properly, insist that it be kicked up to the organised crime teams, people who had the resources to deal with it. On the other hand, he could keep Elaine's situation to himself and deal with it personally. But then, deal with what exactly? Lombard would need a lot more information than he currently had, and that again came down to resources.

He sat down on a bench only a couple of hundred yards from his office at the Palais de Justice and finished his brioche. Screwing up the paper bag packaging, he tossed it towards a rubbish bin where it hit the rim and fell to the floor. A passing student, as usual under headphones, glared at him with a look that said Lombard was *all* the world's problems in one. Apologetically he put the paper in the bin. The same thought came back to him. If he didn't tell Aubret and something happened to Elaine...

He turned on his phone and found Aubret's number quickly. His conscience, as things stood, and despite good intentions, was not a safe haven for anyone right now.

'Juge.' Aubret's tone was flat.

'We need to talk, Guy.'

There was a sigh. 'Yes, we do.'

'She's terrified of someone. And doesn't want to get involved, and reading between the lines...'

'What we thought?' Aubret interrupted. Did Lombard hear relief?

'Yes.'

'OK. Look, I'll get the *dossier* completely updated and we'll present it to Monsieur le Procureur later.' It still felt like a wrench to Lombard, even if it was the right thing to do. 'Still there?'

It was Lombard's turn to sigh, but it was with frustration. 'Yes.'

'Are you in a gym?'

'No.' Lombard forced a laugh.

'Good, because Monsieur le Procureur has been chasing you all morning. He wants to see you.'

'Why did he not just ring my phone?' Lombard shook his head.

'No idea. Maybe he assumed it wasn't on you and on the rare occasions it is, that you wouldn't pick it up.'

'That's becoming a thing,' he muttered.

'What?'

'Nothing.'

'Where are you?'

'I'm on a bench looking up at my office window.'

'Yep. Figures. I reckon you might be doing a lot of that in the future if Procureur D'Archambeau gets his way.'

'I need René on my back like I need a hole in the head.'

'At least you still have a head. He's saying you've mis-handled everything – two deaths, no witnesses and all that.' Lombard grunted. 'And that you have shown no inclination to look for the Daucourt girl, no compassion – I made a list – thoughtless insensitivity, bad decisions not worthy of the role of, etc., etc. We both know where he's heading with it, and he's got a point too.'

Lombard sighed. 'I'm not sure I can be bothered to fight back,' he said quietly. 'And you're right, he may have a point.'

Aubret ignored him, which Lombard was grateful for. 'I told him I'd tell you all this when you got back.'

Lombard didn't seem to hear at first, then Aubret's words registered. 'Get back? From where?'

'Rochecorbon, Monsieur le Juge. Madame Daucourt is expecting you. I'll come and pick you up.'

They arranged to meet outside the grand station of Tours, the *monument historique*, fifteen minutes later. Lombard stood, shoulders hunched, under the limestone statues signalling larger cities that Tours was connected to: Nantes, Limoges, Toulouse and Bordeaux. There wasn't a statue for Paris, that was presumably a given. Everywhere in France is connected to Paris.

Aubret pulled up next to the taxi rank, though not in his usual car. This was an official car with darkened passenger windows in the rear doors, a French *marque* naturally – anything else would be sacrilege – and it gave off the correct impression of prestige that presumably the Daucourt family demanded.

He pulled open the passenger door and slumped into the seat. 'This is ridiculous,' he said truculently. 'We've got more important things to do than go chasing after runaway teenagers.'

'What exactly, Monsieur le Juge?' came a voice from the rear seats. 'Perhaps doing the job of organised crime squads?'

He caught Aubret looking at him out of the corner of his eye, giving him an apologetic shrug as he did so.

D'Archambeau leant forward between the two front seats like an eager child on a long journey.

'I think it's time,' he began, with a false, intense enthusiasm, 'that we all had a reminder of our roles vis-à-vis criminal investigation in France.' Neither of the two men in front spoke. 'You, Commissaire Aubret, are in charge of a team at the *police judiciaire*, is that correct?'

'Yes, Monsieur le Procureur.'

'The *police judiciaire*, the clue is in the title I'm sure you'll agree, are under the control of the *magistrature*. Remind me, Commissaire, who controls the *magistrature*?'

'You do, Monsieur le Procureur.' Aubret spoke through grinding teeth, while a half-smile broke out on Lombard's face at the performance of D'Archambeau, and the conversation he and Aubret had had earlier.

'So. When a crime is reported, I am basically in charge. Are we clear so far?' He didn't wait for a response. 'I direct the police and appoint a *juge d'instruction* to work with them. That's you, Lombard. Your job is to find the truth, act independently as both prosecution and defence, wrap it all up nicely before I present it to court. Again, clear?'

Lombard adjusted the rear-view mirror so that his eyes met directly those of the *procureur*. 'You were not here to issue the introductory indictment, so I assumed control of the investigation as the only other person you could give the case to is in hospital. You couldn't be reached in Lausanne and as far as I can gather, you weren't scheduled to be there at that conference so there was no record of you at the hotel.'

'It was in an unofficial capacity. I represent the state here.' It was clear that D'Archambeau hadn't prepared for any level of fightback.

'Vital work, no doubt.' Lombard's voice dripped with false sincerity. 'But we are in the middle of an investigation…'

'No, Lombard. That is where you are mistaken.' Lombard didn't like the sudden resurgence of confidence. 'You are at the end of this investigation. It is quite clearly a matter for specialist squads. This is organised crime, Lombard, we don't have the resources for this. The death of the man, Barbier, that was a message. A journalist poking about is murdered. You, yourself, attacked. Who is this witness, this Elaine?'

'She was there when the body was found, and I think she's scared.'

'Of course she's scared, you fool! She's a prostitute, and probably in France illegally.'

'I don't think it's that.'

D'Archambeau lowered his voice to a menace. 'You are harassing a witness, no doubt promising the famous Lombard protection in the process. Overstepping your role.' Lombard and Aubret stayed quiet, while D'Archambeau grabbed his motorcycle helmet and opened the rear passenger door. 'I am pushing the murder of Barbier on to specialists, that's my job, to protect the state. Your job, right now, is to find Rosa Daucourt.' He slammed the door behind him, then banged on Aubret's window. 'I want the *dossier* on my desk quickly, Commissaire.' He walked away.

Aubret started the engine and drove slowly through the traffic. 'Sorry,' he said gruffly. 'He was in my office when you rang and then jumped in the car...'

'It's not your fault, Guy.' Lombard sighed heavily. 'But do you know what annoys me most?' he asked. 'The bastard's probably right.'

Chapter 30

'She's frightened.' Lombard's voice was on the verge of pleading as he began to talk to the *commissaire* following a few minutes' silence. 'Terrified even.'

'Who is, the Daucourt girl?'

'No. This Elaine or whatever her real name is. I suspect young Rosa just needs some space. Teenage girls often do.'

'You're really not the expert on that, OK?' Aubret gripped the steering wheel tightly; he was beginning to boil over. 'Look, we've been told to leave it and I've told you already, I'm not losing my job for this.'

Lombard slumped against the window. 'I know that,' he mumbled. 'Just humour me for now though, will you?'

Anyone else and Aubret would just have walked away from the conversation, or shut it down more violently, but Lombard's frustration and annoyance was dominating the car, and he knew from experience that it would not go away easily. 'OK,' he said slowly, 'just for argument's sake, do you think it's a criminal gang that controls her? That would make sense. You say she's East European, she works as a prostitute. Like D'Archambeau said, that all figures. But whoever her mark was, he didn't do anything illegal. He just reported the body.'

This had the effect of animating Lombard as though he'd been given an electric shock and he turned to face the *commissaire* who, despite knowing he was now coming under scrutiny, kept his eyes firmly on the slowly opening Daucourt gates. 'That's just it though.' Lombard had a note of triumph in his voice. 'I showed her the emblem from the medallion found on Barbier, and she recognised it. "You see how lucky he is?", that's what she said. "You see how lucky he is?"'

'Meaning what?'

'Meaning, and I agree before you say it that this is just speculation. Meaning that the medallion didn't belong to Barbier, but to whoever Elaine is protecting. Meaning that at the very least we can get him on tampering with evidence. He didn't just find a body, he may have taken a wallet too.' Lombard sat back, suddenly a little deflated. 'Yes, I know. It's thin.'

Aubret took a deep breath. 'But what difference does it make? It's not our case. If he's organised crime, and that sounds likely, no matter what secret masonic thing he belongs to, and in fact that only makes it more likely that he's organised crime... it's not our problem anymore. It just isn't.'

Lombard stayed silent for a second, deciding to keep his conversation with Maichin to himself for now, to wait until Aubret was in a more receptive mood. He couldn't help himself thinking aloud though. 'If we could just convince her to talk...'

'Bloody hell.'

'I said we could offer witness protection.'

'That's not a system that's covered itself in glory though, is it?' Aubret gripped the wheel more tightly as they drove slowly along the smooth driveway, his patience beginning to run out. 'You know who the experts are in hiding people, giving them a new life? People traffickers, that's who. And she might have already been through that.'

As a *juge* and one of the few privy to the inner workings of the nascent witness protection programme, Lombard felt compelled to try and defend it. 'Is it the system that's at fault, or do people just not realise how hard it will be when you're in it?'

'It's not something I could do,' Aubret conceded. 'The cost is too great.'

'Doesn't that depend on why you've made the sacrifice, what it's for?' Lombard's question was a morose one, defeated.

'Right now, it's OK for you, Juge. I have a wife and three kids. Suppose I'm in a position where I have to go into a witness programme? We get uprooted, change names, all friends gone. My kids' futures completely changed, compromised. I can't talk to my brothers or my parents. My old friends. No one.'

'I get it,' Lombard said softly. 'I really do.'

'You know about loss, you know about grief.' Aubret brought the car to a stop outside the grand house. 'What you know less about maybe is uncertainty. One of my boys went missing once. Christ it was only for a few hours, but that fear, that impotence, it eats you up. Now spread that over years. Not knowing what's happened to someone, where they've gone, why even.' He turned the engine off.

'You're right,' Lombard said quietly. 'It's not the same, I know. But when Elise didn't come back last night... well, it's a responsibility that I'm not built for.' He laughed coldly. 'I think it runs in my family. I ran away once. I was fifteen and I wanted to go back to England, to my grandparents. I think I just wanted to jumpstart my mother into parenting.'

'And, did it work?' Aubret smiled as Lombard turned to him.

'I didn't get very far. I put my tent up in the woods, not far from here actually. Came back after a few days, hungry. I don't think she'd noticed I'd even gone.' Despite the sentiment he smiled warmly at the memory.

Aubret, utterly certain in the sanctity and security of family, wasn't convinced. 'Oh, she noticed all right,' he said. 'Mums do.'

Olivia Daucourt appeared at the top of the steps, the large door left open behind her. She had obviously been crying and she looked older, her real age maybe. Her shoulders were slumped and the strict posture that Lombard had seen before had withered, while both moisturised hands tore at a handkerchief.

'Mums notice.' He repeated Aubret's line. 'We have a prostitute and a billionaire, both mothers, both scared for their kids. The great leveller maybe.'

'You can't compete with a mother's love,' Aubret said proudly. 'I know if I said to Fabienne that we needed to go into hiding and that she could no longer have contact with her mother, she probably wouldn't even come with me.' He tried to laugh it off, but while it was clear that the truth hurt, the effect on Lombard was startling and immediate.

Sitting bolt upright and smacking the dashboard in front of him, he cried, 'Guy! That's it. What if Barbier isn't Barbier, what if *he* was in a witness protection programme? And what if the mother came looking for her child?'

Aubret's mood changed almost as quickly. 'It's not our problem,' he said coldly.

Lombard ignored him. 'We have a victim with a vague history, no friends and no family. His mother died in 1998, yet leaves him a message in 2023.'

'It's none of our business.'

'She found him, Guy. The mother found her son. I'm convinced of it. That's why he changed, don't you see? That's why he smartened up.'

'I am not losing my job over this,' Aubret growled.

'Oh, Commissaire.' Lombard laughed, opening the car door. 'What have you got to lose, really? Your wife prefers her mother anyway.'

Chapter 31

A reluctant Aubret followed Lombard across the gravel drive to the steps, where an anxious Olivia Daucourt waited. He couldn't help but note that there was a slight spring in the tread of the *juge*, a determination but mixed with impatience. Officially the death of Thibaud Barbier was now nothing to do with them, officially they were solely engaged in the search for the missing Rosa Daucourt, but Aubret knew that Lombard's mind did not work like that. He would try to do his best for Rosa Daucourt – that was natural – though he was sceptical that she had even been abducted at all; his thoughts, however, were all about Barbier still. While Aubret hated the position that that put him in, the idea that Barbier wasn't actually Barbier was a compelling one. Dangerous, but compelling.

'Is there any news, Monsieur le Juge?' Olivia Daucourt's voice was weak and pleading as the three shook hands.

'I was going to ask you the same, madame,' Lombard said, his soft, diplomatic tone belying the double meaning of his reply. 'I assume the whole family are here?'

'Yes, they are.' Her reply showed confusion. Lombard strode into the house with the purpose and manner of someone who suddenly had all the answers; there was a certainty, an urgency even that only added, very obviously, to her maternal fears. Standing at the large double doors down the hall, where initially the butler had shown them in, stood Auguste Daucourt. His caricature of a chin, elevated as though he were Mussolini, jutted out in a show of authority but another ill-fitting, though no doubt expensive suit gave him the air of a down-at-heel provincial solicitor.

'Ah, Lombard,' he said. 'I want to have a word with you.'

Lombard said nothing in reply but ushered Madame Daucourt and Aubret into the drawing room, before hanging back to listen to whatever it was the young man had to say. He didn't have to wait long, as Daucourt closed the doors behind him.

'I think you'll find, Lombard, that your position is at risk.' It was a pompously delivered half-threat, a quite awful opening gambit in an argument that Daucourt had no doubt rehearsed in his mind a dozen times, always resulting in Lombard's crumbling admission of simpering incompetence.

Lombard took a step forward, his grey eyes fixed on Daucourt's blue ones, which now blinked behind his round glasses. 'I think you'll find, Monsieur Daucourt, that my position is absolutely none of your business.'

'Ah, well. That's where you're wrong,' he flapped. 'I have some influence, besides the family's position that is. I am not without my own connections in Tours, you know? I am very close to the *procureur* himself.'

'So am I. What are you trying to say?' Lombard felt his temper slip even further away.

'You wouldn't understand, Lombard. People with real power stick together, we look after each other...'

'Sounds like a cosy little club.' Lombard smiled, and that caused Daucourt to blink rapidly. Stepping back, the *juge* reached into his pocket and produced his phone. 'I have some connections too,' he said threateningly. Daucourt blinked some more. Lombard showed him the medallion emblem found on Barbier's body; the pseudo-Masonic imagery and Christian livery still, to Lombard's mind, was too pat, just the symbol of a weak male debating society from people who wanted more. It was worth a gamble on this particular weak male, he concluded.

This time the meaning was clear. 'I am one of you,' Lombard was saying, and the effect was immediate.

The younger man's eyes moved comically from side to side. 'I didn't know you were with us?' His surprise was mixed with anxious dismay.

'I know, right?' Lombard's cold eyes didn't leave him. 'There goes the neighbourhood. Where's yours?'

Daucourt pulled the pocket square out of his breast pocket, and hanging from it was a medallion exactly like the one pictured on Lombard's phone. 'I'm surprised the *procureur* didn't tell me,' he whined like a scolded child.

'And each member only gets one?' he asked.

'You know they do!' The confusion on Daucourt's face gradually moulded itself into a mask of pain at his naivety.

'You haven't done your "Keep a Secret" badge yet have you, Monsieur Daucourt? I'll borrow that if you don't mind.'

'You have no right!' he protested, while at the same time trying to not raise his voice.

'Oh, I really do. I may give it back at the end of school, but I'll talk to you about this another time.' He started to move away, then turned back slowly. 'We could also talk about why you were starting fights down by the river last night. Now, open the doors.'

Defeated, almost on the verge of tears, Auguste did as he was told revealing the family. It looked like none of them had moved: the outfits were different, but everybody was in the same position as the last time he'd been in that room, even Aubret stood in the same corner. They were like waxworks, which was inevitable, Lombard concluded, given the amount of plastic surgery on display. Were this lot, the clearly distraught Olivia Daucourt aside, incapable of showing emotion because of their aristocratic upbringing or Botox injections? He walked around the family photos again, letting the tension in the room deliberately increase but also to try and guess who had had what done. He noticed a portrait of Olivia with her then two young sons standing either side of her, all of them holding glasses of champagne in their hands. Two old before their time and one refusing to grow old at all. Already, and though clearly a few years younger, Jules was taller than Auguste but Olivia Daucourt never changed.

Next to that a portrait only of the mother. The clothes were different suggesting a decade in between the two pictures, but her face, the jawline, the shape of the nose, the wrinkle-free neck, nothing else had changed or aged. The hairline was a touch straighter, but nothing else. The eyes were sadder too; no amount of surgery could mask emotional pain but it was all very macabre.

'Excuse the informality,' he said without turning around, 'but as you are all Daucourt, first names might be easier.' Nobody said anything. 'Jules, when did you get back from the Amazon?'

The youngest son was different from his brother; he wasn't startled by interaction for one thing, he had a confident manner that Auguste tried and failed to project. He'd been socialised maybe, rather than groomed as the successor to his father.

'Just a few days ago,' he said quietly.

'And how did your sister seem?'

'I wish I knew.' His tanned face was downcast as he spoke. 'I got back very late on Sunday, slept in nearly the whole of the next day. When I did surface, Maman told me she couldn't find Rosa.'

'Are you close?' It was Aubret who asked the question.

'There's ten years between us,' he replied apologetically as if that were his fault. 'And with me being away all the time... so it's six months since I saw her last.' He chuckled at a memory. 'Still skinny as a rake, still lovingly bonkers and all over the place like most teenagers, I guess.'

'Skinny!' Nadine repeated caustically.

'She had got worse,' his older brother said coldly.

'As Jules says, like all teenagers,' Olivia confirmed.

'And you?' Lombard directed his question at Auguste Daucourt who was seated, as last time, opposite his wife Nadine, and not beside her.

'We aren't close,' he said, making it sound like that wasn't part of his job remit. 'I am very busy with the company, trying to build it back up. I'm afraid we don't spend much time together.'

While Auguste Daucourt spoke, Lombard watched the old man in the wheelchair. The sheer despair in the eyes was a force that consumed his body.

Lombard put a hand on the man's shoulder which went unnoticed or ignored by Charles Daucourt. 'We are looking for Rosa,' he said gently.

'Rosa!' The old man shouted immediately. 'Where is she?' Agitated and rocking sideways in his wheelchair, he repeated his cry of 'Rosa!' as Olivia, with a stern, reproving look at Lombard, rushed over to comfort her husband. She put her arm around his shoulder, and nuzzled her head into his neck, making soothing noises. He half-smiled and whispered the name again, 'Rosa,' before settling back into his vigil, watching the gardens at the back.

It occurred once again to Lombard that if Charles Daucourt had feigned the effects of Alzheimer's disease to gain early release from prison, it had taken revenge and got him for real. Without a word, Olivia retook her seat on the sofa, her emotions hidden behind a debutante's poise and a protective wall.

'He seems very aware of her absence,' Lombard remarked softly.

'Rosa is the only one of us he now recognises.' Olivia's voice was quiet but firm. 'When she is here, he sees us again, as if she is his eyes. Without her, he is blind to us.'

'They must have had a special bond,' Lombard replied.

'I've asked this before,' Aubret filled the ensuing silence. 'But did Rosa have any friends you might know of, somewhere she might go?'

Nadine stood up; unlike her mother-in-law, she didn't seem as practised at hiding her feelings and the family tension was becoming unbearable for those who hadn't grown up in it.

'How *could* she have had friends?' she cried rhetorically. 'None of us have! Poor Rosa wasn't allowed out, none of us are without asking permission.'

'It's for our own protection, Nadine,' her husband explained without warmth. 'We are a target, have been for years. We must consider our security.'

'Yet you do go out?' Lombard directed the question at no one in particular, throwing it out, hoping someone might pick it up.

'Of course they do!' Olivia cried. 'Don't be ridiculous, Nadine. It's just important we all know where we are.'

'Olivia is right,' Auguste said with attempted authority.

'I'd rather live a little than be imprisoned, dear husband. He's allowed to go where he pleases!' She pointed at Jules.

'Only on a different continent though,' the younger brother laughed. His humour was genuine, but it spoke volumes.

Nadine approached Lombard, meeting his eyes directly. 'We're really not allowed to go out.' She made it sound like a plea for freedom, but Lombard knew exactly what she meant. She had broken the rules, please keep it to yourself.

'You exaggerate, Nadine,' Olivia said sternly.

'But surely Rosa was allowed out?' Lombard's eyes silently answered Nadine's plea. She was safe for now, but he knew where to find her.

'Everybody is allowed out. It's nonsense to say otherwise. It's just, as I say, important we all know where each other is. Auguste has his political meetings all the time, Nadine comes and goes. Shopping, no doubt, picking up what she needs,' she added, with a barb.

'And you, madame?' Lombard asked softly.

'I don't like to leave Charles.' She shut the line of enquiry down immediately, standing as she did so. 'Why don't I show you Rosa's room?' she said forcefully. 'The *commissaire*'s team have seen it, maybe you would like to see it too?'

Chapter 32

Elegantly and silently Olivia Daucourt moved to the double doors and opened them. It gave the stifling atmosphere some release, like a slow tyre puncture from a family, if not at war with itself, then certainly ill at ease. Lombard followed her out into the hall. Walking a few steps in front of him she climbed the wide central staircase, past yet more valuable antiques and paintings. They passed no staff as they climbed, nor when they walked, still without talking, along a surprisingly dim corridor. Madame Daucourt stopped at the last door on the right, grabbed at her distorted image reflected in the shiny brass handle and pushed the door wide open, revealing inside an entirely different world.

It was a surprisingly small room, though its place on the corner of the chateau gave it a double aspect, therefore two windows and a lot of light. It felt though just like the rest of the house, that it was a museum piece from a different century. It was almost entirely pink for a start. Though the walls were white, there was a shocking pink dado rail that divided them making it look like they were wrapped up as a present. There was a white desk with pink handles at the window. The carpet was pink. The duvet cover was pink, though the pillows were white. There were cuddly toys, largely pink, and a collection of dolls, all wearing pink. Two things struck Lombard immediately: it looked like it had been designed by someone in the 1950s who was told to make the place look suitable for a girl, and also, more importantly, this did not look like the private space of a twenty-first-century eighteen-year-old.

Olivia closed the door softly behind them. 'Can we talk in English?' she asked quietly, wringing her hands in front of her.

'Of course,' Lombard replied, still a little in shock at the surroundings.

She sat on the chair at the desk, adjusting the inevitably pink cushion. 'My daughter never really grew up, as you can see? After what happened before, you know... before. We received threats and needed security. I was frightened for Rosa, she was so young.' She waved her hand around the room. 'I'm afraid she was kept that way. My husband insisted on it and I agreed.'

'Do you think,' Lombard paused to make sure he got the right words. 'Do you think she has escaped then?' He was being deliberately provocative.

Her eyes briefly flashed in anger, but once that reaction had died down, she began to sob. 'I don't want to think that,' she said simply.

He let her cry a little, before she composed herself taking a pink tissue from a box on the desk.

'Tell me about what happened before, in Besançon?'

She stood and looked out of the window, at the same patch of lawn that her husband was still no doubt guarding on the ground floor. 'Poor Charles,' she whispered. 'He was a brilliant man, you know? Then I suppose all wives say that about scientist husbands.'

'I wouldn't know. I guess only other scientists are qualified to make that claim.'

'Perhaps you're right. My background was medicine too, though more physical reconstructive surgery than neurological which was his speciality. We met at some crossover conference somewhere, Philadelphia, I think it was. He was keynote speaker. I was only there for a free holiday. His brilliance changed my mind.'

'And now he's reduced to a child.' Lombard this time wasn't being deliberately provocative, but the response showed how much the comparison angered and upset her.

'I don't see it that way.'

'Have either of you been married before? Sorry to ask, but these things may be relevant.'

'No,' was her firm response. 'Charles was engaged when he was very young, but it wasn't serious. You know how men are?'

'Not really.' He smiled. 'And, sorry to ask this, but you are the mother of the children?'

She didn't appear angered by the question, though she did blush a little. 'I am Rosa's mother. Auguste and Jules are both of different mothers, insignificant affairs, he called them. The women I mean, not the boys.'

'And you accepted them as your own?' Lombard did well to hide his shock and amazement.

'Yes,' she replied stoically, before shrugging. 'Charles always said I brought order to this family, where before there was chaos.'

He gave her a moment, digesting how the fractured family, eventually thrown together, were now, it seemed at least, retrospectively trying to look like each other too. 'So Besançon...' he prompted eventually.

'Charles knew he was ill. He's always been worried about his health and he was diagnosed with a neurodegenerative

disease, onset of early dementia. In his case hereditary. He...
we decided that we could pool our talents to look for a cure,
not palliative care, not giving patients an easel and some
paints, like they're five years old. A cure.'

'Was that likely?'

She ignored the question. 'Do you know how Alzheimer's
disease is described by the Institut Pasteur? As a social
burden, Monsieur le Juge, a social burden. Horrific. Imagine
if that *burden* could be removed?' She sighed and smiled
at him, but only once her anger had dissipated. 'To answer
your question honestly, I don't know. Charles felt we were
close, hence we moved – yes, illegally – on to non-human
primate testing.'

'And would that have worked? Are non-human primates
close enough neurologically?'

'Charles thought so.'

'But you'd still have to test any treatment on humans
presumably? So your methods, sorry your husband's
methods, come to light.'

She looked at him pleadingly. 'If we'd found a cure,
do you really think anyone would care how? The damage
terminal illness causes, you know that...' She held her gaze
at him.

'And someone found out?' he asked, turning his eyes
away.

Again she shrugged. 'They did. Who knows how close
we really were though? We were a perfect team, pushing
each other to new discoveries. Discoveries that would have
changed medicine and lives forever. The fire in his eyes, the
sheer brilliance.'

'What happened?'

She sat down, clearly upset. 'Charles had arranged a
new intake of primates.' Lombard guessed that the word

primates made them sound unreal, less human-like, when in fact they were sourced specifically for their human properties. 'I don't know how, there's a market for everything I suppose. Anyway, activists got to the delivery driver. They were the primates that arrived in the truck… and they destroyed everything in a fire, even killing some of our staff. Horrendous.' She looked at him, strength and defiance in her face. 'We paid the price. Prison broke Charles as you can see. For that, and that alone, I regret what we did. Do you know what it is to watch a loved one waste away?'

It was Lombard's turn to stare at the garden. A sprinkler sent jets across the immaculate lawn; hydrangea, spirea and abelia bloomed in colourful synchronisation while a gardener tended to the beds. He ignored her question and concentrated on why he was there. Had they paid the price, the Daucourts? It was difficult to argue in that direction, even if their motives were driven to remove a social burden. 'What happened to the driver?' he asked, suspecting he knew the answer.

She looked confused. 'I've no idea,' she said, shaking her head.

'OK, back to Rosa. What about friends? School friends?'

She shook her head. 'We couldn't risk her going to school. Our family is quite notorious now with certain people, we couldn't risk it.'

Lombard shook his head. 'It seems out of place that Rosa would be allowed to go to Tours on her own then.' He made it sound like he was talking to himself, hoping it would push her into opening up more about the present. After a moment it did.

'We started to clash, to argue all the time. She told me that she felt like a prisoner and though I told her it was for the best, for now… I knew how she felt. I feel the same.'

There were inevitable comparisons with Elise and her decision to run away and he had a great deal of sympathy for both of the young women.

'Do you feel like a prisoner?'

She tore at the tissue in her lap. 'You've met them.' Her voice was almost inaudible, but he could hear the bitterness. She turned to him. 'Rosa is our only daughter. Charles's favourite, my bridge to him.'

'He obviously misses her.' Lombard's tone was equally soft. 'He calls for her often.' She didn't reply. 'So you started to let Rosa go out on her own when she became too much indoors, is that it?'

She nodded. 'I was terrified to do so. I even followed her the first few times.'

'And?'

'She did what any young woman would do. She went to the shops, to cafés. She bounced, she no longer walked, almost danced. I could see that she was so happy and the difference it made to Charles when she came back from these trips. It brought him back briefly.'

Lombard sat on the bed opposite her. 'Did she meet anyone?'

Olivia looked out of the window. 'Part of me hoped that she would, but I don't know if she did. She certainly never told me.'

Lombard lay back against the wall and looked around him. It was hard not to conclude that, just like Elise, a young woman, feeling trapped and controlled had decided to break free. He admired her spirit for that and felt like saying so, before something caught his eye on a girlish notepad on the bedside table. He picked up the notepad. On it was what looked like a scribble. It was a stark, mountain range-like pencil drawing.

'What's this?' he asked sharply.

'I don't know,' Madame Daucourt replied, surprised by his sudden change of tone. 'I've not seen it before.'

'I have, madame,' Lombard said. 'I certainly have.'

Chapter 33

Commissaire Aubret's crunching of the gears matched the crunching of his Gaviscon. His stress levels were rising again. He hadn't really known what to expect from the latest visit to the Daucourt château; some lead as to the girl's disappearance would have been top of his priorities for sure, a seemingly direct link to the murder of Thibaud Barbier would have been low down the same list.

'I'm not letting this go, Guy,' Lombard said, not for the first time since he'd sat energetically in the passenger seat, and they hadn't even reached the end of the driveway yet.

That much was obvious. Aubret knew that Lombard was unlikely to have let the Barbier thing go anyway, despite orders from above to do so. That wasn't his style and something about Barbier had got to him; Lombard wouldn't abandon the man the way the rest of the world had apparently done so.

'If that scribble on the girl's notepad is the same...' Aubret began.

'It is.'

'Then this could be the second case in one afternoon that's taken away from us. She may very well have been kidnapped by the same people who did for Barbier?' The *commissaire* knew he didn't sound very convincing, but his role in some ways demanded that he counterbalance the *juge*. Act as water on his flames.

It wasn't working. Lombard's eyes were bright, he had a tight smile and for once wasn't slouched in the car seat like a teenager being driven to a dentist's appointment.

'Let's suppose you're right. For whatever reason, for something in the past perhaps, Barbier is executed by *le milieu*, organised crime. Maybe not even the past, let's say, hypothetically, the present. He was a low-level dealer, say, operating on his bus route line eleven through Tours, the perfect cover. He skimmed, he paid the price. Message sent. Right?'

'Right.'

Lombard turned to him. 'Why abduct Rosa Daucourt?' His smile and his eyes were now working together, not in triumph exactly, it was in vindication. 'Is she a user? Unlikely. A fellow dealer? Even more unlikely. A witness?'

'It's possible.'

'Yes,' Lombard conceded. 'It is. But circumstance isn't their connection, is it? How likely is it really that their paths would cross? No. This is their connection.' He held up the girl's pencil drawing. 'Whatever it is.'

'Well, Lemery couldn't get a match for it. You feed that image into Google and you get Apple shares, inflation…'

'Your blood pressure.'

'Very funny.' Aubret turned the car on to the main road, heading back to town.

'It's something that's rising though.' Lombard drummed his fingers on his thigh before reaching for his phone. 'Sea levels maybe? That might fit.' A few seconds later, he put his phone back in his pocket.

'No?'

'No. This image has highs and lows, it's going up but it dips occasionally too. Sea levels are just rising.'

'I still don't see Barbier as some kind of environmental campaigner, I know he had that book, but I've looked through it and it doesn't look like he even read it.'

'No. But maybe whoever came into his life was reading it?' Lombard drummed more quickly with his fingers, a sure sign of frustration. 'Can I borrow that book? It's been checked over by forensics.'

Aubret took a deep breath. Their recent history was always going to make a request like this hard to deal with, but at least this time it had been a request. 'I can't do that,' he sighed. 'It'll have to go via the *procureur* to whoever takes over.'

Lombard looked surprised. 'Really, Guy?'

'If Rosa Daucourt's disappearance is linked to Thibaud Barbier's murder, then that gets kicked to another department as well, surely? We're off both.'

'Because of the crime link?'

'Exactly.' If Aubret felt he'd convinced the *juge*, it didn't last long.

'You see, that's not how I reckon it at all. If Rosa Daucourt's disappearance is linked to Thibaud Barbier, I think that makes it *less* likely that there's some all-powerful mafia-style gang at work. Much less.'

'They might have taken her for ransom?' Aubret knew it was weak.

'Where's the demand then?' Lombard didn't even look at him.

'She might be a witness and she might already be dead.'

'There's no evidence of that, which means there's no evidence to give the case to someone else. No, Guy. Rosa Daucourt, and whatever this scribble is, they're our ticket to stick with Barbier.'

Aubret snorted in something approaching derision. 'You don't really think our dear *procureur* is going to go for that, do you?'

Lombard placed Auguste Daucourt's medallion on the dashboard. 'Let me deal with René,' he said calmly before sensing that the *commissaire* was about to explode at Lombard for once again removing evidence. Hurriedly he explained where he'd got the trinket and how.

'So we're looking for someone who's lost their club chain then?'

'That's my feeling too. Someone Daucourt would regard as very powerful or they wouldn't be in the club.'

Aubret shook his head sadly. 'Messy,' he muttered. 'Very messy.'

'It needn't be.' Lombard grinned. 'Have the *dossier* and physical evidence at my office tomorrow morning and I'll go and speak to the *procureur* about organised crime, or the lack of it.'

'What are you going to say?' Aubret was understandably dubious.

'I'll make him an offer he can't refuse.' Lombard grinned again, while Aubret rolled his eyes and swallowed the last morsel of Gaviscon. A grieving, morose, fragile Lombard was hard work enough; a pixyish, over-confident trouble-maker could be even worse.

Within thirty minutes Lombard was sitting at the Café de Bonté having already caused something of a stir among the staff. The *juge* was well known in the café, situated as it was opposite his offices across place Jean-Jaurès. 'Bonté' itself was a vague synonym of justice, and it was one of Lombard's favourite bars when he wasn't hiding. There were plenty of bars he could hide in; he could write a tourist trail around the centre of Tours just hopping from one to another, but the

Café de Bonté was an extension of his office, he did serious work there and he hadn't been often in recent months. His sudden appearance isn't what had the staff gossiping however, but his order. The *juge*'s drinking habits could be unpredictable – beer, rosé, gin and tonic, on occasion even a cocktail if he saw someone else having one – but they all had one thing in common; they were alcoholic. The *juge* this time, and after saying a warm hello to the staff that he knew, had sat down at an outside table, finding shade from the evening sun, and had ordered an espresso. The waiting staff couldn't work out if it was a good sign or bad.

Lombard, though vaguely aware of the interest his order had aroused, was nevertheless concentrating on a report from Commandant Pouget on the search for Rosa Daucourt. That it was thorough was no surprise; that it had elicited very little response from the public beyond the usual cranks, more so. Rosa Daucourt had simply vanished, and though her face was by now on the front of newspapers and local TV, the nationals were oddly restrained so far, there was so little to go on. Lombard studied the photo of the young woman – girl he concluded. She was technically the age of *majorité*, but he had seen her childish bedroom with its shades of pink and soft toys, and her face wasn't that of an adult. This was the most recent picture that the family had, and it was less posed than those in the drawing room at the château. The girl was unguarded and looked nervously at the camera. Did he see fear there, or was he reading that into her look? Having concluded that she was, in effect, still a child, the eyes, framed by a sensible bob haircut and a ribbon in her hair, actually looked older. Not that they spoke of experience or wisdom, or fear. There was a vacancy there, a disorientation that was older than her years.

He placed the photograph back in the file and inevitably thought about Elise. She wasn't much older and at Rosa's age, not looking too dissimilar, had decided to change things, to get out while she still could. She was now a confident and happy young woman, but she had had to break ties with her family to get to that stage. *Had Rosa Daucourt done the same?* he asked himself again. Had she even, by coincidence, taken exactly the same route as his niece and was holed up in some squat somewhere, as he had suggested all along?

He sent a text to Elise asking if she would be around for dinner, and then, when an immediate reply wasn't forthcoming, impatiently sent a message to Aubret asking if the squats had been searched. This time the response was instantaneous and sarcastic, but basically saying yes, they had. Lombard sat back; the sun had moved and he leant his back to catch the warmth on his face, taking stock of the busy scene in front of him. She was out there somewhere, he concluded, and that's where she might want to stay.

His phone beeped and he sat forward expecting it to be a reply from Elise. It was from Chrétien instead. 'Can I call you?' Lombard had almost forgotten about Elaine.

Chapter 34

Lombard had tried and failed to sleep, but now, at nearly 2 am, he'd given up trying and was shuffling around the shadowy antique shop downstairs, his mind racing. Partly, it was concern for Elise. She had eventually replied to his message, but it was clear also that she was having far too much fun to be spending time with Uncle Matt. What fun, he didn't enquire. He hoped it was legal, for both of their sakes. He felt a touch of guilt that he actually wished she had never landed on his doorstep in the first place, and wondered if she'd done the same with other distant relatives. He felt like he'd been handed a responsibility that she didn't feel herself, and he wondered again if it was too late to contact – even anonymously – Madeleine's brother and his wife, her parents.

But the burden of Elise was only a part of the problem, and not even most of it. The real reason he was finding sleep so difficult was excitement – pure emotional adrenalin mixed with anticipation that was giving him a buzz. Neurons were firing around his head like bubbles in a shaken can of fizzy drink and he could barely keep still, let alone lie down and rest. The cliché would be a child on Christmas Eve, but he couldn't remember ever having this level of feverishness.

The plan was to be at the *procureur*'s office for ten o'clock. He ran through it in his mind again. He had concrete evidence that the murder of Thibaud Barbier and the disappearance of Rosa Daucourt were linked, much stronger evidence in fact than that Barbier's murder was the result of a gangland feud or a hit. He had further evidence that Procureur René D'Archambeau had used his position and influence to help the Daucourt family, certainly into pressuring Lombard. Furthermore, though he was aware that this was tenuous and pure supposition, D'Archambeau knew who had found the headless corpse and was protecting him because he was a fellow member of some secret society. The fact that he wanted to kick it up to a specialist organised crime unit meant that he could bury the case, leave it in review knowing there would be no pressure to find Barbier's killer and also, possibly, that the person he was protecting was a well-known criminal.

Lombard's trained legal mind knew which elements of his argument were weak, and which weren't. He knew what he could prove and what he couldn't. René, of course, would know the same but they both knew that the case, presented as a whole, would leave a very heavy cloud of suspicion and impropriety hanging over the *procureur* – possibly not enough to completely derail future political ambitions but enough to put them in a siding for a while. There were two big 'Ifs', as Lombard saw it. First, he had to be capable of this type of political game himself – blackmail to give it its proper name – and the second hinged on whether René *believed* he were capable. It would need both to work. Lombard was hanging a lot on his new-found reputation for the dark arts, but if he was to retain control of the Barbier case, which he was desperate to do, he would have to be willing to follow it through.

His edginess had got to the cat, who curled around his ankles looking for food even though its bowl was still full.

'I'm keeping you awake too, am I?' Lombard picked the cat up and then sat down with it purring on his lap. Sitting down didn't suit his state of mind however and he was soon back up and pacing. It was no good, he needed air and to stretch his legs properly and the bright, fullish moon outside was enticing for a nocturnal stroll around literal old haunts. 'Fancy a walk, cat?' he asked as the creature stretched languidly before clawing at the already distressed legs of a Napoleon III armchair. 'Maybe not.' He answered his own question with a light laugh. 'I may not know quite who I am right now, but the *juge* who walks his cat around the streets of Tours at night isn't what I'm aiming for.'

A few minutes later, he closed the door behind him and stepped into the moonlight that gilded the baroque outline of the Opera House at the end of the street. He had no idea where to go, but he walked with purpose anyway and decided that the heart of Tours was the place to start. The place Plumereau was the beating social heart of the city and its arteries led in all directions from there. A few people were milling about, serving staff wandering home after long shifts, slow and hunched, treading carefully on tired feet. Occasionally the silence would be broken by the sudden smashing of bottles as recycling banks were filled with the night's empties. There were a few late-night stragglers too, reluctant to give up the fun and turn in; with them came laughter, arguments, aggression and tears. The spectrum of post-party emotion. It felt thrilling to walk the quiet, narrow streets, sink into the shadows occasionally, watch the bright bar lights turn out as Tours went finally to bed.

He had an idea where he wanted to go and walked quickly down rue Briçonnet. From there he zigzagged down the back alleys, past lovers in doorways and those that hadn't made it back to their own bed and lay where they'd fallen, like casualties in a battle for hedonism. It was the Tours he loved, a mixture of gothic shadowy mystery and bleak dystopia. It made him feel alive, he realised, and his sense of adventure grew as he stood opposite the Parking Napoléon, where it had all started.

After the conversation with Chrétien earlier, how could he possibly have ended up anywhere else?

'You'd think she'd want to rest more during the day, wouldn't you?' Chrétien had joked cheaply to Lombard, after filling him in on Elaine's movements. She had been far and wide, and done very little. Initially she'd caught a train from Tours to Saumur, had sat in a café on the river for an hour, flicking about on her phone without any great intensity, then caught the train back. All in all a four-hour round trip for, in Chrétien's words, a poor substitute for coffee and to boost her score on Candy Crush. On returning to Tours she had taken the tram back up to Tranchée, where she'd got on that morning, bought some groceries which looked like she was making a nice meal – a bottle of wine, fresh salmon, and so on – and gone to wait at the Écôle Primaire Sycomores. She was very friendly with a few other mums waiting, most of them the same age, nearly all very attractive too. Here, Chrétien had wondered if they might share the same profession, suggesting that that would solve any childcare issues. The thought had never before occurred to either of them that childcare even was an issue in prostitution when of course, obviously it would be, as in any profession. France is a very family-orientated society, they'd concluded, why wouldn't there be a crèche system for streetwalkers?

Having picked up her young daughter, the two had walked the half a kilometre or so back home. 'And this,' Chrétien had offered sardonically, 'is where I realised I'm in the wrong job.'

Monika Albescu – he'd got the name from the doorbell entry – lives in a top-floor apartment in the Complexe Rivoli, a collection of expensive modern apartments, set in a few acres of parkland, with a private gym, and so on. She has a large roof terrace, expensive-looking potted olive trees on each corner and an awning that, Chrétien added with surprisingly little bitterness, is 'bigger than my front room alone'. His overall conclusion, and more typical of the man, was that 'she must be bloody good'.

'Did she go out again?' Lombard had skated over the policeman's tartness.

'Ninety minutes later, she dropped her daughter and a small overnight bag off at a house around the corner. One Irina Dascalu. From there, she made her way back home to her apartment, presumably to get ready for work.'

It was a thorough job by Chrétien and Lombard made a mental note to pass that on to Aubret, who always felt that the man was being carried by the rest of the team. He crossed the road and descended the stone steps into the eerie, ill-lit car park. There was movement in the shadows and though he didn't feel threatened exactly, he was aware of his heart rate quickening significantly, which it rarely did these days. A black woman in a tight dress stepped out in front of him. 'Are you lonely, *chéri*?' Her voice was warm, bordering on concern rather than salacious.

'I'm looking for Elaine?' he replied, trying to hide his nerves. 'Is she here tonight?'

'Why?' The woman's voice had changed, it had a threatening edge. 'She's getting popular these days.'

'I arranged to meet her here.'

'Well, she's not here. She probably went home hours ago, quiet tonight.'

'Thank you,' he said, trying not to look at the woman's ample figure.

'I'm still here though.' Even in the darkness, she knew he was looking anyway. 'And I've got everything Elaine has. And more.' She stepped forward.

'Yes,' he stammered. 'No doubt... another time maybe?' He walked quickly away and back up into the light and relative safety of the main road.

That had been twenty minutes ago and he now stood outside the large gate of the Complexe Rivoli high on the north side of the River Loire, having walked briskly, even for him, up the hill. There were still a few lights on in the apartments. The design of the whole place was of the same ziggurat style as the other new apartment compound he'd encountered near the Fostan gym, the one that had offended him so much. Why had he not noticed these monstrosities before? They were on a scale to be noticed yet, certainly at night, they were almost discreet, like architectural stealth bombers. He watched from across the road at a world totally alien to him, not in cost, though that would be a stretch, but in emptiness, in solitude. He was a lonely man, a loner even at times, he was prepared to admit, but these constructions were designed so that you didn't have to see another soul, angled in clever ways to avoid eye contact with a neighbour in the apartment opposite. Privacy, yes, but it bordered on the insolent.

The lights on Monika Albescu's terrace were still on, artfully lighting her olive trees and the lights from an obviously large television bounced colourfully off a wall. Her blinds or curtains weren't shut. The fear he had seen earlier had gone, or she felt completely safe at home. The ceiling light came on and he clearly saw a figure, a woman, rise from the sofa and stretch as if waking. It was the woman he had met earlier – Elaine, Monika – and she was completely naked.

This was not a woman in fear.

He felt guilty watching her as she patted around her open-plan room; she was putting on smaller lights, creating an ambience, perhaps setting up for a late client. Turning the ceiling light off, she went into another room and a light went on. There were closed blinds in this room, presumably a bedroom, though she emerged quickly wearing a black silk nightshirt. It was open at the neck and well into her cleavage and barely covered her behind. Her curvaceous, old-fashioned body looked all the more enticing and erotic for being partially covered. She sat on a chair and started to put on a pair of stockings.

Lombard's mouth was dry and he realised that he had stepped forward and was no longer in shadow. He stepped back again just as the engine noise of a powerful motorbike came slowly up the hill. Its low throaty growl sounded like a lion pacing before its pride. It stopped before the gate and without getting off a figure in black leathers pressed a button by the gate. He saw Monika, or was she now Elaine, stand and move out of sight. A second later the gate slid back and the motorbike growled into the complex. The lady in the apartment closed an electronic blind on the outside world, the man in bike leathers demanding more privacy than she did.

Chapter 35

In the end Lombard got no sleep at all, lying on his bed waiting for his alarm to go off, watching the antique clock tick slowly away. He felt disgusted with himself. Yes, he knew who 'Elaine' was protecting now and maybe should have realised his involvement earlier, almost since that first accidental meeting at the gym. But his regular forays into hands-on police work were meant to exhilarate him, relieve him of desk-bound boredom, not make him feel grubby and small. He sat on a deliberately uncomfortable chair outside the *procureur*'s office, a large clear filing box on his lap, like a boarding school pupil about to be expelled by the headmaster. It brought back memories of the exact same thing.

In both cases, it was exactly how he had wanted it to play out.

It obviously wasn't the usual form to hand over a case like this, but Lombard wanted to make it a big deal. That way, he figured, René D'Archambeau would feel obliged to hear him out. Inevitably Commissaire Aubret hadn't liked it at all. Lombard hadn't told him of his plans; if he had Aubret probably wouldn't have handed the case box over to him. As it was he'd walked him all the way across the top floor of the Palais de Justice, guarding the box from what he saw as Lombard's light fingers. They'd moved slowly like pall bearers. He had told Aubret about Victor Fostan arriving late at Elaine's apartment and, interested though he was, he didn't see it swaying D'Archambeau in any way. The case, as far as their involvement in it went, was closed. Even so, the *commissaire* had been reluctant to leave Lombard alone when he was called away to follow up yet another crank 'sighting' of Rosa Daucourt.

'I'm sure he won't be much longer, Monsieur le Juge.' Lombard had known Madame Trossard, D'Archambeau's secretary, for nearly ten years. She had been secretary to D'Archambeau's father when he was *procureur* up until his death, but she and Lombard had never gone beyond stiff formality, though she wasn't cold, just very proper. He guessed that she was completely unaware of her nickname in the *magistrature* of '*la nourrice*', the childminder.

'He might be when he remembers it's me that's waiting for him.' He smiled sarcastically at her, not expecting a flicker of the same in return.

'He does not have his father's punctuality, I'm afraid.' She noisily shut a filing cabinet and returned to her immaculately kept desk. It was as close as he'd ever known her come to showing any sign of disloyalty but she spoke in a way that not only admonished her boss, but Lombard as well.

Something buzzed on her desk and she pressed a button in response. 'Send Lombard in please, Madame Trossard, I have a spare five minutes.' Madame Trossard blinked in embarrassment and, avoiding any meaningful eye contact, nodded towards the door. *The poor woman*, he thought, *the son is very different from the father*.

'He'll miss me when I'm gone,' Lombard joked, standing up and making his way to the heavy oak office door. He knocked unnecessarily, to just separate his own manners from those of his superior, and entered D'Archambeau's office. The *procureur* stood with his hands behind his back, looking out of the window at the offices on the other side of the road. Lombard preferred his own office view and had often used that as a way to deflect comments on his lack of ambition, or interest in becoming *procureur* himself. This office didn't have the light that his own did, there were far more shadows and that didn't suit him, though it was certainly ideal for René D'Archambeau.

'Why this pantomime, Lombard? It's childish,' he said, without turning around. Lombard placed the box on the large desk and sat down, saying nothing, forcing the *procureur* to address him face to face. 'You hear me? It's childish.'

'Possibly.' Lombard shrugged. 'But we have new information and I wanted to present it myself.'

D'Archambeau's eyes narrowed with distrust and he moved to sit down before changing his mind, preferring the dynamics of looking down on the seated Lombard.

'I don't see how anything can change the basic fact that this Barbier was involved in *le milieu* in some way. And that being the case, it is our duty to pass it on.'

'What's the hurry, René?'

D'Archambeau reacted to the informality like he'd bitten on gristle.

'It's not about hurry, Juge, it's about resources, as you know. We do not have the resources, or expertise, to cover that and the disappearance of the Daucourt girl. We do not.' He delivered this as someone who was used to getting his way and having the last word, forgetting momentarily who he was dealing with as he turned back to the window.

'So effectively you're prioritising. Barbier means nothing.'

D'Archambeau swung back round angrily. 'Less than nothing, Lombard. Some loser who gets involved with the wrong people and pays the price. That's your headline. Kick that can down the road to the experts and you'll find it's nothing to do with Tours at all.'

'Oh well.' Lombard stayed calm and hooked on to the other man's eyes. 'If it benefits tourism…'

D'Archambeau snorted in derision. 'Don't be a prig, Lombard.'

Both fell silent, regrouping. Eventually it was Lombard who spoke next.

'Rosa Daucourt's disappearance and Thibaud Barbier's murder are linked,' he said flatly, opening the box as he did so. On the desk, he placed the girl's drawing next to a photograph of Barbier's tattoo.

'What are these?' D'Archambeau asked dismissively.

'This is the tattoo on Barbier's shoulders. This drawing, scribble, whatever, I found beside Rosa's bed.' Their similarity was obvious. 'Now, if you're convinced beyond doubt, René, that it's big city criminals at work, then that goes for both.' Lombard was choosing his words carefully. 'And I don't think that your friends, the Daucourts, would appreciate the potential delay in debriefing a new team, do you?'

D'Archambeau nodded, not in agreement, but in thought. 'I don't like the way you said "friends", Lombard, you need to be careful here.'

Lombard smiled. 'I am being very careful, Monsieur le Procureur, very careful indeed. But I spoke to Auguste Daucourt. I know you are part of some secret society. It strikes me that you probably have a duty to "look after" each other. That's usually the point of these things.'

Whatever he thought René's reaction might be, a big grin followed by genuine laughter wasn't it – and it was unnerving.

Lombard fished out the medallion and pushed it forward. 'You know what this is?' he asked quietly. D'Archambeau shrugged. 'It was found on Barbier's body.'

The *procureur* picked up the envelope. 'Yes, of course I know what it is and it could belong to any number of people,' he explained, as if to a child. 'This society, as you call it, the Compagnons de Saint-Martin to give it its proper name, is a collection of individuals convened to protect the good name of Tours.' He laughed. 'It's a childish conceit that I was asked to join and I think it's my job to keep a close eye on these things, don't you? Especially, and listen carefully to this, Lombard, you may learn a little about how the world works, especially *because* there are some very unpleasant characters involved.'

'Like Victor Fostan?'

'Is he a member? I don't know.' René didn't flinch.

'Why have you not reported it?'

'It's an ongoing investigation. I have been working with Juge Dampierre.'

'Do you have a membership list, because one of your group...'

'Not *my* group...'

'Someone in the Compagnons de Saint-Martin was involved in Barbier's death.'

'I will of course provide that information to whoever takes over the investigation. Do you have anything else?'

Lombard realised he had been horribly naive. He'd played his only card and it hadn't worked. People like D'Archambeau have more time than ordinary people, they constantly move forward covering up their footprints as they do so and remain three moves ahead. He felt like a fool.

'Oh, my dear Lombard.' René shook his head. 'Do not, ever, go into politics, please, you'll be eaten alive. Is that why you brought this box here? You thought you could blackmail me into letting you carry on the investigation, is that it? You know, for a son of Albion, you are surprisingly lacking in perfidy.' It always came to this with René: Lombard was English, not French. 'Do you really think that I was somehow moving you off this case because of "close friends"?' Again he laughed before adopting a much more official tone. 'That is a very serious accusation, Monsieur le Juge. So serious, in fact, that it forces me to ask for your resignation. I'm sure you understand.' He feigned distress. 'What else can I do, old friend?'

The same equipment that had buzzed on his secretary's desk, now buzzed on his with perfect theatrical timing. 'Yes, Madame Trossard.'

'A reminder, Monsieur le Procureur, you have a meeting at eleven o'clock in Chambray.'

'Thank you, Madame Trossard.'

It was a prearranged ruse to cut their meeting short, Lombard knew that, but he couldn't find it in himself to move. He didn't mind being thought of as naive. He'd never pretended to be much else when it came to the dark arts of realpolitik, and it was almost laughable that he would attempt to outmanoeuvre D'Archambeau, a Machiavellian expert of the game.

'I'll make it as easy for you as possible, Lombard,' the younger man said, disappearing into a small annexe room. 'Still grieving, and so on, Madeleine's death destroyed his willingness to continue in such an important role, etc., etc.' He popped his head around the door. 'It leaves a massive hole, and so on. Ironically, Lombard, I suspect if Madeleine had still been alive, you wouldn't be here. She'd have told you not to become embroiled in things that are above your station.'

Lombard didn't see the grin; he remained seated, looking at his hands in his lap. D'Archambeau came up behind him and clicked his fingers. 'Wake up, Lombard. Time to go. You have a resignation letter to write. I'll reluctantly accept it this afternoon.'

He moved back around to the other side of his desk, zipped up a leather jacket and put a black motorcycle crash helmet down between them. Lombard looked at it and his eyes suddenly focussed like someone coming out of a trance. Slowly he leant across the desk and pressed a switch on the phone system. 'Madame Trossard, this is Juge d'Instruction Lombard. Procureur D'Archambeau asks if you might postpone his eleven o'clock meeting? Something's come up.'

Chapter 36

Aubret sat on a low stone bench opposite the Cathédral Saint-Gatien and watched as Officer Benbarek tried to interest people in his photo of Rosa Daucourt. He was having far less luck than those selling bottles of cold water – probably without a licence to do so – or the ticket sellers for the tourist train. It was a steaming hot late morning and the *commissaire* sipped from his illicit bottle of water and tried to avoid his eyes catching the sun as he tilted his head back. Screwing the bottle lid back on, he muttered to himself. 'What a waste of time,' he growled.

The high-profile nature of the Rosa Daucourt disappearance – the media feeding frenzy got more exaggerated every day she was gone, especially in a slow news summer – meant no lead could be ignored, no matter how tenuous it might be. It doesn't get much more dubious than 'I saw someone who looked a bit like her near the cathedral', yet here they were. Texeira, Pouget and Chrétien were following similarly weak possibilities while Lemery was using her skills to hack into CCTV around the city centre. Part of him wanted Lombard's theory that her disappearance was linked to the death of Barbier to be true; that way they could get rid of both cases which were equally draining and equally bogged down. Then the other part of him, the competitive copper, wanted her found by his team. A further part of him, the father, wanted her found alive and unharmed. Maybe Lombard had been right about that too. She hadn't been abducted or attacked, she'd escaped.

'We're aren't getting anywhere with this, sir.' Benbarek took a swig from his own bottle. 'One lady over there was sure she'd seen her, positive.'

'And?'

'In her dreams. Rising on angel's wings in rapture.'

Aubret rolled his eyes. 'OK, let's head back.' He got up with difficulty from the low wall. 'Did you get a description of the wings?' he growled, as they went to seek shade in the backstreets.

A few minutes later their pace slowed as they enjoyed the cooler shade on rue de la Cloche, passing small shops all of which advertised 'Salle Climatisée' above their actual commerce. Benbarek stopped opposite a dingy-looking place that actually looked closed.

'What's up?' Aubret asked, with a touch of impatience.

'This is a tattoo place, we should ask them about this design. It might be a fashion thing only a few people know about.'

Aubret shrugged. 'A fashion thing?' he repeated dubiously. 'One that appeals to middle-aged bus drivers and eighteen-year-old heiresses?'

Benbarek smiled widely in return. 'Shall we go back and stand in the sun, wait for the second coming?'

It was Aubret's turn to smile. 'Lead on, kid.'

It was gloomy inside but blessedly cool. There was a low buzz of electronic needles from cubicles out of sight of the casual visitor, but it was the smell that Aubret noticed the most. It smelt like burning rubber or melting PVC, like a plastic chair left out in the hot sun.

'That's the ink,' Benbarek informed him. 'That other smell is medical-grade soap.'

'Why though?' Aubret whispered. 'Why have it done?'

Benbarek shrugged. 'It's a form of art. It's also a permanent ID. A fashion statement.'

'Fashion changes, these are permanent. My wife can't wear the same dress two days in a row; who'd be happy stuck with the same permanent picture?'

Before Benbarek could answer, a painfully thin young woman approached them, smiling. She wore a short skirt and a vest, her black hair was piled on top of her head and almost every conceivable and visible part of her pale body was covered in ink. Fantastically intricate designs and colours swirled and plunged and weaved. Aubret couldn't take his eyes off her, yet felt uncomfortable for staring. He had to admit that the whole effect, apart from the less artistic black studded raised boots she was wearing, was like that of a tapestry. It was mesmerising and impressive and he was very grateful that his daughter didn't look like that. 'Can I help, gentlemen?' Her voice was very calming, giving the place more of an air of mysticism than a backstreet tattoo parlour. They showed their ID, which immediately put the woman on the defensive; her previously warm eyes became cagey and furtive.

It was Benbarek who spoke. 'Really, we just came in on a hunch and for the AC.' His warmth didn't have an effect on the woman. 'We're trying to find out what this tattoo is, what it means...' Rather than show her the photo of a dead Barbier, he showed her the image from Rosa's bedroom. 'Any idea?'

Relieved that it was nothing to do with her premises, she looked carefully at the picture. 'Is that it?' she asked. 'It's not part of a larger design?'

They both shook their heads.

'It's not something I've seen. Hang on, I'll ask my colleague.'

She disappeared into the back room and for a moment the sound of the needle stopped and they could hear whispering. The woman reappeared with a small man in tow. He looked more like an Italian barber than a tattoo artist, his dyed black hair and moustache glinting off the low-level light.

'I refused to have anything to do with it!' he said dramatically. 'I said she is too young, no ID, no ink.'

Aubret leant forward and very slowly said, 'Who and when?'

The man became less flustered and sat on a chair in what looked like the waiting area. 'It was two days ago. A man and a girl. He had this design and I said, "What is it?" It looked like nothing, a squiggle, nothing. No art.'

'And?' Benbarek didn't want to let the artist get carried away.

'He says it's private. A private joke. A joke! A tattoo is no joke! And I say that I must have ID because the girl might be too young.'

'What did she look like?' Aubret asked, holding Benbarek's arm down before he could show Rosa's photo and influence the man.

'She has dark hair, cut like this.' He indicated shoulder length. 'And she had big dark glasses that covered most of her face.' Aubret let Benbarek's arm go.

'This her?' the young policeman asked.

The man squinted as he looked, then shrugged. 'It could be, it's difficult to tell. But it could be. Anyway, I refuse. I sent them away. This is a respectable place, with a good reputation.'

'Are there places like this that aren't respectable?' Aubret asked. 'I mean specifically in Tours. Places they might have gone where they didn't ask for ID.'

The man was happy, gleeful even, to list a number of other tattoo parlours in the centre of Tours, competitors no doubt and there was more than likely an element of mischief about the list, but they were further on than they had been.

'What did the man look like?' Aubret asked.

Again the tattoo artist shrugged. 'Tall, like you,' he pointed at Benbarek. 'Smart, but dressed for a colder day, a beard on his chin like D'Artagnan. But he had glasses too.'

'A couple more things,' Benbarek asked as Aubret was turning to leave. 'This list – do any of them offer prison-style tattoos, you know, homemade ink, not so deep into the skin?'

The man looked unimpressed at the question, in the way Aubret looked the exact opposite, making a mental note to ask his young colleague where he'd learnt this stuff. 'That is just homemade stuff, anyone can do that. Charcoal, water, baby oil. Pah! Why pay?'

'To make the tattoo look older than it is?'

'Anyone can do that,' he repeated. 'It's not art.'

Benbarek nodded. 'And lastly, where was the tattoo going to be, did they say? I mean where on the body?'

'Between the shoulder blades, on the back here.' Needlessly he pointed to his own back, then picked up the mountain range-like image again. 'A good place to hide something so dull.'

Chapter 37

Procureur René D'Archambeau sat down opposite Lombard. There was no real surprise on his face at Lombard's actions; he looked more like he'd been waiting for the challenge and was not only up for it, but relishing it.

'I hope you know what you're doing, Lombard,' he said calmly, his eyes unblinking like a snake. 'I was prepared to let you go quietly, full pension, full honour and all the trimmings, but I'd say you're about to make that generosity very difficult.'

Lombard put his hands on the table between them. 'The thing is, René, you were right.' D'Archambeau raised his eyebrows in sarcastic fashion. 'I am no good at politics and Madeleine would have undoubtedly talked me out of trying to intimate blackmail or suggest there's a whiff of corruption.'

'Of course she would, fine woman.' D'Archambeau always spoke like a much older man.

Lombard tried to keep his temper. 'Indeed. She would have suggested something entirely different.' He paused, and picked up the crash helmet. 'She'd have told me to go right for the jugular, don't let up. She'd have told me to become *embroiled*, René.' D'Archambeau looked at Lombard, confusion at his emphasis of the word furrowed his brow. 'It was you with the prostitute Elaine, you who found the body, and you who, belatedly, reported it. You then fled to Lausanne on some pretext or other. This medallion from the – what did you call it? The Compagnons de Saint-Martin is yours, not Thibaud Barbier's. You went back to look for it, probably the morning after, knowing you had dropped it somewhere nearby. Maybe you were seen leaving the car park the second time. Whatever, something spooked you.' D'Archambeau stood and went back to the window, less sure of himself. 'Did you take anything from the crime scene, Monsieur le Procureur?'

'No, Lombard,' the man's voice was quiet, and without its usual cynical edge. 'I leave evidence tampering to you. This prostitute, it was a one-off…' he began to add, before Lombard interrupted.

'Elaine? Or, Monika Albescu to give her proper name. That's the name she is registered in at least. I have her address too, but then you know the address already, don't you, René?'

D'Archambeau turned around slowly, a wry, defeated smile playing weakly on his ashen face. He leant back against the windowsill, his hands in his pockets. 'What do you want?' he asked quietly.

'I want the Barbier case. I think I know why you want it moved elsewhere, it's easier for you to hide Monika. I assume you're paying for her apartment?' He added an unfamiliar snide touch to the question, which was out of character, but then his features changed. 'The child,' he said slowly. 'She's yours, isn't she?'

D'Archambeau ignored him and instead circled the room, his nervous energy calling for movement. 'And all you want is to keep control of the murder of a nobody?' His question was derisive. 'I don't understand you, Lombard. You have my pants down, my hands tied behind my back and me bent over a barrel and all you're capable of doing is kissing me on the neck.'

Lombard shrugged, wincing slightly at the crudeness of the imagery. 'You really don't get it, do you? I'm not like you, René. I'm not interested in games or politics. My job is a simple one, remember, a *juge d'instruction*, I just want truth.' He immediately regretted how pompous he sounded.

D'Archambeau stopped circling and let out a half-laugh. 'We're not that different, Lombard, we're both as vain as each other in our own way.'

This time Lombard moved to the window. 'I know I'm regarded as an oddity, distrusted even, because I have no ambition. And that's your biggest problem with me, René, isn't it? I can't be beaten because I won't fight. There's no sport for you. We have some similarities, vanity maybe, but we want different things. You'll never be satisfied, never be happy because you're either looking over your shoulder for perceived enemies or your eyes are on the next rung on the ladder. I'm not interested in that, so stop fighting me. I'm not worth your effort.'

'You're not happy either,' René sneered.

'No. But I have been.' Lombard shrugged. 'I can draw from that well when I need to.'

'And does it do you any good?'

'Not always, no. But I'm not hiding anything the way you are.'

'What's that supposed to mean?'

'Your relationship with Monika. I'm choosing to make it none of my business, but I say again, I know the child is yours. This isn't a one-off, the child has got to you. Of course, you being you, then publicly you must stay in the marriage of convenience that you're in, like royal households from the age of enlightenment, it is… advantageous.'

'Don't overdo it, Lombard.'

'I'm right though, aren't I? You married into a wealthy politically connected family. It will get you where you want to go, but not sometimes where you want to be. That place is with Monika and your daughter.'

D'Archambeau came to the window to stand next to Lombard, where they stood side by side. 'Her name is Jessica. And she does not know that I am her father. My marriage wasn't always so obviously contractual, but it certainly became so when we found we couldn't have children. Do you know what's worse than not having children, Lombard? Having a child you can't call your own.'

'For her safety, I presume.'

'Yes. If the media, or my non-*perceived* enemies, found out, Monika would be deported along with our daughter.'

'Damn you, René.'

Lombard's anger took D'Archambeau completely by surprise. 'What?'

'I have no idea if any of what you're saying is true or not, none at all. Lying for you isn't just second nature, it's an addiction. But I can't test that out here, can I? If you're being honest with me, there is no way on earth I, and you know this very well, would, could tell another living soul. And if you're lying to me about protecting Monika and… and your daughter…'

'If I'm lying to you?'

'I'd have to tell someone else to find that out, wouldn't I?'

D'Archambeau smiled coldly. 'Checkmate. What a predicament for you. You see, even someone as straight-forward, non-game-playing as you has to make moral decisions occasionally. Go and find your killer, Lombard, I hope you do. The reflected glory on the Tours *magistrature* will be very useful.'

Lombard took a deep breath, went back to his chair on the other side of the desk and sat down. 'Let's get to business then,' he said calmly, placing the medallion back in the box of evidence. 'Obviously I can't give this back to you because Commissaire Aubret would miss it. It's been in the water anyway, there is nothing to tie it with you.' He closed the box and then, without looking up, said, 'I take it you and "Elaine" meet as you did as part of some role-playing game?'

'Are you suggesting she is still working as a prostitute? Are you trying to be insulting in that sanctimonious way of yours, Lombard?' He leant on the desk, demanding eye contact, which he got.

'No. I just want to know all the facts, Monsieur le Procureur. It's my job. Now, I have a few other questions. Charles Daucourt. Was he genuinely ill when you and Dr Cloutier signed his early release from prison?'

D'Archambeau sat down slowly, not taking his eyes off Lombard, as though wary of him. 'Yes, he was. In my opinion. And in poor Cloutier's too.'

Lombard paused. 'Poor Cloutier?'

'You didn't know? Odd, when you have so much in common. He's tolerated because of his grief too, trades on it still.' Lombard looked blank. 'His son was drowned in an accident. He was twenty and Cloutier was called to the scene…'

Something in René's face changed suddenly; there was pain that Lombard couldn't remember ever seeing in the man before. Maybe Monika and the child really had developed another side to him?

'I didn't know.'

'I've used him occasionally as a locum on the rare occasions Dr Sebourg is away. He's a drunk, but a good doctor still. He's the family doctor to the Daucourts now, a one-patient practice. I got him that job when he couldn't handle anything more strenuous.'

'And is there much to do with the family apart from Charles Daucourt's dementia?'

'Cloutier thinks they're all insane, if that helps; runs in the family according to him. They use plastic surgery like it's a change of clothes. Like Auguste's ridiculous chin. You've met Auguste? Of course you have. Nasty man. Very ambitious.' He chuckled. 'And that's coming from me! No, credit where it's due to me, Lombard, I have ambition and the talent to match it. Auguste is just nasty. What is he, thirty? He doesn't just pull the wings off flies, he pulls the heads off butterflies.'

'They're not a family renowned for their kindness towards animals.'

'No. You're talking about Besançon? Charles Daucourt liked to play God. All those experiments just to develop some mascara or something. I know you think I'm cold, but really. And whatever he was working on was lost in the fire anyway.'

Lombard leant forward and put his hands on the desk. 'René, I think Thibaud Barbier was involved in the thing at Besançon. I think he was the driver.'

D'Archambeau shrugged. 'I don't know the case well enough, but what makes you think that?'

'I don't know for sure, call it a feeling I have. But I think Thibaud Barbier is an alias and whoever the driver was, was put into witness protection. He's not named in the case or trial reports.'

The *procureur* took a deep breath. 'Two things,' he said. 'I can't go asking favours about who's in witness protection on a hunch, you know that. And second, even if you had evidence, if anyone sniffs around witness protection the case will definitely be taken away from you. Neither of us could stop that.' Lombard reluctantly nodded in agreement. 'So you think that Barbier, or whatever his name was then, has been found by these animal rights people and dispatched?'

'I think it's possible. Revenge. Down to killing him like a *foie gras* goose.'

D'Archambeau winced at the detail. 'And Rosa Daucourt?'

'It's all a part of the same thing. Everything has to do with Besançon, the Daucourts and whoever Clovis is now. I'm sure of it.'

D'Archambeau shook his head, not really taking in what was being said to him but not taking his eyes off the *juge* either. 'Why does the death of this Barbier mean so much to you anyway?'

Lombard stood up and gathered his things. Slowly moving towards the door, he stopped and turned around. 'I want to know why he was so unhappy,' he said quietly. 'Where did his pain come from and who had he lost?' He turned to the door.

'Lombard.' D'Archambeau's tone was the friendliest he had ever known it. 'You're right, you know? These kinds of games aren't for you. So take some advice from someone who lives them every minute of every day. Ask yourself this question. When you stumbled on the body of the journalist, why were you allowed to live? That's the question, Lombard. Why are you still alive?'

Chapter 38

Despite René's stark and portentous warning, Lombard walked back to his office with something approaching a jaunty stride. If he'd become a pessimist by circumstance, there were still remnants of the old Lombard that could occasionally break through like sunlight through a leaden sky. He was determined now to find out who Thibaud Barbier really was and to get him some justice.

'Are you supposed to still have that box?' a sceptical Muriel asked as he came into view.

'Don't you start,' he replied. 'I get enough of that from the *commissaire*. Whatever happened to trust?' he added, smiling.

She looked at him askance. 'Are you saying the *procureur* is letting you keep the case?'

'With his blessing and his best wishes.'

'Perfect timing then.' She smiled warmly.

'It is?'

She shook her head. 'We're going out to dinner tonight, remember? You owe me from when I rescued you at the pizza place.' He looked blankly back at her. 'I knew you'd forget!'

'I haven't forgotten. There's a table at Café Bleu for eight o'clock.' She looked dubious, but kept smiling anyway. 'Won't the other single ladies miss you?'

'Ha!' she snorted. 'We don't meet every night.'

'Tonight it is then,' he said over his shoulder, closing the door to his office. After any meeting with Procureur D'Archambeau, Lombard always needed a few minutes to take stock, almost to check that everything was intact. He sat at his desk and gathered himself. He had what he wanted: the death of Thibaud Barbier and the disappearance of Rosa Daucourt. It was a chance to start over again.

A few minutes later, he put the box back under his arm and, exiting his office, was relieved to find that Muriel wasn't there. He left her a note. 'Off to see Aubret. Can you book a table at the Café Bleu for eight? Lombard.'

The *commissaire* and his team were listlessly lounging around their office when Lombard came through the double doors. They were like a firefighting crew waiting for an alarm to push them into action. Even the endlessly energetic Commandant Pouget had her feet on the desk. Aubret appeared at the door of his office, leaning on the frame, his tie loose and a defeated look on his face.

'You brought my box back at least,' he said without any emotion. 'I suppose our *procureur* preferred to arrange the evidence in a velvet-lined trunk with a wax seal?'

'Not quite, you'll find everything still there,' Lombard replied and walked into the centre of the office. 'We have the Daucourt search and the Barbier murder; full rein to do it our way and not worry about other departments or potential organised crime links,' he declared simply.

Pouget stood up immediately, Texeira threw some empty coffee cups in his bin; even Lemery looked up from behind her bank of screens, a rare thing indeed. Only the languid Chrétien looked unmoved while Aubret walked slowly up behind Lombard and tapped him on the shoulder. Benbarek chose that moment to come through the doors with a tray of fresh coffee.

'Just in time!' Lombard was enjoying himself.

'Are you sure that's what happened?' Aubret's voice wasn't menacing, he had too much respect for hierarchy to try that, but nonetheless there was a stern, no-nonsense undertone of weary belligerence.

'Ring him if you like, Commissaire, I'll understand.'

Aubret's eyes narrowed. 'I trust you,' he said quietly, though neither man truly believed it.

'I simply appealed to his better nature,' Lombard said brightly. There was silence in the room. 'OK, I appealed to a particular side of his nature, then. Namely, if we can clear these things up, and I think we are all agreed the two are related, the *magistrature* and the Tours Brigade Anti-Criminalité will bathe in righteous glory.'

'You mean D'Archambeau will bathe in righteous glory?' a bitter Texeira muttered, before catching the eye of the *commissaire* and bowing his head in apology before gratefully taking a coffee from Benbarek.

'So,' Lombard spread his arms wide and addressed the room. 'Where are we?'

'Benbarek, tell them about this morning.' Aubret sat down on the edge of a desk, sipping, then wincing at the coffee.

'The tattoo,' Benbarek said to the room, and walked to the wall-mounted investigation boards at the end of the room.

'We only know it's a tattoo on the dead guy.' Texeira was the cocky kid in the class who had to say something.

'Maybe not,' Benbarek shot back. 'Hear me out.' He repeated to the team what he and Aubret had gathered at the tattoo parlour near the cathedral.

'You got lucky,' Texeira reluctantly acknowledged.

'Maybe, maybe not.' It was Aubret who intervened and Texeira took that as a signal to be quiet.

'I rang around half a dozen other tattoo parlours in town,' Benbarek continued. 'They've all had the same thing, a man and a young woman come in with this design. They have no ID, the tattoo parlour turns them away.'

'It seems obvious to me that they're trying to be seen.' Pouget's observation was agreed volubly by the group.

'Any hint of coercion?' Aubret demanded.

'Of the girl? None. I asked.' Benbarek was back to being the centre of attention. The team stayed quiet. 'I have a theory.' Benbarek looked at his *commissaire* for permission to continue, which he got. 'I think it's branding. I still don't know what it means, what the image means. But it's like a club badge on a football shirt. It's their team. Even where it's positioned on the body.'

'Between the shoulder blades.' Lombard nodded at Benbarek, impressed. 'Lemery, can you find details on the death of one Lucien Delaunay, please?'

'Who's he?' Aubret asked.

'He was the leader of a group of eco-nihilists, for want of a better term. He was pulled out of the Garonne a few years ago, minus a head but with a, possibly this, tattoo.'

'OK, get on it, Lemery,' Aubret needlessly repeated the order. 'Now, tell them about your prison ink theory.' Aubret threw his attention back to Benbarek.

'I asked about prison ink at one of the tattooists because I think, on the dead man, it's been made to look old; a prison tattoo would do that, the ink fades and isn't as deep in the skin. Also it hasn't healed.'

'Meaning?' Pouget asked.

'Meaning, Commandant,' – Lombard walked around the back of the group – 'that Barbier's tattoo is not only recent, it might even have occurred after death. Is that right, Benbarek?'

'Yes, sir.'

'Excellent work.'

'Another thing too. On the girl's drawing there're three dots after the last peak, suggesting there's more to come. Barbier's just ends.'

'So whatever the image is, she has more of it to come, you mean? Whereas Thibaud Barbier's had come to an end.' Lombard nodded towards Aubret. 'In other words, time.'

'We need to find this couple as soon as possible.' Aubret stood up suddenly. 'Trying to be seen or not, it's likely it's Rosa Daucourt and she's in serious danger.'

It was just like Aubret to become immediately paternal, though Lombard wasn't as convinced as his colleague. Rosa Daucourt was in trouble, that was quite likely, but none of the tattoo parlours had reported coercion. At this point she could be just as guilty as whoever she was with.

'She's not in any of the squats, not the usual ones anyway.' Texeira stretched as he stood up.

'Chrétien, ring all the tattoo parlours, tell them we want to know immediately if this couple come in. Immediately.' Aubret carried on giving swift instructions to his team while Lombard wandered into the *commissaire*'s office. He felt his phone vibrate in his pocket and found it was a message from Elise. 'I'm at the shop, fancy lunch?'

He felt torn by the invitation. The adrenalin was flowing from the surge in activity among Aubret's squad, but more than the excitement, he felt he should remain there. Opposed to that, he still felt a responsibility towards Elise and he hadn't seen her in a couple of days.

'I'll take the Barbier side of things,' he shouted above the office hubbub. 'I have a couple of leads I can follow up.' Lombard went quickly down the stairs without looking back, not seeing an exasperated Aubret's shoulders slump as he left.

Elise had gone to some effort. A table cloth had been laid on a nineteenth-century *table de bistrot*, with a couple of purloined antique plates and exquisite art nouveau cutlery set on top. The collection, with the addition of a couple of Alphonse Sieber designed dining chairs from the 1920s, came to about six thousand euros, or six thousand and three euros if you factored in a baguette and some partly sliced saucisson.

'I thought as we hadn't seen each other for a couple of days, we should have lunch,' Elise said brightly, joining him at the table.

'It's a nice idea,' he replied. 'I like the set-up, all that's missing is some Piaf songs.'

'I did look.' She laughed. 'You don't seem to have any music down here.'

He cut some saucisson. 'No, Madeleine thought it would be corny, trying too hard.'

There was a pause. 'You must miss her so much,' Elise said quietly and he could see the tension in her forehead, and back on to her shaved scalp. There's no hiding place with no hair, he thought.

'Of course I do, but she's here.' He would prefer not to get into the subject for now, guiltily he realised because he had so much to do.

'Looking out for you, you mean?'

He laughed. 'More like admonishing me when I screw up.' Again, there was a silence while they ate, apart from the sound of cutlery on plate; they could hear the cat snoring nearby. 'So what have you been up to?'

'Having fun!' was her quick reply.

'And has your boyfriend saved the world yet?'

She sighed in mock boredom. 'I know he came across as a bit intense the other day, but he's actually not like that all the time. He's very funny, likes a joke.'

'But he is your boyfriend?'

This time her tone was serious. 'You sound like my dad, or your *commissaire.*'

They fell back into silence, but this time it was a little more tense.

'And are you both in a squat?' Lombard asked, then seeing the look on her face immediately apologised. 'Sorry,' he said, lifting his hands in the air.

'We're not, no. He has an apartment north of the river. Anyway, there was another reason I wanted to see you,' she said, changing the tone. 'I have an apology to make.' She stood and went to get her rucksack which the cat was using as a pillow on a nearby divan. 'Our books must have got mixed up. I think this one is yours.' She produced from her bag a copy of *L'humanité en péril*, it's now familiar blue-and-orange cover again clashing with its background, this time faded refinery of the dining set-up.

'Why do you think they've been mixed up?' he asked, not seeing any superficial difference between the two books on the table side by side.

She flushed and gathered herself. 'Louis is dyslexic,' she said, with a touch of defiance. 'I've been helping him to read and he puts his finger under each word… he noticed a few… holes, pinpricks. They weren't in my copy, I'm certain.'

Lombard snatched up Barbier's book and rifled through it. There weren't many pinpricks, but there were enough. Enough to signal a basic code, a simple steganographic cipher. 'I've got you,' he exclaimed and ran upstairs.

Chapter 39

The train moved slowly through the Paris suburbs as it approached its final destination at the Gare Montparnasse. Lombard wasn't a huge fan of Paris, it was too big for his tastes, too sprawling, and though he recognised that his ambivalence came from not knowing it well enough, he'd never been inclined to get to know it either. It was a place that actually made him feel less French and while ordinarily that wouldn't bother him, his identity was his business. Try telling that to Parisian waiters though who could smell Anglo-Saxon DNA like sniffer dogs recognise drugs mules. Lombard's French was naturally perfect, no hint of an English accent, yet waiting staff in a Paris bar never failed to respond in English to him in their endless game of one-upmanship. Fortunately he wouldn't have time for such annoyances.

The metro was busy even ahead of the usual evening rush hour as people headed early into the weekend, and he had to rush across the concourse at the Gare de Lyon to make his connecting train, which was also packed. Lombard was not a great traveller. He had an issue with timetables; leaving and arriving at someone else's arrangement didn't suit a man who had grown used to keeping other people on their toes.

It's why he liked to walk everywhere as much as he could, though even he realised that walking the four hundred and forty-five kilometres across France to Besançon was out of the question. He settled himself into his solo seat by the window and once again watched the Paris suburbs slide past. He put his book on the table in front of him and, seeing as he'd left in a hurry and brought nothing else to occupy his time, decided to actually read *L'humanité en péril* and see what all the fuss was about. So far, he had read very little, just enough to decipher the pinprick code. A simple enough cipher to break providing you knew it was there in the first place, which he did thanks to Elise's boyfriend and his reading difficulties. There were fifteen pinpricks in all, small holes under letters or numbers that spelt out a hidden message. The first five had spelt the word MAMAN; the next ten were numbers beginning with 06, giving a mobile number. Barbier had access to his mother's number, strictly against the terms of his place in the witness protection programme and which presumably she had given him. He had rung the number immediately Elise had left and an old woman had answered the phone after a few rings.

'Yes?' she'd said nervously.

'I am Juge d'Instruction Matthieu Lombard of the Tours *magistrature*,' he'd replied, trying to sound warm and friendly despite the grandiosity of the statement.

'Ah.' Her interruption was immediate. 'I have been expecting your call, Monsieur le Juge.'

She didn't give her name and he hadn't asked for it. Instead she had told him simply where and when they could meet and he'd run to the station in Tours to begin the journey to the east of France via Paris.

The opening line in the book was certainly arresting, '*Mais bon sang, dans quel bourbier ai-je été me fourrer?*' 'Good grief, what mess have I got myself into?' Before continuing he skimmed through the rest of the thing first; he was always keen to see a book's structure before reading it, to get to know it almost physically before the intimacy of absorbing what it had to say.

The first thing he noticed was the absence of chapters; it was one long denunciation of the state of the world, though with over four hundred reference and research points at the back. Sighing, he put the book down. It was Madeleine in paperback form. An uninterruptible fulmination on mankind's disgraceful past, dangerous present and doom-laden future. A no doubt beautifully constructed argument, forensic in its detail and heartfelt in its passion, backed up with research, incontrovertible data and righteous anger. He remembered being on the end of countless examples of her harangues, not that she blamed him directly, but just that he was there. He missed them and he missed Madeleine terribly, and fell asleep thinking of her.

It was nearly half past five when he arrived in Besançon, feeling crumpled and stiff from the journey. He went first to the toilets to splash water on his face and so was one of the last to emerge at the front of the station. A formidable-looking old woman was standing smoking a cigarette. She was wearing a brown woollen skirt and a faded pink blouse. Her tights were too thick for the season and her blue sandals were worn thin with age, but she had pride in her eyes and a defiant comportment that suggested she was expecting trouble.

'Madame…' Lombard was only able to get in the one word as he approached her.

'Monsieur le Juge?' she snapped. When he nodded that he was, she barked at him again. 'Let's go then, your return train is in two hours, and I live in the sticks.' She opened the door to her tiny microcar, the kind that can be driven without a licence, and then added, 'But then you'd know exactly where I live, wouldn't you?'

'We can just go to a nearby café.' Lombard's tone in response was charming. 'I don't want to put you to any trouble.'

'It's no trouble, Juge, and I want you to see where my son lived before you lot took him away from me.'

Silently he did as he was told and got into the car, though not without some difficulty. She didn't say a word as she turned on the ignition and the thing spluttered into life, and then she stayed silent for the fifteen-minute journey out of the centre of Besançon and up into the small hamlet of Chapelle des Buis. The view was stunning but Lombard was concentrating hard on how to approach this meeting. She seemed angry with him, or at least what he represented: that is the people she deemed had taken her son away from her. There was no mention of his death though, and that puzzled him. The opening line from the book that had brought him here came back into his mind, 'Good grief, what mess have I got myself into?'

It was difficult to know which house was hers as they pulled into what looked like the ruins of a farm, long ago abandoned. Roofs had fallen in on hay barns; rusty machinery lay upturned, protruding from the weeds like dinosaur fossils just unearthed. It was eerily quiet, and for a moment Lombard wondered if he'd been set up. His fears were allayed as an old, grotesquely overweight Jack Russell waddled up to him, growled half-heartedly and then rolled on to its back, looking for a belly scratch.

'You're lucky,' the old woman said, shaking her head at the dog. 'He can be vicious with strangers.'

It looked an unlikely claim.

'What's she called?'

'He!' she shouted angrily, then seemed to admonish herself for being angry. 'He. He's called Asterix. Come on, boy, you must be hungry.' Her tone was lighter as she opened the door. 'And you too, Asterix,' she added mischievously.

She was difficult not to like.

'Right, before you start with the lecture,' she said wearily, pulling a dusty dark bottle from an even dustier dresser. 'I know. All right, I know. I shouldn't have gone, I shouldn't be in touch, I should just grieve like my poor boy is dead.'

Lombard stood with his back to her, which was fortunate as he wasn't sure if he'd have hidden his surprise. Whatever he might have prepared for this interview, the idea that the mother didn't know of the son's death had not been anticipated. It would have been a difficult situation anyway; now it was a moral question. He looked down on the dresser top at some unopened bills and he saw the name 'Lisette Bellecamp' through opaque envelope windows.

'Madame Bellecamp,' his voice was quiet, his mind still undecided. 'Tell me all about it.'

She looked up at him first in surprise; then slowly gratitude softened her eyes where moisture now gathered at the corners. She blinked hard and wiped her nose with the back of her sleeve and downed a glass of whatever fiery liquid she was serving. Then she coughed. She was obviously putting up a front of defiance for the man from the state. 'Normally I just get a bollocking.' She tried to sound collected, but it was obvious that Lombard's warmth had upset her own preconceived ideas of him.

He sat down and poured himself a drink. 'You found him again?' he ventured, filling in the gaps.

'People tell me I put him in danger, but you don't know my son. He can't cope on his own!'

'Why did he agree to go into the programme then?'

'Because,' she poured another drink. 'Because he's not very bright and he wants to please. He always does as he's told. So he signed a load of stuff without my help and that was it, my little Dani was gone. Taken.'

'You found him before then? How did you find him this time? Was it the monster truck rallies?' Asterix pawed at his ankle and he picked the dog up with difficulty and put him on his lap. He smelt terrible.

Madame Bellecamp looked at him. 'Of course. He can't help himself. He loves those things. I can't stand them myself, so noisy.' She sipped at her drink this time, which Lombard was grateful for as she had to drive them back to the station. 'I travel all over France, go to those wretched things...' She rocked forward slightly. 'Just on the off-chance, just for a glimpse of him.'

She stood up and went to a bureau where, in the shadows, Lombard hadn't noticed a large collection of photographs and pennants, medals and magazines. A shrine to the late, lamented Daniel Bellecamp. Only she didn't know he was late and lamented. She brought a framed photograph back to the table and placed it gently in front of Lombard. A podgy, young man in mechanics overalls stood on the edge of a group gathered around a trophy in front of a battered car. The youth stood slightly apart, but nonetheless there was no hiding the pride and the joy in the young man's face. Lombard smiled. He'd found Thibaud Barbier, or at least Daniel Bellecamp.

'He looks very happy,' the *juge* said.

'He was.' She poured herself another drink. 'He was. Before he got in with the wrong crowd.'

Lombard poured himself another drink too. 'Do you want to talk about it?' he asked warmly. 'Or have you done that enough?'

She puffed her lips out and shrugged. 'I don't mind. There's no one left to talk to anymore, and I'm sure Asterix could do with a night off.'

Lombard turned his phone to mute and settled in with Asterix snoring on his lap.

Chapter 40

Her eyes lingered lovingly on the photo of her son and she sniffed again.

'He loved being part of all that.' Her voice was wistful and tinged with regret. 'Oh they used him, paid him a pittance and never really allowed him to join their gang, you know? He wasn't one of *them*. But he was happy, you see, so I said nothing. He was too innocent to see how they treated him, but I knew. I saw it.'

'Did he have any close friends?'

'A few. All of them loners in their own way, they all took off weeks before the Besançon thing.'

'Maybe they're also in the programme?' It seemed logical to him.

'No, I don't think so. Dani thought they'd all gone abroad, that's what he was told at the lab. He believed that, I don't.'

'He sounds like a trusting young man.' Lombard took another sip of the *eau de vie*. 'What is this?' he couldn't help himself from asking.

She shrugged. 'It gets you where you want to go,' was her enigmatic reply.

Lombard coughed. 'I'm not sure I want to go there,' he spluttered and Lisette Bellecamp laughed. 'What do you think happened to the others then?'

She looked at him, making up her mind whether to open up fully to him.

'They're dead,' she said eventually.

'What makes you think that?'

'A gut feeling, that's all.'

'They're sometimes the best.' He coughed again as he sipped.

'You're not like the others.' She nodded as she spoke and Lombard felt he had passed a test of some kind. 'Do you have children?' she asked, swilling the drink around her glass.

'No. It just never happened.'

'Married.'

'Widowed.'

She nodded again. 'I thought so. Grief is like a smell after a while. It stays on your clothes like cigarette smoke. I grieved for Dani when they first took him, then I thought, why the hell am I doing that, he's not dead! So I made up my mind – I'd find him. Wherever they put him, I'd find him.'

'How did you find him this time?' Lombard poured them both more drink.

'Pure luck!' she snorted. 'I went to Tours, another one of those stunt car things. I thought I'd have a look about and I got on a bus and blow me! It was him. Dani. Older, balder, fatter and those lovely eyes had gone.' She paused, seemingly trying to fight back tears. 'Then he recognised me and the eyes you see in this picture, they came back. They came back, Monsieur le Juge, you see? Whatever his name is now, Dani came back.'

'It must have been very emotional for you both.'

She shrugged again, it was her initial reaction to everything. 'It was like visiting someone in prison,' she said coldly. 'He was behind this screen and I could see he was too frightened to come out and give his mum a hug. He was always afraid about upsetting someone, doing something wrong. And I saw the fear come back then. The unhappiness. I'm not soft, Juge, but it was a broken heart I saw.'

'And you gave him your number in this book.' He put the book on the table between them and she read the cover as if she didn't recognise it.

'Yes. Some other woman, posh type, handed it in to him, said a passenger had left it behind on a seat. "Oh, that's mine," I said. She didn't believe me, but what was it to her? I put my number in, gave it to Dani and got off. "I'll see you tomorrow," I said, "same bus line. Think of your old Nana Agathe."' She leant in conspiratorially. 'Old Nana Agathe taught us the code; she used it during the war.' Lombard had to stop himself from mentioning that it was principally a code used by the Nazis, but he needn't have bothered. 'Horrible old traitor, she was!' The woman laughed.

'Why did you get off the bus when you'd been looking for so long?' Lombard was keen to get off the subject of Nana Agathe.

She looked down at her lap. 'I could see I was upsetting him,' she said in barely a whisper. 'I was forcing him to make a choice. The choice was his mother, or whoever he'd promised that he wouldn't break the rules. You can't rush these things,' she added, tapping her nose, 'a mother knows. But I stayed the week, saw him every day and at the end, I said I'd be back soon and that I'd know where to find him now.'

'He must have been upset to see you go.'

'And relieved,' she smiled. 'I told him to lose weight and get a girlfriend. Well, what else are mothers for?' She laughed and poured more drinks. *Thibaud Barbier/Daniel Bellecamp always did as he was told*, Lombard thought.

'Tell me about what happened here in Besançon.' He looked mournfully at his glass, knowing he had to drink it or risk ruining their connection.

'Pah!' she responded viciously. 'You'd have thought he was the guilty one. He had various driving jobs, deliveries and stuff. And it was always him that got the worst ones, the ones no one else wanted. The overnight stops in lay-bys, taking animals to the abattoirs. And he'd be the one shouted at and abused by protestors at the abattoirs too. He hated it, but he did as he was told.'

'He delivered monkeys to the Daucourt laboratory.'

She sighed and shook her head. 'I told him he shouldn't get involved. "It's my job, Mum," he'd say. But I knew something was up. He got hijacked – is that what they call it? Some of these protestors… mind your own business is what I say.' She slammed her glass down. 'They threatened Dani, "Drive us through the gates and drop us off. And don't say anything, or you'll end up like the turkeys you take to be slaughtered." All this came out in court, and they thought they were really clever, that my Dani wouldn't say anything, but he couldn't help himself.'

Lombard smiled. 'Dani always does as he's told, and he was under oath.'

'You know how easy-going he was? He even helped them! One of these saboteurs,' – she spat the word – 'said it was too dark to read the words on the plans he had, so Dani read them for him.' She shook her head. 'Silly boy. Silly, simple boy.' Lombard didn't know what to say. 'He nailed the bastards though.' Her voice was heavy, and didn't have the pride he would have expected. 'And they all went down, most of the saboteurs and the billionaires. Extortion, violence, bribery, animal cruelty, illegal experimentation, you name it. They all went down. Only they all got nice prisons, more like hotels if you ask me. Dani was the one in a real prison. Taken away from his home! Taken away from me!' She stood unsteadily and turned away from Lombard to hide her tears. 'They never found the one who was the leader though. He just vanished. So they said he would likely be the victim of reprisals, best to go and hide away, Dani. I'd have liked to see them try with me around!'

'Did they try?'

'They sent messages. Birthday cards. "Hope you're OK, Dani? We're watching you!" He wasn't here; they'd taken him by then. Look.'

She opened a drawer behind her. It was a crudely drawn turkey and a speech bubble saying *'Bon Anniversaire!'* The writing was disguised: left-handed, letters back to front, sloping, childlike characters. He handed it back and she looked at it, though not with hate. Its motives aside, it was a link after her Dani had been taken away from her.

She sat in the corner on a dingy sofa and cried for a few minutes with Asterix on her lap. Lombard left her alone to do so, sitting quietly and taking in the simple, dark room.

Eventually she stopped crying, wiped her eyes and stood at the table, bottle in hand. 'So, Juge, do what you have to do. Give me the telling off you came here for, threaten me with court orders and the like, then get out. You won't tell me where he is now, I know that. But,' she leant in closely and he could smell the alcohol on her breath. 'I'll find him again and you won't stop me looking. However long it takes. I'll see my Dani's smiling eyes again.'

It took Lombard an hour to walk back to the station. He'd cut the interview short, realising that Madame Bellecamp's warmth towards him had been short-lived and that she'd never drive him back, even if she'd been capable of doing so, which was something he strongly doubted.

He sat in his seat in a first-class carriage and watched the summer evening sun wash over the spectacular country-side as the train headed back to Paris. Should he have told her about the death of her son? The question reverberated around his head. What difference would it really have made? Would she have believed him? Her son was all she had and while she thought she could find him, she had something to live for. Thibaud Barbier was dead, but Daniel Bellecamp was living on in the woman and in her next search. That was one side of his thinking. The other was that not only did she have a right to know, he was effectively playing God with other people's children, and that included Elise. Was he saving them? Or was he saving himself from having to confront emotion he didn't feel strong enough to handle?

He soon fell into an alcoholic sleep and woke just as the train arrived at the Gare de Lyon, which was still busy, even at just after 10 pm. He had an hour to kill before the last train back to Tours, the slow-stopping service, and decided to walk the short distance to the Gare d'Austerlitz. He crossed the Pont Charles de Gaulle and only then remembered that he hadn't turned the sound on his phone back on, smiling at the thought that Elaine had been right. There weren't a lot of messages. Aubret was naturally wondering where he was, Elise would not be back for dinner, that was no surprise, and there was a voice message from Muriel. He rolled his eyes in the moonlight. 'It's now eight thirty-five,' she said, sounding more disappointed than angry, the tinny, remote answer service adding to the smallness of her voice. 'I take it you aren't coming.' He leant on the bridge wall and thought about calling her back, but his battery was failing and the screen was dimmed though still clear enough to be tempting. 'It was difficult to read in the dark,' he said to himself, remembering that's what the old woman had said; 'Dani read them for him.' *He couldn't read!* he thought, slamming his hand on the still warm stone of the arch. 'Why am I so slow?' he said angrily to a blanket of stars, some of whom seemed to wink back in mockery.

He turned and walked quickly in the direction of the Gare d'Austerlitz; he couldn't afford to miss that last train back to Tours.

Chapter 41

Bursting with unaccustomed adrenalin, Lombard tried to settle himself into a carriage at the very front of the train. He was trying to save himself time when the train eventually arrived in Tours at about half one in the morning, but such was the energy running through him, he felt he could probably run there quicker. It had come late, hopefully not too late, but nothing and nobody were what they seemed in this investigation; everyone was wearing a mask including, he realised, himself. The whole investigation was like a masquerade ball – characters had been adopted and roles played out.

He'd been inured to it himself, protected for so long by the cosiness of an inward-looking marriage, that he hadn't fully realised the extent to which people played roles in their own lives. Sometimes hiding themselves from the truth, sometimes hiding their truth from others, but always hiding. And that was something that now, as the fog of intense grief over Madeleine was starting to dissipate, he could see that he was as guilty of as anyone. His own problem lay in not knowing who the real Lombard was, not without Madeleine at his side at least, but too many people in this case knew exactly why they hid and what they were hiding and it was time to tear down those veils.

He had urgent questions that needed answering, questions which only Officer Lemery could answer quickly. Questions about Auguste Daucourt and the entire clan: how all the players in the Besançon incident had ended up in Tours? Who followed who? He would have contacted Lemery too, despite the late hour, knowing that she would jump at the chance to help, but then he looked down helplessly at his dying phone, cursing the potential of modern technology and the frustration of its limits. As if to compound his impotence a youth bounced through the carriage, past his seat, listening to music via his own mobile phone at a volume so alarming and so designed to offend that Lombard felt it belonged in a cinema. The young man, late teens the *juge* guessed, was a white boy wishing he was black. Oversized baseball cap on top of a bandana, oversized trousers and oversized trainers – he stood in the middle of the carriage willing the attention to be on him. Having found that it inevitably was, he nodded to himself in self-congratulation and sang along to the music. It was hard-core rap, laid over a music bed of at least a half a dozen other genres and the lyrics told a tale of how violent life really was in the suburbs of south central Los Angeles. The kid was a walking cliché, a wannabe gangster out past his bedtime but looking for confrontation on a quiet, late-night train.

He took a seat a few tables down in a position where Lombard could watch him reflected in a dark window. The music was relentless as were the mutterings from the few other passengers. During the day, on a busier train, someone would have said something, but this was late-night Paris and the kid was aggressive so people just grumbled from the shadows, aware of the potential risk. The kid was cocky for sure and well aware of the effect he was having as Lombard watched him plug his phone in to the seat charger and swig on a bottle of Pepsi, delighting in loudly repeating some of the coarser lyrics of the music. Two things crossed Lombard's mind: one, he could not put up with this for the next two and a half hours and two, he wanted that charger.

He stood up and nestled himself in noisily opposite the surprised youth.

'I really like that,' beamed Lombard. 'The music, I mean. What is it?'

The young man ignored the question, and instead mouthed something pretty obscene in tune with the lyrics and directed at Lombard who smiled patiently back.

'It's PNL isn't it?' he said brightly, delving into his vast bank of trivia knowledge. The kid looked at him in disgust either because it was PNL, a well-known French rap group, and this grandad had no business knowing about them, or it wasn't PNL and this grandad was just another old bloke trying to fit in. 'I love PNL!' Lombard was keen on playing the full madman, if nothing other than to release his own tension and burn some adrenalin. 'Their second album is my favourite, *Dans la légende*. You know it? I have the Pink version with 'Cramés' as the bonus track. Where are you going?' All of this was delivered breathlessly and wild-eyed as if Lombard was high on something and therefore erratic.

The kid stood uneasily, not taking his eyes off Lombard as he did so; the *juge* had clearly hit a nerve and knocked the youngster's confidence.

'This is my stop,' the youth said quietly, his street *argot* fading and his middle-class accent coming through. Lombard snatched up his phone and handed it to him.

'You better hurry,' he said, the kid doing exactly that and forgetting about the charger, which fortunately was compatible with Lombard's own phone. Plugging the phone in, he found himself automatically and loudly humming the tune to whatever it was that had been playing. He wouldn't have recognised a PNL tune from any other, but he knew how to win a quiz. From another part of the carriage, somebody told him to be quiet and he smiled at the bravado now the empty threat had gone. *Again*, he thought, *everybody is hiding*.

He watched the battery indicator climb slowly on the screen and as soon as he thought it manageable texted Lemery. 'Apologies for lateness of the hour. Can you trace a phone number, find where that phone is now?'

The response was immediate, which, although exactly what he wanted, also saddened him somehow. 'Depends on the network provider. What's the number?'

He typed in Elise's mobile number. He could have rung her himself, but he didn't want her to worry about him checking up on her, or alert Louis Aguirre to the same fact. Then he followed up the message with a 'Don't you ever sleep?'

'Give me a few minutes,' was the swift reply. 'And no, far too busy turning down social invites.' He chuckled to himself. Lemery had been silent for three years and in that time, people – and he was as guilty as anyone – seemed to have forgotten that there was still a personality there, still a smart young woman who just chose not to speak, that's all. 'One more thing. Can you send me details of Lucien Delaunay? Education in particular. Was he a scholar?' He leant back into his seat and waited, closing his eyes as the long day finally started to take its toll. He thought about Lisette Bellecamp and the sheer will and determination of a mother to track down her son, her conviction that he was still alive even though Lombard knew different. He thought of Olivia Daucourt too, gradually falling apart after trying to maintain a stoic façade for the sake of appearances. Again it was a mother's love, the power and intensity of a tie that nothing else could break. He thought of his own mother and her on-the-surface diffidence towards him that he realised, possibly too late, was an act and then he thought of Elise's mother, his own sister-in-law – was she resigned or frantic? Proud of her daughter for escaping a stifling existence or angry that the nuclear family had been blown up? He had no idea of the strength of such a bond; he and Madeleine had been equals, adults; he had not been responsible for her, and she'd have given him a titanic roasting if he'd suggested that he was. He did feel responsible for Elise though. He hadn't seen the danger early enough and now she was in thrall to a fanatic, a violent killer. Had Elise invented an alibi while her boyfriend had attacked him? Then René D'Archambeau's words came back to him. 'Why are you still alive, Lombard?'

His phone pinged as Lemery came back to him, hopefully with some information. 'Easy-peasy' the message read, before giving him an address in the north of Tours. 'And no, Delaunay dropped out at lycée level, some form of dyslexia.'

The train pulled into Tours slowly and he ran out of the concourse and picked up a taxi outside at the largely deserted rank, giving an address to a morose driver. Morose taxi drivers had become Lombard's favourite kind as it meant he was left in peace with his own thoughts, time that, despite spending the last two and a half hours uninterrupted, he now needed. He had no real idea of what he was going to do. At a minimum he was going to confront Louis Aguirre and remove Elise from his grip. If he was right the man had a brutal and violent past, was quite possibly responsible for the revenge killing of Thibaud Barbier and may have abducted Rosa Daucourt. There was absolutely no evidence of that, but Lombard had his suspicions and getting the man alone was a priority. The taxi dropped him not far from the gated estate where D'Archambeau's Elaine lived, though the house he was seeking was further up the hill. As he got nearer he could hear the noise of a raucous party coming from the end of a secluded cul-de-sac, specifically from a house hidden behind a high wall. Angry neighbours had gathered at the gate, protesting at the noise, so Lombard skirted them in the shadows looking for a way over the wall around the corner.

Cursing his lack of fitness and seriously considering whether gym membership might not actually be long overdue, he dropped into the garden unseen. From his hidden vantage point, he could see a couple of dozen people, some drinking, some dancing, some just lounging around on the *terrasse*. It was a typical party from his point of view, and the noise wasn't as extreme as the irate neighbours were making it out to be. Keeping to the shadows he approached a ground-floor window and peered in, ducking down immediately as Louis Aguirre walked directly in front of him. Aguirre stopped and stood with his back to the window, inches from Lombard, who watched as a woman's arms wrapped themselves around the man's midriff. The two embraced and swung round so that the girl had her back to the window. She was a slender young woman wearing a striped Breton-style navy shirt with a wide crew neck. Her dark bob finished some way above the collar, showing white shoulder blades and a tattoo. The mountain range tattoo. His heart raced. For now, he couldn't see her face but if this was Rosa Daucourt then his suspicions were correct, she had run away. Her prison had become too much, though she may have swapped one for another.

He wondered whether he should just go in by the front door rather than lurk outside, but he wanted to be sure it was her. The couple were locked in a never-ending embrace, while Aguirre whispered in her ear. She pulled away and turned to the window, a beaming smile below tired but happy eyes.

Lombard sank to his knees, not to avoid being seen, but in shock.

The girl with the tattoo was Elise.

Chapter 42

What brought Lombard out of his momentary trance were the blue flashing lights of a police car at the gate. For a second he wondered what he had missed, but then realised that one of the neighbours must have called complaining about the noise of the party. That noise now sunk into the background of Lombard's reality; it was just a dull hubbub in his numbed mind. He looked up at the window again expecting the couple to have moved away, but Elise stood there looking at him, horror and guilt etched into her young features making her seem older than she actually was. He felt a tap on his shoulder and whirled around, his arms raised in self-defence, expecting trouble from an assailant. Louis Aguirre stood there, the light from the window making him look pale and ghostly. He had a benign, cold smile on his face, and an arched eyebrow above those impassive, bottomless eyes.

'Monsieur le Juge?' His voice was smooth like molasses and heavy with sardonic superiority that had Lombard's hackles up immediately. 'It's not my place to invite others, but I'm sure the hostess wouldn't mind one extra. Things are winding up now anyway.' He turned and Lombard followed him up a short path and in through a pair of double doors. People's heads turned as they passed, voices lowered, the two men's funereal pace and sombre faces suggesting that trouble was imminent.

Elise was still standing facing out of the window, and she had her back to them as they approached. She had one hand down at her side and in it, scrunched and held white-knuckle tight, was a dark brown wig.

'Where is she?' Lombard snarled at Louis. It wasn't his way to be aggressive, certainly not to start off that way, but a combination of fatigue, dull pain and betrayal had left him completely empty.

Elise swung around. 'No!' she cried. 'It's not like that!' She looked down at the wig in her hand. 'Tell him, Louis.'

'Yes.' Louis was even more languid than before. 'It's really not what you think. It was all just a joke.'

Lombard took a step closer to him. 'The famous Louis Aguirre sense of humour, eh?'

'Uncle Matt.' Elise tried to step between them.

'Are you Louis Aguirre tonight or are you Lucien Delaunay?'

Louis didn't take a step back and expressed surprise at the question. 'Who?' he asked airily.

A shadow fell over the three of them as a heavyset figure came between them and the light.

Commissaire Aubret coughed theatrically. 'Need any help?' he asked, his tone flat and threatening. An equally menacing Texeira stood at his shoulder, not taking his eyes off the unperturbed Louis Aguirre.

Lombard had his eyes fixed on the man too, but a slight smile was trying to fight its way on to his lips. In truth, Lombard felt a massive wave of relief; fatigue had backed him into a corner and Aubret and Texeira had arrived just in time.

'Lemery?' he enquired, his eyes still locked on Louis Aguirre.

'Yep. She tracked your phone too, she was worried about you.'

Lombard shook his head slightly. 'She really is quite the gossip.'

'Isn't she just? Care to tell me what's going on? Much as I like getting woken in the middle of the night, I do like to be told why.'

'Seems fair.' Lombard's response was cold. 'My niece, Elise Battier, you know. This is her boyfriend, Louis Aguirre…'

Elise stepped forward, putting a hand on his arm. 'Uncle Matt?' Her voice was pleading.

'Juge Lombard,' he replied firmly, though his eyes showed the pain that his response gave him. 'Louis Aguirre, Lucien Delaunay, same thing, also goes by the name of Clovis in his capacity as leader, organiser, chief agitator… how would you describe your role, Monsieur Aguirre?'

The younger man gave it no thought. 'Concerned citizen?'

'I suppose so,' Lombard conceded. 'Whatever, he is heavily engaged in what the state describes as domestic terrorism. Violent environmental protests, sabotage.'

Louis Aguirre nodded in assent. 'You make me sound like a hero, Lombard, but I prefer concerned citizen if that's OK with you?'

'You like to pick out what suits your ego, don't you, Louis? Citizen. A free man under the revolution. Saboteur. Again, a French word with the tradition of resistance. And Clovis, of which Louis is the modern iteration.'

If Louis Aguirre felt threatened, he didn't show it. 'Your knowledge for trivia is well known, Monsieur le Juge, but it's a bit late for quizzes. Come on, Elise, let's go.'

Aubret gave Lombard a look which didn't hide its frustration.

'At the very least, you two can be arrested for wasting police time. Commissaire, this is the pair who rather theatrically toured the local tattoo parlours. Turn around, Elise, show the *commissaire* and his colleague your tattoo.'

Lombard did not like the way his niece then looked at her boyfriend, almost asking for permission to do as Lombard had asked her.

'What does it mean?' Texeira asked.

'Care to explain, Elise?' Lombard snapped.

'You should all know what it means,' Louis said angrily. 'That you don't is exactly the problem.'

Aubret took a deep breath. 'Enlighten me,' he said quietly. It was not a warm invitation.

'It's a suicide note,' was the equally quiet response. 'The earth's temperature, how it has risen since Elise's birth twenty-two years ago.' He looked from one to the other, Texeira to Aubret to Lombard, then back again, his eyes were a mixture of triumph and desperation. 'Can't you see?'

'What I see are the eyes of Thibaud Barbier and the cut throat of Edmund Brunel.' Lombard's voice was heavy with tiredness and disappointment. 'And what I want to see next is the very much alive face of Rosa Daucourt.'

Louis Aguirre shrugged. 'That has nothing to do with me,' he said airily, 'or should I say us.' He stepped closer to Elise and put his arm around her shoulders.

Lombard turned to his niece, feeling Aubret's warning hand on his arm as he did so. 'How much do you know about your boyfriend?' he asked. 'His real name for example?'

Elise tried to look defiant, but she also looked scared.

'My real name?' Aguirre scoffed.

'Lucien Delaunay. A suspect in the bombing of an oil refinery in Bordeaux. His own family's oil refinery.' He challenged the man to respond.

'Am I?' Again, he overdid the mocking response. 'That must have made Christmas awkward.'

Lombard grabbed his throat. 'Three people died. There were more deaths in Besançon, at the attack on the Daucourt laboratory.'

Aubret grabbed Lombard's arm. 'If I am Lucien Delaunay then ring *my* family and ask them to prove my identity.'

Lombard felt all eyes on him. 'They've already confirmed your identity,' he said slowly. 'They confirmed your death.'

'Awkward,' Aguirre sneered.

'They were probably glad, in theory at least, to be rid of you. You changed your identity, your appearance and so on. Everybody's doing that these days, it's like an epidemic, but...'

'But, Lombard, you have no proof at all that I am this Lucien Delaunay, none at all. I should imagine that if Delaunay managed to fake his death so well that his parents fell for it, he'll have pretty much covered his tracks since, wouldn't you?'

In other circumstances Lombard might have admired the bravado of the man. His confidence was part of his breeding but his dedication to a cause – and his sheer chutzpah in obliquely even admitting Lombard was right – was something to behold. Bravado though, or a Messiah complex? *There's a fine line in the zealot*, Lombard thought.

'All I want right now,' – his voice was steady and low – 'is Rosa Daucourt. Where is she?'

Elise looked nervously at Louis, who shrugged. 'I genuinely don't know.' His smug smile didn't waver. 'Yes, we played a game with the tattoo thing, but that was a joke. I am very sure, Commissaire, that you had dozens of sightings, all as wasteful as ours. Will you be following up all of those for "wasting police time"? No. I doubt it.'

'Why do it?' Aubret was getting more irritable the longer this interview went on. 'What's the point?'

'The point?' It was Elise who answered. 'Do you know what that family have done? Do you? They tested on live monkeys and apes. The pain they caused, can you imagine?' She was almost in tears. 'They deserve to feel haunted and that's what we were doing. Haunting them. Never letting them forget that they are being watched, followed, despised.' She looked defiantly at her uncle, who showed no emotion in return.

'And that includes Rosa, does it?' he asked her directly.

'It includes them all.'

'Where is she?' he repeated, then turned back to her boyfriend. 'Where is she?' he shouted.

The party, which had still been going on around them, now changed in mood. Whatever the aggressive group by the window were, they had been ignored as dancing and drinking continued. The bubble they had created for themselves was like an entirely different universe, but Lombard's question delivered with the force of anger and some deep inner torment silenced the room around them. Louis Aguirre shook his head and shrugged.

'We don't know,' a calmer Elise said, though any trust Lombard had in her had gone entirely.

'Commissaire, what do you need to search their residence?' Lombard stood up straight, adding an official edge to his question.

'Written permission from a *juge d'instruction*.' Aubret's answer was immediate.

'Do you have a pen and paper, Officer Texeira?'

Both sets of official eyes did not leave those of Louis Aguirre who, for the first time since the showdown began, showed some signs of unease, though not as much as they would have liked.

'Perhaps first you'd like to write your address for us, Monsieur Delaunay?' Lombard handed him the pen and paper.

'My name is Louis Aguirre and you don't need any kind of search warrant, you have my permission to look around all you like.'

'All the same, write down the address, please?'

'I can tell you the address.'

'Also, it's my birthday. Write *Bon Anniversaire*, it'll cheer me up.'

Louis refused the pen and paper, just smiling quizzically at Lombard instead.

'Later maybe. You see, you were wrong, Elise.' Lombard had now completely recovered his composure. 'Monsieur Delaunay is not dyslexic, he has dysgraphia, a distinct, slightly different, neurological disorder.'

Aubret shook his head; his annoyance at being awake in the middle of the night was being compounded by the fact that, as usual, Lombard hadn't kept him entirely informed of developments. 'I think we should all go to your place and have a look around, see if there are any missing Daucourts, don't you?' he said wearily to Louis.

The party, what was left of it, was pleased to see them go.

Chapter 43

The journey was a short one, a silent, tense five minutes in the car heading east towards the old *quartier* of Saint-Symphorien. They stopped outside a deconsecrated church, set back from the main road and partially hidden by a thick laurel hedge. It was two thirty in the morning and Lombard, despite the adrenalin, was feeling the fatigue eat at him, crawling through him like frostbite.

They parked and Louis Aguirre took them past a complicated alarm system and into a magnificent entrance hall and salon. From the outside, the building still looked like a church; inside it looked like a modern loft apartment, with brushed metal fixings and walls that only touched the floor, giving the impression of a maze. The mezzanine, however, was like an ancient library. Thousands of books keeping insulated guard on the place. Lombard found it comforting in one sense – if he could design a library for himself, it would be this – and disquieting on another. Louis Aguirre was not to be underestimated.

'Feel free to look wherever you wish,' Aguirre said, ignoring the awe that he knew his unwelcome guests felt. 'There is a small crypt which I use as a wine cellar. I'll fetch the key.'

There were a couple of rooms made from the old church antechambers and Aubret and Texeira began their search. Lombard stayed with Elise; his temptation was to search as well, but he knew he would be heavily distracted by the mezzanine library and decided to stay where he was.

Elise sat at a dining table, the centrepiece of the main room. 'I'm sorry,' she said simply.

At first he wasn't sure how to respond – as an investigating magistrate with a witness or as an uncle. 'I hope for your sake that Rosa Daucourt is alive,' he said, shaking his head. 'Your game won't look quite so funny if she isn't.'

She bowed her head. 'She's not here, you know? We have nothing to do with her going missing.'

'Sorry, Elise, but I don't know if I can trust you right now. And it may be that you don't know anything, but that doesn't mean your boyfriend is innocent. He's already killed.'

'You can't prove that!' she shouted, before lowering her voice and repeating herself.

'I can't prove it or I'm wrong?' His voice was tired, and her response heartbreaking. 'I'll have to tell your parents,' he added.

She shook her head sadly. 'Oh, you are so naive.'

'What does that mean?' He sat down beside her.

She looked at him, tears forming in her eyes. 'They know. They've always known. I told you that story because it was exactly the kind of thing you wanted, needed to hear. Poor little Elise, I can protect her. You needed to feel needed. I could see that from the start.' She wiped a tear from her eyes and took a deep breath. 'Anyway, they know.'

'So you spun all of that out of pity for me?' He was surprised at how angry it made him as he stood and walked around the table, trying, though battling exhaustion, to gather his thoughts. Naturally what Elise had said, her deception, hurt him badly, wounded him. Also, he knew, she was right. He had been looking for exactly that. They had both got what they needed, an emotional transaction.

Aubret appeared from around a corner and looked at him in frustration, shaking his head. 'Unless there are hidden rooms or something like that, possible in a place like this… she's not here.' His voice was dripping with disappointment, not just for the lack of success but for Lombard. The *juge* sat down, looking like a hollowed-out version of himself. Elise looked down at the table in front of her, saying nothing.

'I'll prepare a full search warrant tomorrow morning, Commissaire,' he said with forced energy. 'Also to include medical and financial records.'

Elise gave him another pleading glance.

'Do you want me to take them in?' Aubret asked, unusually feeling awkward because of the family element.

Lombard shrugged and shook his head. 'What's the point? Look around. Louis, Lucien, Clovis, whoever he is, is a very rich man. You take him in on "wasting police time" and he'll have the best *avocat* in town on our backs within an hour and be back here ten minutes later.'

Aubret nodded. 'If you say so.'

'There's no choice, is there? We do this exactly by the book or we lose him. Even then…' He looked at Elise and made sure she was looking at him. 'Even then, he'll find some disciple to cover for him. He probably always has.'

Within twenty minutes, Lombard, Aubret and Texeira were outside standing at the car. Louis Aguirre stood, silhouetted in the lit doorway, waving as though to friends after a pleasant evening, adding to the fury of the three of them. Elise was not playing that game, however, and Lombard at least felt some relief for that.

'Can I drop you off?' Aubret asked as he opened the passenger door.

'No. Thanks. I need to think and walking helps.' He turned away.

'Go home, Lombard.' Aubret's tone suggested it was an order. But Lombard ignored him and turned into the darkness.

He had walked half a kilometre before sincerely regretting not taking the offered lift home. If his head felt heavy, his limbs were so tired they could barely understand the messages about mobility coming from his addled brain. He sat on a low wall and thought about calling Aubret to tell him of his change of mind, that he did need a lift after all. More than that, he hurt. His pride was hurt – Elise's deception, preying on his grief so that she had somewhere to hide while she searched for her violent lover. Whatever her parents knew, they surely didn't know that about her life? He did, and yet he had left her there. He stood uneasily and made his way back up the hill to Louis Aguirre's expensive residence.

He was too tired to give much more coherent thought to the investigation; everything was rushing at him as if he were a child on a ghost train. Images, names, events, bodies, severed heads, Asterix the dog – it was a jumble of facts and inferences and theories that he no longer had the means to sort out. And probably wouldn't be able to until he'd had at least a fortnight's sleep. The one positive he had was that, because of Elise's deception, albeit altruistic deception, he hadn't been harbouring a runaway. That guilt could be passed aside.

He turned the corner and the smell hit him first. All the lights were on in the old church, but it wasn't electric light. This light had a redder, fiercer glow and danced as though moving to some terrible tune. The place, inside the solid, ancient stone walls, was an inferno. He ran to the door and banged on it, shouting Elise's name as he did so. He ran around the building looking for a way in, eventually finding an open wooden door at the rear. He put his jacket over his head and dived in, still shouting 'Elise', though if she was there she could never have heard him. The noise was as intense as the heat. Disorientated, he reached a wall of flame and knew it was hopeless. Turning back the way he had come, he tripped on the uneven floor. Trying to gather the strength to get back up, his limbs gave way. He had reached empty, and he could go no further. He closed his eyes waiting for the inexorable wave of fire to take him.

The last thing he remembered was being dragged by the feet and dumped on the dew of a summer lawn. He didn't know how or by whom, the only thing he had left in his mind was one question: 'Why are you still alive, Lombard?' it repeated, 'Why are you still alive?'

Chapter 44

Lombard coughed repeatedly as he made his way downstairs to the shop. He was half awake, half dressed and carrying what felt like half a lung. He had no recollection of anything after passing out in the early hours of the morning on a damp lawn, but seeing as he was at home, alive and almost standing upright, he concluded that things could have been worse. He had a headache, but as he'd had that headache for nearly a week now it would be almost more worrying if it wasn't there. He leant against the wall on the bottom step and tried to get his bearings. On the divan where he'd first found Elise asleep was a portly figure slumped and snoring lightly. He lifted his hand to cover his eyes from the sunlight which was piercing through the metal shutters and tried to focus. Once he had focussed, he focussed again just to make sure.

'Doctor Cloutier?' he asked, not trusting his own senses.

Cloutier opened his eyes; a slight confusion in the brow was the only other movement. He looked as surprised as Lombard was that he was there.

'Ah, Lombard,' he said eventually, sitting up slightly and looking at his watch rather than at the *juge*. 'How are you feeling?'

'It's too early to tell,' Lombard replied, making his way to the kitchenette at the back of the shop.

'Really? It's ten to four in the afternoon.' There was a pause. 'Oh, I see what you mean.'

'Can I get you a coffee, Doctor?' Lombard spluttered, trying to suppress more coughing.

Cloutier stood, almost managed to tuck his shirt in and stiffly made his way towards him. 'Let me have a look at you first,' he said, and took a stethoscope from his pocket.

'Much need for a stethoscope in your line of work, Doctor?'

The doctor put his ear tips in and placed the bell on Lombard's chest. 'I don't always deal with the dead,' he said. 'Breathe deeply.'

Lombard did as he was told. Then he opened his mouth, stuck his tongue out and, with a little difficulty, said 'Ah'. Then the doctor checked his ears, nostrils and eyes before shaking his head mournfully.

'Bad news?'

'Far from it. You're a very lucky man. You'll have a sore throat for a couple of days and don't go running any marathons, but yes... very lucky.'

Lombard filled the kettle. 'Who do I have to thank for that?'

Cloutier shook his head. 'No idea. I was just told to keep an eye on you, make sure you didn't do anything stupid, and wait for a call. See if I'm needed.'

'The fire's out then?'

'Yes. The place was destroyed, but they're making it safe for forensics to go in, and me, like I say, if I'm needed.' He turned away.

'Coffee?'

Cloutier sat back down. 'Just half a cup, please.'

'What do you mean, half a cup? An espresso?'

'Yes, an espresso but in a mug. Half a cup.'

Lombard thought about querying it, but decided to leave it. There were far too many other things that were bothering him.

He handed the doctor his half-mug and sat down opposite. The doctor looked around for somewhere that wasn't an expensive-looking antique to set his mug down and eventually opted for the rug between his feet. Lombard watched him intently. Every movement looked like the result of a slow committee process, options weighed before a decision was finally made. Then the doctor reached inside his jacket and pulled out a silver hip flask, filling the cup with a dark liquid which had the sweet and nutty aroma of strong brandy. He then held the hip flask up and, for the first time Lombard could remember, made eye contact as he offered him some of the brandy.

Lombard tipped half of his own coffee out into a nearby *toile de Jouy* chamber pot and gratefully accepted.

'So you don't know who saved my life then? Or if a young couple were at the scene?' he asked, the smooth, warm drink feeling like a balm on his dry throat as he tried also to hide his worry at what might have happened.

Cloutier shook his head. 'No. All I know is a neighbour saw the flames and called the *pompiers*; they arrived quickly and found you on the lawn. One of them recognised you and Commissaire Aubret was fetched.'

'He'd have loved that.' He took another long sip of his fortified coffee. 'This is perfect, thanks.'

'Well, I am a doctor, you know?'

Lombard weighed up whether to say what was on his mind. 'I asked Doctor Sebourg about you,' he said eventually.

'I would have done the same.' Cloutier shrugged. 'I'm good but, to be fair, not always reliable.' He poured some more brandy in both of their cups.

'So she was right then.'

'Eh?'

'We're not that dissimilar.' Cloutier shrugged. 'I heard about your son,' Lombard continued, feeling a little dizzy. 'I'm sorry.'

'And I heard about your wife.' They clinked mugs as though they were champagne flutes.

'I met a remarkable woman,' Lombard continued. 'She said grief is like the whiff of cigarettes on your clothes, you carry it around and other people can smell it too. Almost like a warning, I guess.'

Again Cloutier shrugged and looked, unfocussed, into the far distance. 'I think largely women cope with these things better,' he said quietly. 'For men, a close death is an insult. An affront to their masculinity and control. For women, it's just another bloody obstacle.' He poured himself more brandy. 'Take Olivia Daucourt. For the last however many years she's been trying to keep her family together. Her husband has been fading for much longer than she cares to remember, her eldest son can't cope with any responsibility and her youngest son runs away the minute any responsibility rears its head. Yet, look at her strength.' For the second time he looked directly at Lombard.

'And now Rosa's missing too.'

'Poor girl.' Cloutier shook his head.

'Why do you say that?' Lombard asked after a pause.

Cloutier pursed his lips and handed the hip flask over. 'I guess I'm not betraying any Hippocratic oath to tell you this.' He lowered his voice cautiously, however. 'Rosa has something called Sanfilippo Syndrome, a childhood dementia, not dissimilar to Alzheimer's in that it affects speech, mobility, and so on.'

Lombard took this in and tried to organise his questions, of which there were many. 'Is it a hereditary condition?'

Cloutier nodded sadly. 'They're both going downhill quite rapidly. Charles is only lucid when he sees Rosa. In truth he barely knows her, but her face... it seems to bring him back, however briefly.'

'Are Auguste and Jules affected?' Lombard's voice was equally low.

'There are signs of psychopathic tendencies in Auguste, but Olivia, Madame Daucourt, watches him closely. She watches them all closely. She has to.'

'That must be very difficult.'

'I don't know how she copes. Not only that, but watching her husband and the youngest child wither like that, fade before you... and then someone takes her away, out of what? Spite, revenge... you tell me, Lombard?' The doctor clenched a fist and out of anger and frustration, punched his own thigh.

'It looks like spite,' Lombard replied, the effects of the brandy beginning to revive him. 'A grudge that Clovis won't let go of.'

'Clovis?'

'That's the... brand name, I guess you'd call it, of Louis Aguirre, once known as Lucien Delaunay. I'm certain he was responsible for the destruction of the Besançon laboratory.'

'Ah,' Cloutier shook his head. 'And all the research that was lost with it too.' His phone rang, a sombre series of tuneless beeps, which he answered once he'd located the correct pocket. 'Yes, he's awake and in pretty good form considering, Commissaire ... I see ... yes ... we can be there in twenty minutes. OK.'

'News?' Lombard was almost afraid to ask.

Cloutier sighed and shook his head a little. 'They've found a body,' he said sadly.

Chapter 45

Commissaire Aubret was there to greet them as Cloutier parked his 4x4 behind one of the *pompiers* vehicles whose lights were still flashing. Lombard could see elements of the rest of the team dotted around the area; Benbarek and Texeira were talking to obviously concerned neighbours while Pouget was in conference with a tall, heavily built fire officer of similar rank.

'How are you feeling?' Aubret asked, showing genuine concern and holding his hand out.

'Lucky to be alive,' Lombard replied with a wan smile. 'Again.'

Aubret nodded. 'Yeah, that's becoming a habit.' He nodded at Cloutier. 'Doctor.'

Cloutier recovered his medical case from the backseat and nodded back. 'You have another body for me, Commissaire?'

Aubret threw a quick glance at Lombard, whose eyes betrayed the fear he was feeling over the news.

'Follow me,' the *commissaire* said.

Having dressed in full forensics suits, a scene of crime officer led them into what was, until the previous evening, the entrance hall. It was now just a blackened hollow. Smoke and damp from the hoses gave it an apocalyptic feel – the aftermath of a terrible battle that no one had won.

Aubret turned to Lombard as they walked carefully towards the far corner of what had been the salon. 'You don't have to do this, you know?'

'I do,' he answered, with a touch of gratitude in his voice anyway.

'It can't be good for your lungs after what you've been through.'

'Thanks, Guy, I'll be fine.'

'Oh dear.' It was Cloutier talking as he knelt awkwardly next to the remains of a charred corpse, sitting with its back resting on what was left of a leather and chrome sofa that Lombard recognised from the night before. It was a horrific sight, and one of the worst that Lombard could remember. There were no arms or legs, the thermal heat having amputated them in the fire, and what remained of the head was tilted to the side as though in resignation or exhaustion. This charred torso had once been a living, breathing person but it looked like that had never been the case.

'OK.' Cloutier sighed. 'I know the *juge* likes to hear educated guesses, so here's my early theory. First, this is a woman, that is self-evident.' It wasn't anything of the kind to either Lombard or Aubret. 'And I would say that, given her position sitting up, she was killed before the fire was started.'

'How can you tell?' asked Lombard, trying to lay his fears to one side by concentrating on the detail.

'Because she's sitting,' Cloutier answered clearly. 'If she'd died as a cause of the fire, carbon monoxide poisoning for instance, she'd be on the floor. She'd have crawled, I mean, and we'd find her in what is called the procubitus position. A bit like downward dog in yoga. Sorry.'

'Can you give her an age?' Aubret asked awkwardly.

'Not yet, no. Not old though – again, a guess.'

From the corner of his eye the *commissaire* looked at his colleague who had his own eyes shut.

'Lombard! Aubret!' A shout came from outside the forensic ring and the two men, with some relief, made their way outside the ring and through the tent. Procureur D'Archambeau stood with his hands in his pockets next to Commandant Pouget who looked distinctly uncomfortable.

They re-emerged through the tent, having removed their professional garments.

'Monsieur le Procureur,' Aubret said, almost as if standing to attention, while Lombard simply nodded. 'There's the body of, we think at this stage, a young woman, who was likely dead before the fire started. That's all we have so far.'

'Christ. OK, gentlemen, we need to talk.'

The small, willowy figure of D'Archambeau led the stout Aubret and the languid *juge* to his large car, parked behind the doctor's own vehicle. He nodded for them to get in.

For a while they sat in silence, Lombard and Aubret still recovering from the horror of what they had just seen and D'Archambeau with the sense to let them do just that. 'Do you believe me now, Lombard?' the *procureur* said eventually. 'You are lucky to be alive. We have three other corpses, two you have effectively stumbled upon, and both times you've been spared.'

'If you're going to ask me why,' – an exhausted Lombard barely had the energy to speak – 'I'm afraid I don't know.' Even now, he was unwilling to think Elise was involved.

They resumed their silence. 'The dead girl in there...' D'Archambeau nodded at the burnt out chapel. 'Is it Rosa Daucourt, is that the theory?'

'It's possible,' Aubret said quietly.

'Who else is it likely to be?' D'Archambeau snapped irritably.

'It could be Elise Battier.' Lombard spoke without emotion.

'Who is she?'

'My niece.'

'Christ,' D'Archambeau said again puffing out his cheeks and shaking his head as he did so. 'What's going on?'

Lombard stared out of the window, almost hypnotised by the smoking charred mess of the former chapel. 'It goes back to Besançon,' he began, 'and the attack on the Daucourt laboratories.'

'That's old news, surely?'

'I don't think it is, not by a long way.'

'And do you agree, Commissaire? Or has the *juge* not kept you informed?' D'Archambeau's unblinking eyes watched Aubret in the rear-view mirror.

Aubret was quick to respond. 'I'm fully aware of Monsieur le Juge's conclusions so far, and I agree with them. Someone is targeting the Daucourt family and we believe it to be Lucien Delaunay, or as he's calling himself now, Lucien Aguirre. He led the original attack on the Daucourt labs.'

'He'll be in prison then.'

'He died before he was caught.'

'He died?' The question hung in the air. 'Sorry, are you saying your main suspect is dead?' Lombard would have expected D'Archambeau to sound more caustic than he did, and certainly try to distance himself more from an investigation that had such a weak, downright incongruous central plank. Instead he just shook his head again.

'The family, a rich family from Bordeaux, identified the remains of their son,' Lombard argued weakly.

'They also had him immediately cremated after begging the local *procureur* to release the body for mourning.' This was news to Lombard and didn't sit too well with René either. 'I had Lemery check the files this morning,' Aubret added, by way of explanation.

'And presumably he's now gone missing again?'

'He denies everything of course,' Lombard interrupted. 'We spoke to him last night. The only thing we could have pulled him in on was wasting police time; it just would have wasted more.'

'And your niece, Lombard?'

'His accomplice.'

Again Aubret leant forward. 'I spoke with her parents this morning, sir. They're fully aware that in recent months she had fallen in with the wrong crowd, and they were aware she was here in Tours.'

'With you, Lombard?'

'Staying with this Louis Aguirre,' Aubret confirmed immediately.

'Thibaud Barbier was in the witness protection programme,' Lombard explained. 'His real name was Daniel Bellecamp. I spoke with his mother yesterday. She found Daniel, Thibaud, by accident and in doing so may have blown his cover. This Louis Aguirre, as he's now calling himself, knew she was looking for him and was having her watched. Daniel was taken hostage during the Besançon attack and was able to identify the group, Louis in particular.'

'And was murdered as a result.' D'Archambeau pursed his lips. 'He's clearing the decks of everyone involved in that attack then? Including the Daucourt family.'

'That's the theory,' Aubret confirmed once more. Lombard remained impassive, staring out of the window but focussing on nothing in particular. 'There's a full manhunt in progress for him and, er, Elise Battier. I have asked for police protection for Lisette Bellecamp and the Daucourt house is also under protection.'

'But you also – sorry, Lombard, but this is a feeling I'm getting – you think that he may have turned on his accomplice and covered over his tracks again?'

'Yes, sir.'

Lombard opened the passenger door suddenly and leapt out spewing the contents of his intimate meeting with Doctor Cloutier into the pavement gutter, falling on his knees as he did so. 'Elise,' he managed through the spluttering. 'What have I done?'

A look of immense distaste came over the *procureur*'s face as Lombard stumbled first one way and then the other, unable to fully control his limbs. 'Take him home, Commissaire. Make sure he rests.'

'I will do, now.'

'And, Aubret, make sure he has protection too.'

'Of course.' He dashed out of the car.

'From himself if no one else,' the *procureur* muttered.

Chapter 46

Lombard lay in his bed staring at the ceiling and, not for the first time that week, wondered how he had got there. Not just an existential question that he posed to himself, he had to admit, with monotonous regularity, but physically. How and who had put him to bed? The last thing he remembered with any clarity was the overwhelming feeling that being sick in Procureur D'Archambeau's car would quite possibly damage their new-found, but inevitably fragile, working relationship, such as it was, based on the dark cloud of blackmail anyway.

He looked at his watch, which said 11.25 am. He was hoping that meant Sunday and not that he had been in some exhaustive, carbon monoxide, high-quality-brandy-induced coma for longer than that. As he lay there, feeling remarkably well considering, it all felt like a dream, a throwback. He would sometimes lie in bed on a Sunday long after Madeleine had risen, just listening to her movements. He would first hear the shop bell as she went out for all of the Sunday newspapers, bread and croissants. On her return, if the weather was good, she would open the stiff, rusting door-length shutters that led to their roof terrace above the shop, overlooking the rue Buffon and the Théâtre de l'Opéra, the sun shining directly on the terrace from the east. She would wind down the squeaky green striped awning so that she could later sit in the shade with her papers, before returning to the kitchen to prepare the coffee. A few minutes later, he would hear the bedroom door open.

'*Chou?*' she would say. 'I know that you are awake. You can get up now, everything is done!'

The memory was so vivid, it hurt. He could hear the noises and smell the breakfast, for a moment his heart leaping before settling sadly back to the knowledge that that life had gone. He turned on his side and even thought he saw a strip of light under the door; the only light that could possibly do that was from the roof terrace which hadn't been open for nearly eighteen months. Everything came back to Madeleine: any low point, any setback, any despair. They came back to her. She clouded his mind and his judgement. In his pain, in his loneliness, and seeking something that was no longer there, he had behaved like a naive teenager. Madeleine, if she were there now, would comfort him, but chide him too. Then the bedroom door opened slightly.

'Monsieur le Juge,' a woman's voice said softly. 'If you're awake, I have prepared some breakfast for you. Sorry, but I need to go soon.'

Muriel Fauvion closed the door gently behind her, leaving Lombard not much the wiser than he had been before. As soon as the door shut, he leapt out of bed and took a quick shower in the en-suite bathroom, then dressed quickly choosing from his extensive array of summer linen suits.

'I'm so sorry to have kept you waiting, Muriel,' he said emerging blind into the summer sun and the smell of fresh coffee. For a moment he couldn't quite locate her then his eyes adjusted and he found her underneath the green striped awning. Madeleine's green striped awning that, like the terrace, hadn't been opened since before she died.

'The excuses you come up with to avoid dinner with me!' she stood and laughed, kissing him on the cheek. 'Anyway, you haven't really kept me waiting, but I've known you a long time and if I let you sleep through the end of this, you'd never forgive me,' she added, pouring him a coffee.

He relaxed a little and returned her smile, gratefully taking the coffee. 'Are we near the end then?' he asked, with a certain relief.

She picked up her iPad that lay on the table, which was thankfully a clear break from the image he had of Madeleine surrounded with traditional newspapers. 'I've just received this from Commissaire Aubret,' she said, tapping the screen. Then she began to read:

'There's no sign yet of either Louis Aguirre or Elise Battier. All CCTV has been checked, though they may have been disguised and separate. Nothing at the airport, bus and train stations or vehicle hire. They could have had an accomplice and been away even before the pompiers arrived at the blaze.

'There is still no positive ID on the corpse found at the scene of the fire. We are awaiting dental records. It could be either Rosa Daucourt or Elise Battier; both families have been notified while a full media blackout is in place until a positive ID has been made.

'Lisette Bellecamp is fine and undisturbed.

'Madame Fauvion, tell this to the Juge when he wakes up. It's all under control, go back to sleep.'

'So they're likely still in Tours then,' he said, waving a dismissive arm at the last sentence. 'I'm surprised Elise's parents haven't been in touch with me.'

'They have,' Muriel said. 'I told them you were injured in the fire and were resting. They said to tell you that Elise fell in with the wrong crowd a few years ago and they hope you'll be OK.'

He shrugged. 'A wrong crowd to some is the right crowd to another. Even Nelson Mandela was branded a terrorist, you know?' He walked to the edge of the terrace and leant over, looking at the slow Sunday meanderings of the tourists.

'But this Louis, Lucien Delaunay has killed before?'

'Oh yes.' He turned around. 'Manslaughter of those who died in the refinery at Bordeaux and the workers, if they were that, though I have my doubts, who died in Besançon. Probably Thibaud Barbier because he betrayed him, possibly Edmund Brunel because he knew somehow that Delaunay was still alive. By any means necessary, to coin a phrase. And all because the Daucourts experimented illegally on animals.'

Muriel put her iPad away. 'Well, it seems a warped set of priorities to me,' she said, while he hid a smile from her. 'Now, I do have to go. I'm taking Léo to the circus, a twelfth birthday treat.'

'It's his birthday? I completely forgot!'

'Why don't you come then?' she said brightly. 'Aubret has things under control and Léo hasn't seen you in ages.' He began to shake his head and generally communicate negative body language to get out of the invite. 'Besides, you owe me.'

'Ah, there is that.' He smiled at her, though inside he was squirming at the idea and wondered where Aubret was now and whether he had any news.

'Also,' Muriel began, 'the circus has animals. Léo's choice not mine. There's bound to be a protest. You never know who you'll bump into.'

He thought about it. He could sit around and wait for any news, or he could walk the streets with no direction.

Either way, he would, as he had done so far, just make things worse, get in the way. Or, and a thought came into his head, he could look for an extreme animal rights protestor at a likely animal rights protest.

'Give me five minutes,' he said to a surprised and delighted Muriel.

Almost immediately after they had left the car behind and started walking towards the circus, they could see a small protest was beginning, centred on the caged animal wagons that were to the rear of the tent itself. The wagons, inevitably painted a mixture of red and yellow, housed various bored, scrawny-looking beasts totally unperturbed, and probably quite used to small bands of well-meaning, placard-waving activists shouting for their freedom. The male lion, lying next to its bars, yawned and looked like freedom was the last thing on his mind.

'I don't know why they're here,' the precocious Léo said with all the disgusted affront of a teenager. 'Circus animals will be illegal after 2028 anyway. What are they supposed to do, just let them go?'

It was difficult to argue with the logic and instead Lombard began to tell the tale of Fritz the Elephant who had escaped from the Barnum & Bailey Circus in 1906, running amok in the centre of Tours before he was slain and his remains put in the museum. They both lost interest in the story, however, and certainly Lombard became distracted by one particular protestor wielding her heavy placard with some difficulty. *'Plaisir pour Vous, Prison pour Eux'* it read. 'Pleasure for you, Prison for them.' He made his way over.

'Bonjour, Maman,' he said with a mixture of disappointment and guilt. He hadn't asked her previously about her possible connection to Clovis, because he hadn't wanted to admit it to himself that she might be involved. He tried to hide his feelings though. 'Not as many as usual, are there? Is it too warm for a protest?'

'As long as our presence is registered!' she spat back angrily, incongruously offering her cheek for a kiss as she did so, which her son accepted. 'It is disappointing though, I'll give you that,' she added sullenly. 'Some hotshot campaigner from the south apparently too. He never even turned up!'

'Louis Aguirre?' he asked, affecting nonchalance.

She tutted. 'I might have known you'd know him! Secret state spying no doubt.'

'Is everything OK, Madame Lombard?' An elderly man in a straw sunhat asked after her.

'Oh yes, monsieur,' she answered coquettishly. 'It's the law harassing me, that's all!'

Lombard smiled at her, rolled his eyes and strolled off to rejoin Muriel and Léo in the queue. 'How is she?' Muriel asked.

'Feisty,' was his distracted response. He was thinking about Louis Aguirre who had clearly at least ingratiated himself with local groups beforehand, if not organised the protest. Was it a cover? Had he never planned to show up? Having met him, Lombard felt that unlikely. He also suspected that Elise would be there too. If she could. So whatever plans he, and possibly Elise, had had they had been changed at short notice, and that's if poor Elise was even part of his future plans and not dead.

They took their seats on rickety raised benches, three rows back from the front. Close enough to get a good view of the show and close enough to be virtually knocked out by the stench of previous ones. The animals – the bored lion, a few camels and llamas, those that were contracted to see out the last few years of legal performance – were carrying the smell of history out with them and Lombard, suddenly feeling the week's physical exertions, would have been grateful if they would do it quickly. It seemed to pass Léo by, though Muriel had a polite handkerchief over her mouth trying to repel it, as did most adults in the humid tent. After an overhyped introduction by an elderly ringmaster, the artists elicited a few oohs and aahs before the lion, with a noticeable limp, was paraded as a taster to be enjoyed later in the piece.

Before that, however, a small troupe of clowns tumbled into the ring, bouncing off each other with ease and precision that felt surprising given what were quite tawdry surroundings. Léo laughed heartily as they slapped each other and fell. 'Every clown has a unique face,' he cried above the noise of the applause. 'No two are the same.' He seemed to regard it as the most incredible fact.

'And do you know they copyright that face?' Lombard shouted above the din.

'They paint it on an egg,' Léo replied as if talking to a halfwit.

'We need a volunteer!' One of the clowns cheered. 'Someone from the audience to help with a special magic trick! Who will it be?'

Lombard felt Léo look at him and deliberately looked the other way.

'You, sir!' The clown singled out a large, very reluctant individual on the front row who was then goaded by his companions into accepting the challenge. Lombard breathed a sigh of relief.

The man gave his name while one of the other clowns tickled his head and generally unnerved him. The lead clown then said to the audience, 'I'm going to show you magic, but this guy won't see it!' There was a round of applause. 'Do you have good eyesight?' he asked the man in a stage whisper.

'My eyes are excellent,' the man said, trying to recover some dignity.

'You still won't see it!' Cue more laughter as Lombard watched Léo lean forward, hooked. Muriel smiled proudly on the other side of him.

'I'm going to show misdirection,' the clown shouted. 'You, ladies and gentlemen, will see it, you will see it all. He will not. So don't point, don't say anything or you'll spoil everything! Let him find out for himself.' The clown then placed some coloured tissue on the man's lap, while again he was distracted by the other two clowns at his shoulder. The clown chatted to the man, wishing him luck, as he tore one of the tissues in half and rolled it into a ball in one of his hands. The clown explained everything that was going on, everything that he was doing. He asked the man to lean forward so he could get a better view. 'Every time I open my hand the rolled-up tissue is there, see?'

'Yes,' said the man, with no confidence at all.

'Now concentrate. You see the rolled-up tissue in the hand, I close my hand, I open my hand the tissue is there!' He opened his hand and the tissue had gone. The audience had seen him throw it behind the man and a few sniggered. The man looked confused.

The clown did the trick again. Then again. He even put one piece of tissue in the man's shirt breast pocket, under his nose. The audience saw it and the man did not. The audience were beside themselves, all applauded and laughed. The man looked upset and uncomfortable. The applause got louder and louder, the laughter more mocking.

Léo had tears of laughter rolling down his eyes and he mouthed the words that the clown, feigning disappointment with the man, said to the audience. 'Misdirection,' he cried with triumph. 'You relax the body, you relax the brain! You fool the brain, you fool the eyes!'

Lombard barely heard the rest of the sentence. He climbed across annoyed audience members, apologising half-heartedly as he did so, his phone in hand. 'Commissaire!' he shouted. 'I know where they are!'

Chapter 47

The young *gendarme* threw his speeding police car around the impossibly narrow rising bends of the backstreets of Rochecorbon. So far he had narrowly missed crashing on at least three occasions and earned the anger of many a lunchtime-baguette-carrying local in the process.

'I'd like to get there in one piece.' Lombard tried and failed to sound relaxed as he held on to the handle above the passenger door.

'So would I, sir!' the young policeman replied, missing the point entirely. He still couldn't believe his luck at being hauled out of the group of police by the famous Juge Lombard, just as an old woman was threatening to split his head open with her anti-circus placard. He skidded to a halt next to a group of cars parked randomly at the entrance to a field of vines, causing the three people standing there to jump back in alarm and annoyance. Commissaire Aubret was just putting his orange 'Police' armband on when he saw the car approaching, while Pouget and Benbarek had theirs already in place and guns at the ready.

'Whose side are you on, kid?' Aubret snarled after he'd opened Lombard's door, and then not bothering to wait for any answer continued with, 'OK, Juge, care to fill us in?'

Lombard gratefully slid off his seat and stood, stretching as he did so. 'You spoke to Lemery?' he asked, as if that were answer enough.

'I did. There's a place just down the road, used to be a second home for some Parisiens, became a squat and was bought cheaply by one Victor Fostan. And?' Aubret wasn't being aggressive, just business-like with no time for needless conversation.

'There's no such thing as bought cheaply in Rochecorbon, Guy. Where does Fostan get his money?'

'Maybe the gym is doing well?'

'It probably is. But who paid for the conversion from the original bar? Who paid off his cousin's sizeable debts?' Before Aubret could answer, Lombard continued. 'Who do we know has the money for that? Who has the funds to completely reinvent themselves and pass themselves off as something else, wiping the past away?'

Just as the *commissaire* was about to offer a reply, Pouget stepped forward. 'Texeira says that Fostan is definitely in the house, sir. And looks to be alone…'

Aubret shot a quick, intense glance at Lombard and then, with half a smile and a glint in his eye said, 'Right. Let's go!'

At the end of a short dirt track driveway stood an unkempt, pavilion-style house. There was moss on the roof and a few heavy plant pots which contained nothing but weeds. All of its shutters were closed too, except for the main double doors that led on to the front balcony. A motorbike was on its stand at the foot of the stone steps leading to the front door as the team – Aubret, Pouget, Benbarek and Lombard – crouched at the roadside watching Texeira. The officer was on his haunches by the open sliding doors of the garage at the side of the house and which led under the building itself. He was gesticulating that the target, Fostan, was inside.

'So, do we think the three of them are in there?' Benbarek's adrenalin was getting the better of him and it needed feeding.

'Close by,' Lombard replied.

Aubret leant in close to his young colleague. 'It's a question of geology kid,' he said. 'Lower Rochecorbon borders the river; upper Rochecorbon, where we are, is cliffs and they're riddled with caves.'

'More viticulture and history than geology, Commissaire.' Lombard couldn't help himself. 'The caves were used as dwellings but also to store wine. The property at the bottom of this cliff used to be the Domaine Sandrier.'

Benbarek looked from one to the other. 'And?'

'And it's now the home of the Daucourts,' Pouget explained.

'Right, thanks,' Benbarek said, rolling his eyes at Pouget, 'that's really all I needed to know.'

'What's he doing?' Aubret erupted as Texeira, his gun drawn, kicked the already open garage door aside and walked slowly inside and out of sight. 'Bloody cowboy!'

The three police rushed to the entrance while an unarmed Lombard hung back slightly. A moment later Texeira re-emerged, a look of confusion on his face. 'I swear I heard him in there,' he said, shaking his head. 'But the place is empty.'

'You're forgetting your viticulture and history mate.' Benbarek put his gun back in its holster.

'Eh?'

Lombard walked through the group and turned the light on inside. The place was empty apart from a few old cans of paint and a bucket. Also, in the far corner, stood a large wardrobe. 'Anybody fancy going to Narnia?' he asked breezily.

Aubret ignored the reference. 'Hang on, Juge, let's do this properly,' he said. 'Right. If this is the entrance to the caves, let's be careful. I'm looking at you, Texeira. Also, we don't want to flush them out the other end and cause a shooting match. Commandant, you take Texeira and go to the Daucourt house. Have a quiet word with the officers on watch and be ready.'

'Yes, sir. How will we know where the cave entrance is down there though?'

'Good point. Lombard?'

'Just follow the gaze of the old man in the wheelchair.' Lombard was examining the wardrobe closely and put his ear to the door. 'This is definitely the entrance,' he confirmed.

Aubret shrugged at Pouget and Texeira and sent them on their way. 'Stand back, Juge, just in case.' He pulled his gun and slowly opened the door, revealing a well-lit chamber that became significantly wider the further it got from the wardrobe opening. 'Benbarek, you stay and keep watch here,' Aubret whispered. 'Lombard, follow me.'

'Don't worry about me, Commissaire,' a cool Lombard replied, walking through the redundant furniture. 'They need me alive, remember. All of this is, to some extent, done in my name,' he added enigmatically. 'It's about family.'

Aubret shook his head and followed Lombard down a staircase and through a couple of galleries. Both were extremely well lit and cold, the walls of limestone at times rough and dusty and at others polished and shiny. The two men trod carefully, aware that any sound would send an echo some considerable distance into the depths, and so to anyone waiting below. Aubret stopped beneath a light and took out his phone and began to type on it. He passed it to Lombard to read.

'We need to know who's in the house and if anyone has come out the other end. BUT I HAVE NO SIGNAL.'

Lombard nodded and shrugged, causing Aubret to start typing again.

'I'm going back up to speak to Pouget. You wait here. I MEAN IT. WAIT. HERE.'

Lombard feigned hurt at the idea that he wouldn't wait, but Aubret gave him a look basically saying 'Don't be an idiot'. He also tried to give Lombard his gun, which the *juge* refused. Quietly then, the *commissaire* began to make the short journey back to the surface leaving Lombard in the damp and eerie silence, with just a few hundred years of troglodyte history for company.

Aubret had been gone for five minutes when the judge, his senses heightened, heard voices below: a man's and a woman's. It was difficult to gauge just how far away they were, though they were definitely below his own level. He strained to hear what they were saying but any clarity was just out of earshot from where he stood, in the shadows, his back to a cold wall. He looked at the last set of stairs he and Aubret had come down and thought about retracing his steps as a precaution, to move away from the danger, but then he heard laughter. It was clear and distinct. A man's superior, mirthless cackle, rendered even more hollow and caustic by the echo. It tripped something in Lombard. After all he had witnessed and been through, the deaths, the violence and the quiet, stoic despair of Lisette Bellecamp, her son's crushing solitude… this heartless, sadistic braying was too much for him. He stepped silently out of the shadows, and began moving slowly towards the noise as if drawn by a magnetic force.

He climbed down two further iron spiral staircases and found himself in a tunnel about three metres wide. It was high enough to stand up in as well and lit on one side with bare bulbs. He pressed himself against the wall that was unlit and sidled along the passageway. Every few metres, on either side, there were single-chamber rooms with iron bar gates at the entrances, some open, some shut. All the rooms contained wine racks, which were mostly empty and all covered in dust and cobwebs. It seemed obvious that he was approaching the ground entrance and that this was the old Domaine Sandrier 'grand cave'. He heard the voices again, much closer, though it was still difficult to fully make out what was being said, the echo continuing to dull the sharpness of the speech. Then he heard footsteps approaching and sank into one of the wine chambers. The footsteps passed close by the entrance as Lombard instinctively closed his eyes and turned his head away. He opened his eyes and immediately had to suppress the urge to cry out in horror. Beside him was a metal shelving unit and sitting on the top shelf was a large glass fermentation jar full of yellowish liquid and a pale severed head, the head of a fat man whose dull lifeless eyes looked wearied by Lombard's revulsion. He stepped back and fell out of the doorway, landing on his back and looking up into the barrel of a gun.

Chapter 48

'I knew we should have killed you.' Auguste Daucourt sounded more inconvenienced than threatening, the light reflecting in his glasses as he arched his eyebrows. 'Get up,' he ordered.

'It was you who saved my life in the fire?' Lombard pulled himself up.

'You were supposed to be on our side, the famous *grieving* judge. Now be quiet and move.'

Silently Daucourt marched Lombard down the corridor, before telling him to stop at another open limestone room. This one seemed empty but was irregularly shaped, with recesses and crevices that looked bigger than they probably were thanks to shadows created by the glare of the single lightbulb hanging from a low ceiling. Daucourt pushed him on to the floor and closed the gate behind him, locking it and putting the key in his pocket. He was still wearing the same oversized suit that he always seemed to wear which made him, oddly, feel even more threatening to Lombard, more unhinged.

'I'm not alone,' Lombard said quietly.

'Indeed you aren't.' A thin, cruel smile opened like a wound on Daucourt's face, forcing his absurd chin to jut even further out. 'You have company here, and so much in common.' He cackled to himself – the same hollow laugh that had drawn Lombard to this level in the first place – and turned off the ceiling light. Lombard heard the footsteps fade into the distance and a door close.

He stood up, as erect as he could at least, crouching slightly to allow for the low ceiling. The gate was a proper jailor's door leading Lombard to think that the room may even have been used as a cell long ago. An unofficial correction room for poachers, thieves or recalcitrant servants, anyone who got the ire of the local landowner, even as far back as the Romans when Rochecorbon was called Vodanum before it came under the protection of Corbon, first king of *Les Roches*, in the early eleventh century...

He took a deep breath, he was panicking and he knew it. He needed to think straight.

Daucourt's overconfidence meant that he hadn't even searched Lombard before shutting him away, and Lombard gratefully retrieved his phone from an inside pocket. Cursing that there was still no signal, so no way of letting Aubret know where he was, he at least had the torch on his phone and panned the smallish room for anything that might help an escape. The place looked even more medieval thanks to handheld twenty-first-century technology and the shadows were even more pronounced. Shining the torch at the ceiling and at the walls, he began to circle his cell, counting his steps to get his bearings. Then he positioned himself to the right of the door, determined to follow the irregular wall pattern until he made his way around to the left-hand side. When he was close to shuffling through the lap, his foot kicked into something soft and he shone his torch downwards. A body lay slumped against a wall, head bowed, resting on arms that were in turn resting on knees. Lombard recognised the deep black hair and bent down to wake Louis Aguirre.

At first gently shaking the shoulder, he pushed a little harder causing the body to fall to one side. The dead man rolled and stayed stiffly in the slumber position thanks to rigor mortis and it was now that Lombard could see the terrible head wounds inflicted on the man. A piece of his skull had been removed on the left-hand side just above the ear and what looked like cigarette burns inflicted on the brain itself. This time he didn't fall away in horror. Not that the sight wasn't horrific, but that this was a man who had not only killed, but who had already died. Lombard's thoughts were elsewhere; his priorities were with the living. They were with Elise. He sat on the other side of the room and waited.

He didn't have to wait long.

The bulb was switched on and his eyes shut tightly at the sudden explosion of light.

'Get up, Lombard.' Victor Fostan was confident enough in his own physical abilities to not feel the need for a gun, and Lombard had to reluctantly admit that his confidence wasn't misplaced. Instead of allowing him to stand of his own free will, as he'd instructed, Fostan grabbed the back of his neck and lifted him like he was a puppy, throwing him out of the doorway. 'Turn right and keep walking,' he said, showing no emotion at all. 'Then stop at the door.'

Lombard did as he was told, slowly though, trying to think of a plan as he went. For some reason he doubted his guardian angel would continue their – so far – good work, and he was now very much more dangerous alive. They walked in silence until a sudden loud metallic crash came from behind the door as they approached it, followed immediately by a woman's short, piercing and agonising scream. Forgetting that he was a prisoner Lombard rushed at the door and flung it open, an equally surprised Fostan with him at his shoulder. Olivia Daucourt lay on the floor a bleeding wound to her head, but alive. Auguste Daucourt stood above her, fear and pain on his face. In the middle of the neon-lit room, on a metal table – presumably once used as somewhere to bottle and label wine – lay Elise.

She was either unconscious or dead, it was impossible to say from where he stood and Auguste Daucourt still had a gun.

'I didn't touch her!' he wailed.

She lay with her eyes shut under a thin white bed sheet and on her face were a series of black dotted lines in marker pen. Some on her cheek bones, others just below the eyes, also on the nose and chin. Olivia Daucourt managed to stand unsteadily and rushed at Lombard, throwing her arms around his neck, sobbing as she did so.

'Thank God,' she said in English. 'Thank God you're here, they tried to kill me!'

'What did she say?' cried her son, as Fostan slipped quietly away. 'What did she say to you?' He raised his weapon, his own tears blinding his sight. 'Talk in French damn you!'

A shot rang out and Auguste Daucourt screamed in pain, dropping his gun to the floor just as Commandant Pouget stepped into the room holding hers still directed at him. She was closely followed by Aubret and a defeated Victor Fostan.

'It really would help if you spoke in French, madame,' the out-of-breath *commissaire* said.

'My own son!' Olivia Daucourt continued her plea, theatrically straightening her hair. 'A murderer.' She turned back to Lombard. 'They said they would kill me if I didn't change the way she looked. They wanted to turn her into Rosa! They told me… to keep Charles going.'

Lombard disentangled himself from her arms and rushed to Elise. She was alive, but presumably under anaesthetic, awaiting surgery and her new face.

'No, madame.' He turned around angrily. 'This was your doing. It has been from the start. I should have seen it – the convenient drawing of a tattoo in Rosa's room.'

'No!' she cried back, then turned to Aubret. 'You must believe me!'

Aubret looked to Lombard for an explanation. 'Go on, Juge.' His voice was quiet, but hard as granite as he grabbed Olivia Daucourt's arm tightly.

'It goes back to Besançon.' Lombard stared down at Elise as he spoke. 'The deaths in the warehouse weren't of workers at all. They were people being experimented on – victims, loners, friendless individuals that wouldn't be missed. Madame Daucourt and her husband weren't just experimenting on apes and monkeys, Commissaire, but people. Real living though sadly pathetic human beings. Check missing persons in Besançon, all about Barbier's age.'

'All of this for make-up?' Aubret couldn't hide either his revulsion or his disbelief.

'No. Not make-up. A cure for dementia, isn't that so, madame?'

Olivia Daucourt stopped crying and looked at Lombard, like a lover looks at a much-missed ex. 'You must let me go,' she pleaded. 'He cannot cope without me.'

'He barely knows you exist!' Lombard's almost crazed response acted like an electric shock on the woman who looked at him in pure hate. 'It's Rosa he misses, not you! You may have been his muse, his inspiration, whatever you want to call yourself, you may have been that once, but when Rosa actually began to resemble her mother, her real mother that is, not this plastic caricature that you turned yourself

312

into, this mannequin, you lost him. He was only lucid when he was with her, not you anymore. That's why you wanted Elise. From a distance he would think Rosa had returned and you could use that.' She began to plead once more. 'You lost him years ago, and even as he went he saw through your fake shell.'

In an instant, she changed. 'He ignored me!' she screamed. 'I did everything for him. I bought off all of his mistresses, paid for their children and he threw me aside. I wanted him back, but he was the only one who could fix himself. He had to continue his work. We need a new Rosa.'

Lombard shook his head at the madness of it, while the rest of the room – apart from a simpering Auguste and a resigned Fostan – were in shock.

'So that's why Barbier's head was removed,' Aubret half-whispered. 'To hide the operations and experiments.'

'Not quite, Guy,' Lombard said softly.

'Madame Daucourt began to get messages, didn't you? Your nemesis from Besançon, Lucien Delaunay, wasn't dead after all and he was letting you know. He came to Tours, you even saw him on one of the occasions you were following Nadine Daucourt.'

'Nadine Daucourt?' Aubret asked.

'Oh yes, Commissaire. Nadine has a specific taste in men: gentle loners, needy souls and not sadists like her husband. Madame Daucourt – and her daughter-in-law wasn't, I don't think, aware of this – could not let this happen. But rather than simply coerce Nadine to behave, she used it as a source of recruitment. Then one day, and this is just a guess, but an educated one, one day Nadine found Thibaud Barbier. Olivia Daucourt recognised him, and she had an idea as to how to incriminate Lucien Delaunay and get him off their backs. She could clear the decks of everyone who knew too much. Poor Barbier, who probably didn't even know he knew anything, and Brunel, who was sniffing around. Classic misdirection. They gave us motive, opportunity, even a suspect with a previous history of violence.' He paused. 'Poor Thibaud Barbier. He did exactly as his mother told him, he found a "nice girl" in Nadine, a bit of hope in his life, but he got caught up in an old ideological turf war instead.' Lombard shook his head.

'And the girl in the fire?' Aubret was still shaking his head at the cruelty of it all.

'Rosa Daucourt,' was the simple reply. 'I've no doubt she died of natural causes having inherited a neurological imbalance from her father. She suffered from Sanfilippo Syndrome, childhood dementia. The poor girl was probably kept alive for as long as was possible. She would be walked here to this makeshift lab, pumped full of whatever and walked back. One day, she didn't come back. Charles Daucourt noticed that. "Where is she?" he asked. "Where is she?"'

Aubret tightened his grip on Olivia Daucourt's arm, even though she gave no resistance. By now, he was effectively holding her up.

'So they placed her corpse in the chapel, set it on fire and kidnapped this Lucien character and your niece?'

'Yes. He's dead, by the way. You'll find him in a cell down the corridor. And Barbier's head is preserved in another room.' Lombard shook his own head sadly, before his eyes welled with tears and angrily he addressed the limp figure of Olivia Daucourt. 'And you really thought that I would support your work, madame? That your repulsive, psychotic ambition to treat terminal illness would be suited to me? Why? Because of my wife? That's why I was spared? That's how self-righteous and deluded you were. I would go after Lucien, Louis, Clovis – whatever he called himself in your vile feud – because I would have some sympathy with *your work*? No.'

Finally Olivia Daucourt raised her head. 'I don't believe you,' she sneered. 'You're famous for it, for mourning, wallowing... you'd do anything to bring your precious Madeleine back. You'd have done anything to save her!'

Lombard shook his head again gently, even allowing a wistful smile to come to his face. 'No, madame, because she would not have wanted to live with that knowledge. She was better than you.'

Juge Lombard took a deep breath and left the suffocating room in search of fresh air.

Chapter 49

Charlotte Lombard sat under the green striped awning and pursed her lips so tightly they looked sewn up. 'Unbelievable!' she exclaimed, and tossed her iPad aside on to a cushion, narrowly missing the sleeping cat. Lombard sat on the wall of the roof terrace watching the scene below and sipping from an antique champagne flute of dubious provenance. Then the elegant old woman picked up the discarded tablet, re-read what had caused so much consternation and repeated her vexation. 'Unbelievable!' she cried again.

'Is it though?' Lombard contentedly closed his eyes, his mind and body still exhausted. He had that wonderful feeling of a fatigue well earned, and the sparkling wine, a very fine bottle of Domaine Sandrier he had picked up, was having the desired tranquillising effect.

'Is it?! Have you read this?' She was furious. 'A dramatic conclusion was reached this evening to the two gruesome killings that happened in Tours this week. Olivia Daucourt and her eldest son, Auguste, were arrested, along with local businessman Victor Fostan, for the murders of journalist Edmund Brunel and bus driver Thibaud Barbier. The case was solved in no small part thanks to a secret investigation by Procureur de la République René D'Archambeau into the activities of an underground society... I can't read anymore!' She threw the tablet to one side again.

'Well, it's not entirely inaccurate, you know?' Lombard teased.

'What are you talking about? You were beaten, burnt and, and I don't know what else... the disgusting weasel!' She stood angrily and poured herself a glass of wine.

'Weasel?' Lombard replied with a hint of mockery. 'I thought you liked animals?'

'Oh, you're impossible!' She flounced back to her seat.

Lombard closed his eyes again and smiled contentedly. His phone hummed quietly on the table and he went to pick it up. It was Aubret.

'Do you want the good news or the bad news?' the *commissaire* asked without preamble.

'Will I be able to tell the difference?'

'Good point. Well, anyway, your niece is unharmed and in hospital. Her parents are with her.'

'Good. I should go and see them,' Lombard said, though he had no intention of doing so.

'Also, we have a full confession from the Daucourt mother and son. Well, I say confession... it reads like more of a boast actually.'

'I can believe that, yes.'

The *commissaire* paused, Lombard even thinking that the line had gone dead. 'Hello? Guy?'

'Are you sitting down?' was the curt reply.

'Go on.'

Aubret sighed heavily. 'That head you found. It wasn't Thibaud Barbier.' Lombard sat up. 'It was Gilles Fostan. As was the body in the river. The tattoo was a hook, added after death, to get us looking for Clovis. More revenge, this time a cousin's.'

'And they killed him like a *foie gras*?'

'Fitted a gastric band, then force-fed him.'

'And this was Fostan, not Barbier?' Lombard was too tired to be surprised.

'Madame Daucourt said they had Barbier lined up, like you said, as bait for this Clovis bloke, and knowing you wouldn't let it go. But Barbier disappeared, just vanished. They had his licence and used Fostan instead who they had languishing in the caves. Sick when you think about it – and convenient.'

Lombard put the phone back on the table and walked back to the wall, his features deep set in concentration. He leant over the edge and shook his head, before returning to his phone. He looked back through his calls and dialled Lisette Bellecamp.

'Are you OK?' his own mother asked, trying to hide her concern.

After half a dozen rings the phone was picked up. It was a male voice.

'Lombard,' it said. 'We've been expecting your call. Madame Bellecamp is no longer on this number.'

'Where are they?' he asked coldly.

'They?'

'They.'

There was a pause. '*They* are back together and that is all you need to know.'

The line went dead and Lombard returned to his seat on the wall, and managed a celebratory sip of his wine.

'This place is too big for one person,' his mother declared, plumping a cushion. 'And it needs a woman's touch.'

Lombard, possibly still reeling from the fairy-tale like news of Barbier and his mother, nodded in agreement. 'There's room for you here, Maman,' he said simply.

'Oh good God, no!' Charlotte Lombard's face was a mask of horror. 'What a terrible idea,' she said. 'Just as we are getting on so well?'

A relieved Lombard turned back to the street scene below him and, in what seemed like a lifetime, raised a glass to the future.

Also available by Ian Moore

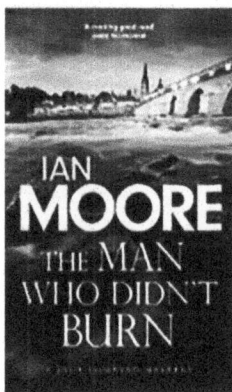

The Man Who Didn't Burn
(A Judge Lombard Mystery, Book 1)

A KILLER. A SAINT. A TOWN FULL OF WHISPERS.

When an English expat is brutally murdered, his charred corpse left on a Loire Valley hillside, the police turn to Juge d'Instruction Matthieu Lombard to find the killer.

Instead, Lombard discovers a wealth of secrets, grudges and feuds in the idyllic town of Saint-Genèse-sur-Loire. He begins to suspect that the remaining members of the Comité des Fêtes know more about the death than they are letting on.

But rather than towards an arrest, each clue he uncovers seems to point in one, unexpected direction: Joan of Arc. Is the answer to the murder hiding in the barroom gossip of the Lion d'Or? Or in another century altogether?

OUT NOW

About the Author

Ian Moore is a leading stand-up comedian and writer. He lives in rural France and commutes back to the UK every week. In his spare time, he makes mean chutneys and jams.

He is the author of the bestselling Follet Valley series of mysteries, as well as two memoirs on life in France contrasting with life on the road in the UK. *À la Mod: My So-Called Tranquil Family Life in Rural France* and *C'est Modnifique: Adventures of an English Grump in Rural France.*

Acknowledgements

This has been a labour of love for me, Lombard is someone I believe in greatly. He is as infuriating as he is inspired and keeps me on my toes because of that. If I have any of his qualities it is my capacity to be equally infuriating, so huge thanks for all the love and support of my wife, Natalie, who believes in Lombard as much as I do.

Thanks also to science journalist Michelle Petersen who was a massive help with my initial research, and to Eve Hall for her excellent work on the edits and for being so complimentary. Something I am needy enough to require all the time.

My agent Bill Goodall has been hugely important in bringing Lombard to the bookshelves as have everyone at Duckworth Books, Pete Duncan, Matt Casbourne, Rob Wilding, Josephine Cassaglia and Daniela Ferrante. I am very lucky to work with so many good people and they are the best.

Note from the Publisher

To receive background material and updates on further humorous titles by Ian Moore, sign up at farragobooks.com/ian-moore-signup